MW01139080

Devil's Night

THOMAS STACEY

outskirts
press

Devil's Night
All Rights Reserved.
Copyright © 2022 Thomas Stacey
v3.0

This is a work of fiction. The events and characters described herein are
imaginary and are not intended to refer to specific places or living persons.
The opinions expressed in this manuscript are solely the opinions of the author
and do not represent the opinions or thoughts of the publisher. The author has
represented and warranted full ownership and/or legal right to publish all the
materials in this book.

This book may not be reproduced, transmitted, or stored in whole or in part by
any means, including graphic, electronic, or mechanical without the express
written consent of the publisher except in the case of brief quotations embod-
ied in critical articles and reviews.

Outskirts Press, Inc.
http://www.outskirtspress.com

ISBN: 978-1-9772-5741-3

Cover Photo © 2022 www.gettyimages.com
Cover Design © 2022 Thomas Stacey
All rights reserved - used with permission.

Outskirts Press and the "OP" logo are trademarks belonging to
Outskirts Press, Inc.

PRINTED IN THE UNITED STATES OF AMERICA

For
Sandra

Thanks
to
Diane
for
"The Rainbow Bridge"

Thanks to my son Craig
For editing and encouragement!

Other books by Thomas Stacey
The Sam Browne
Alone, Together, Nevermore
Massacre of the Innocents
1861-D

Table of Contents

1. Devil's Night 1
2. Catalina 11
3. Clubhouse 37
4. Aftermath 43
5. New Family 50
6. Back to School 59
7. Investigation 63
8. Lenny 86
9. Georgie 100
10. Rosemary, Anna, Norman 118
11. Georgie's New Friends, Perro 132
12. Nifty Norman's 162
13. Devil's Night II 176
14. The Gales of November 195
15. Investigation II 215
16. Soft Interviews 226
17. Interrogations 235
18. Adjudications 258
19. A Meal Served Cold 275
20. Lucifer 290
21. Devil's Night III 311

1

Devil's Night

It was Devil's Night, the night before Halloween. They were five close friends, living on the same block in a close-knit neighborhood of Detroit: looking for something to do . . . as usual, on this cool, quiet night with porchlights aglow and garbage cans secured throughout the neighborhood.

The mouth-watering smell of freshly baked bread escaped from Kosta's bakery-chimney and settled over the surrounding area. It was hard to resist. As they opened the door, they heard the familiar bell tinkle over the door and a stoooped-over lady with thinning reddish hair encased in a hairnet, gave them a wry smile. "What'll it be boys? The usual?" She asked rhetorically with a thick Polish accent.

"Pony up guys," Georgie said and they all dug into their pockets and put an assortment of pennies, nickels, and dimes on the glass counter. The woman counted with her arthritic crooked index finger and slid the coins one by one into her open hand next to the counter. She grabbed a fresh, warm, loaf of Polish rye and forewent the slicing machine. She placed it on the counter into Georgie's waiting hand. She knew the boys enjoyed tearing the bread apart and eating it by the chunk.

It was still warm — almost hot. As they tore off chunks, the heat mixed with the cool air and formed a mouth-watering steam. They walked slowly and deliberately down Wesson Street, eating and talking and looking for the ideal prank on this quasi-festive eve.

"What about eggin old man Kowaczik's?" Georgie mumbled with a mouthful of bread. Georgie was the presumed leader of the five. He was the one, along with Jimmy, who usually directed the actions for the night — sometimes harmless and sometimes not so harmless.

"Well . . . any suggestions guys? How about waxing some store windows? I can get some candles. No soaping . . . that's too easy to wash off. Maybe Steve's Drug Store? You know he's a real prick and kicks us out when we look at his comics. Quit feeding your faces and give me some ideas." No one responded. Each waiting for the others to respond. They all continued eating and walking. The twilight was fading as the streetlights flickered on. With the porch lights and the street lights they could see a smattering of jack-o'lanterns and Halloween decorations scattered across some of the porches.

Jimmy Gorski was the first to respond to Georgie's request. "That egging and waxing are getting old and boring, Georgie. We need to think of something new and a little more exciting." Just as Jimmy finished, they all spotted a scarecrow dummy propped on a porch—swing on an eerily lit porch.

"Holy shit! Do you guys see what I see?" Jimmy said as he swiveled his head and nodded. They all nodded with quiet hmmms.

"Keep walking guys. Down to the corner and we can decide what we can do with that dummy," Georgie commanded. They all continued to walk.

The scarecrow was sitting on the large porch that covered the entire front of the house. Lights from the living room and a yellow-bug-bulbed porchlight spilled out onto the scarecrow. It was an unplanned eerie theatric to the Halloween decoration sitting on the swing.

The scarecrow was made by the Father of the household with help from his two preschoolers and his wife. He retrieved an old pair of worn-torn Wrangler jeans along with one of his flannel shirts with holes in the elbows, and safety-pinned them together. The children helped squash up *The Detroit Times* newspapers to stuff into the arms and legs. Now . . . what to do for the head? His wife said she had an idea. She went into her closet and brought out one of her Styrofoam wig heads. Perfect! They all contributed to crayon-drawing a face with coal black eyes against the white foam. Mom added bright red lipstick lips with fake drops of blood dripping from the corners of the clown-mouth and a black mascara pimple-dotted nose. Dad found an old Detroit Tiger's hat and Mom pinned it to the head with some old stick pins. To finish off the scarecrow, Dad stapled a pair of high-top black Keds to the hems of the Wranglers, added a clothesline noose . . . and voila, a perfect scarecrow dummy for Halloween.

When they got to the corner Georgie said, "Okay gang, I've been thinking. We steal that dummy and do something creative with it, like hang it somewhere, where people will think it's a real person. We'll have to wait until they turn the lights off before we cop it. Can you guys stay out late?" They were all 13 and 14 years old and were allowed to stay out a little after the street lights went on and a little later on weekends. This was Saturday. Tomorrow was Halloween and the day after that was Monday, November 1st, All Saints Day and their Catholic grade school was closed for the day! They all nodded their heads with "Yeps." They could wait until the porch lights went out to do their seemingly harmless prank of stealing the dummy and hanging it somewhere.

Georgie Kolpacki was the oldest, 14, close to turning 15. At this age, more than a year older than the other boys, made a big difference. He was tall with coal-black slicked-back hair. Acne was starting to blossom on his European olive complexion. He was an only child in a dysfunctional family, giving him the freedom to roam the neighborhood, almost at will. His four other friends' actions were a little more restricted by siblings and stay-at-home mothers.

Georgie took out a pack of crumpled Lucky Strikes that he had stolen from his father's bureau and shook out a couple of cigarettes. He took one and offered the pack to the others. They all took one and gave the pack back to Georgie. He stuffed the pack into his denim jacket pocket and took out his lighter. He held the brushed-steel Zippo with his thumb and middle finger and squeezed until the Zippo top flipped open, emitting a strong lighter-fluid smell. He flicked the flint-wheel as he snapped his fingers and the lighter blossomed into a brilliant blue and orange flame. He grinned. He loved showing off his little stunt with the Zippo. Holding his head sideways, away from the flame, he lit his cigarette, snapped the lighter shut, and offered it to Jimmy. The Zippo went around the horn taking turns lighting their cigarettes.

As the smoking continued, some were inhaling and spitting tobacco bits, while others were coughing and trying to learn to inhale. Lenny, Stanley and Mark, nervously asked what the plan was. They were the younger followers of the group led by Georgie and Jimmy. Georgie tried to ease their obvious nervousness. "Listen guys. It's Devil's Night and it's no big deal. People expect shit like this. We're just gonna sneak up there when the lights go out and grab that sucker off the porch. Like I said . . . no big deal. I'll tell you what to do when we get there. Jimmy and I will sneak up on the porch and grab it. You guys will be lookouts. Got it?" Georgie said rhetorically.

Georgie and Jimmy were on their second cigarette and the sky had pinched out its last wisp of orange sunset light. They were all staring down the street with particular attention to their target house. As they stared, the first porchlight snapped off, then another, and another, and finally the scarecrow was in complete darkness. "Let's wait a few and be sure they're keeping their lights off and then we'll go," Jimmy said.

Georgie was impatient and anxious. After a few minutes he said "Okay, that's enough. Let's go." He started to walk and the others followed. As they walked with quiet tennis shoes, Georgie instructed the three younger boys that he and Jimmy would creep up on the porch and take the scarecrow. He pointed and instructed Stanley, Mark, and Lenny each to watch up the street, down the street, and across the street. They were all pleasantly nervous, even Georgie and Jimmy.

As they approached the porch steps, Jimmy put his index finger to his lips and faced the rest of the boys. He whispered, "Shhh." Mark, Lenny, and Stanley each took their post of watching up, down, and across the street. Georgie and Jimmy tip-toed up the steps and over to the porch swing. They both grabbed the scarecrow at the same time and the swing began to move giving off an unwelcome squeak. They froze and looked at each other. Georgie raised his hand with his palm toward Jimmy motioning him to back off while he carefully lifted the scarecrow. This time there were no squeaks from the rusty swing chain. As he slowly lifted it, he felt some resistance and noticed that the scarecrow had a clothesline rope with a hangman's noose around the Styrofoam head and it was attached to the swing. He pulled out a black-scaled switchblade knife, snapped it open and surgically cut the rope where it was attached to the swing.

It was only a matter of minutes to get the scare-crow off the porch, but to the three lookouts, it felt like hours.

Since they didn't plan on what to do when they had the dummy scarecrow, they began running. Georgie had the torso and Jimmy grabbed the legs with the dummy's head flopping loosely as they ran toward the newly opened I-94 expressway.

When they got to the corner of the service drive, parallel to the expressway, they stopped to catch their breath. Georgie placed the scarecrow down next to a neatly manicured hedge that bordered the front of the corner house. They all looked at each other and began giggling . . . having succeeded in their little prank.

"What now?" Lenny, the smallest of the group asked as he gasped for air from the run and the giggling.

"I don't know," Jimmy said. "Look around and see what we can do."

They all turned around, looked around and shrugged their shoulders. "Let's just take it to our clubhouse," Lenny said.

No one responded as they continued to look around for a place to hang the scarecrow. Then . . . Lenny spotted a prospect. The Wesson Street bridge going across the expressway had a sturdy steel handrail along the pedestrian walkway.

"Hey guys. Look at that rail on the bridge. We could tie the dummy to the bridge with that rope on its neck and hang it over the rail. That would scare the shit out of the cars. They would think it's a real person. Whaddya think guys?" Lenny moved his eyes from one to the other, looking for a response.

"You might have something there Lenny," Georgie said as he rubbed his hairless chin. "Let me think about this." He pulled out his pack of Lucky Strikes and lit one and passed the near empty pack to Jimmy. The other three boys watched in silence waiting for a plan.

"Okay. I think that's a pretty good idea." Lenny had a satisfying grin. "You agree Jimmy?" Jimmy nodded.

"Same as before. Jimmy and I will walk over to the middle of the bridge with the dummy and you guys stay here and keep watch in all directions. If you see anyone coming, give us a loud whistle. Got it?" They all nervously nodded their heads.

Georgie and Jimmy simultaneously took their last drag on their cigarettes and flipped them into the street. Georgie knelt down and checked the rope around the scarecrows head and snugged it up a bit. As before, he took the torso and Jimmy grabbed the legs and they crossed the service drive leading to the Wesson Street bridge crossing the expressway.

The I-94 expressway was barely five years old and drivers were still getting used to the 65 mph daytime speed limit and 55 mph at night. It was Saturday night and Devil's Night so there wasn't a lot of traffic that evening. As they walked to the middle of the bridge, they gave the occasional look over the rail and down both directions of the expressway. They could see and hear the cars whizzing by and could smell the exhaust fumes. The three boys on the service drive were watching Georgie and Jimmy walk across the bridge with their prize and were paying little attention to their surroundings.

At the far end of the bridge where the traffic was oncoming to the side they were on, they stopped and laid the scarecrow on the bridge's pedestrian walkway. Georgie checked the rope again and took the loose end and tied it to the top of the handrail with two overhand knots. They both lifted the scarecrow and eased it over the side, holding on to the shoulders of the red and black plaid flannel shirt.

"Ready, Set, Go," Georgie shouted. And they let go of the dummy. As the slack of the rope straightened out from the Styrofoam head, the head separated from the shirt and the headless body plummeted down toward the expressway. They heard the screech of tires from numerous cars and the sickening loud crunch of metal smashing into concrete. Without looking, they ran as fast as they could back to the service drive. Lenny, Mark and Stanley were already running down Wesson Street — away from the squeal of tires and the horrific sound of metal meeting concrete.

As they ran, Jimmy shouted to the three boys ahead of them. "Meet at the clubhouse!"

2

Catalina

The Lesko family: Larry, Doris, Rosemary, and Mickey, lived in a Polish section of Detroit for the past 16 years. After living in an upper flat next to a noisy car wash on Michigan Avenue, they felt secure enough and decided to make the big move. Larry was a Korean veteran and secured a GI loan after he was promoted to line supervisor at the Cadillac Assembly plant. Their daughter Rosemary was one year old when they moved there and Mickey was born a few years after that.

The block they lived on was in an open and friendly neighborhood. Neighbors were social and were there to help whenever needed. They looked out for each other's property and children and most were involved in neighborhood and church activities. There was an abundance of teen-agers and most of them were boys. Mickey was smart, short, shy, and a bit on the portly side. He forced himself to be friendly wherever he could in order to make friends. On rare occasions he was allowed to hang out with the other more popular boys on the block: Georgie, Jimmy, Lenny, Mark and Stanley. It was usually when they needed a homework favor or to borrow his bike or baseball equipment.

It was the night teen age boys looked forward to every year – Devil's Night. The night before Halloween when they were allowed to prowl the streets and do mischievous deeds that were mostly accepted by the adults as long as no permanent damage was done. Ringing doorbells and running away was aggravating to residents but entirely harmless. Soaping windows was also harmless, but a little aggravating. Waxing windows on stores and cars and houses was a bit more bothersome, since it couldn't be washed off like soap and had to be scrapped off with a razor blade. Throwing eggs at a car or house was a bit of a mess and hard to clean up, especially when the weather was cold and the eggs froze to the surface and left a permanent blemish on the house or car's paint. The worst and most dangerous was the prank of finding some dog droppings: putting them in a bag, put it on someone's porch, lighting it on fire, ringing the doorbell, and wait and watch as the homeowner came onto the porch and stomped on the bag with the mess inside. Most adults knew the ploy and would carefully grab the bag and drop it off the porch. Those ignorant of the prank would have to remove their shoes to be cleaned later as the perpetrator's stifled giggles were heard from their hiding places in nearby bushes.

Mickey was at that curious age and his fringe friendship with the boys in the neighborhood whetted his appetite to go out with them on this special night to join in the mischief and fun.

"Dad, can I go out with the boys and walk around the neighborhood tonight? Promise not to get it any trouble. I saw them today and they said I could go with them. Please." Mickey had his praying hands held close to his mouth.

"I'm not sure that's a good idea Mickey. Especially if you're talking about Georgie and his crew. I know most of the boys like Lenny are pretty good kids, but that Georgie worries me a bit. His mother and father have some drinking problems and he doesn't have much supervision. I've seen him loitering on the corner and smoking cigarettes."

Mickey had a look of dejection on his face and Larry felt bad for him . . . in a way. But he felt roaming the streets with Georgie and his gang, especially on this night, was a bit bothersome. He felt that the other boys, especially Mickey, would probably be easy to sway by the older more delinquent Georgie.

As he looked at Mickey, he had a thought. Mickey had inherited his tendencies to savor sweets and his physique showed it, as did Larry's. "I got a better idea.

Let's get Mom and you and I and take a ride down to Jim Dandy's on Livernois. I'll let you get a banana split. And I might get one myself. Whaddya say champ? Sound like a plan?" Larry rubbed his son's brush cut head.

"Yeah. I guess so. What about Rosie?"

"Your sister Rosemary is not much into the sweets like we are. But we'll ask her. I think she's in her room. Why don't you go ask her and I'll go tell Mom our plan?"

Larry was hoping that asking Mickey to ask his sister to come and calling it 'our plan' would help Mickey forget about joining his friends on Devil's Night.

The family car was Larry's car — his Cat. It was a 1964 Pontiac Super Duty 421 Catalina coupe with a silver body and shiny-black-vinyl-top. He washed it, at least weekly, and Turtle Waxed it monthly in the summer months. Clean shoes were required and even though his wife Doris was a smoker, she was never allowed to smoke in the "Cat", as Larry referred to it.

"Rosie doesn't want to go. She's gabbing with her girlfriends on the phone. Let's go. Where's Mom?"

"She'll be ready in a minute. You can get in the car and we'll be right out. Make sure Perro doesn't get in the car. They don't let dogs in Jim Dandy's and I don't want him barking for us in the car while we're feasting on ice cream," Larry said licking his lips. Mickey was getting anxious thinking about plucking the Maraschino cherries off of the whipped cream topping on one of Jim Dandy's gargantuan banana splits. He had already forgot about Devil's Night.

As Larry waited for Doris to get ready his mind wandered to what his life had become. He felt blessed that he had a good steady job. His marriage to Doris was lovingly perfect along with the gifts of two wonderful children. He knew Mickey struggled a bit with his weight and his shyness, but he was encouraged that he was making some friends in the neighborhood. As he thought about that, the guilt of denying Mickey Devil's Night out with the boys, he started to second guess himself. *Oh well, he'll get over it once he starts in on that Jim Dandy banana split,* he thought. He thought about Rosemary, his beautiful and mature daughter. She had graduated from Holy Redeemer with high honors and was accepted into The University of Detroit with a plan to get a law degree. He was startled out of his thoughts by the sound of Doris saying, "I'm ready Dear. Let's go. My mouth is watering thinking about a hot fudge sundae at Jim Dandy's."

They all piled into Larry's pride and joy. Mickey in the back and Doris in the front passenger seat.

"I'm gonna take the X-way down there. Maybe

open up this Cat for a bit."

"Don't you dare, Larry. Be careful. There are a lot of crazy drivers out there. And be careful with the kids roaming the streets," Doris cautioned.

"I'm gonna drive down to West Grand Boulevard to get on the expressway. Give us a little time to enjoy the ride."

Larry backed out of the driveway and cautiously made their way down Buchanan to West Grand Boulevard and onto the expressway. The night was cool and dry and the traffic was light. Neither Doris or Mickey had yet to ride on the expressway and it was somewhat of a unique first-time experience. It was like driving in a dry canal with high grassy hills on either side. They were both looking side to side and fascinated by this new experience. It was quite exhilarating to be going fast alongside other cars – with some cars passing at frightening speeds.

Larry thought he might push the old 421 a bit and pressed the accelerator to the floor and felt the passing gear as it kicked in!

"Stop it, Larry. You're scaring the shit out of me. If you keep it up, I'll light up a cigarette."

"Okay, okay. I'll back it down a bit. Just wanted to get a rise out of you. How you doing back there Mickey?"

"I'm doing great. I like going fast like that. Mom . . .

you're a stick in the mud."

"Never mind stick in the mud. Do you want to get us in an accident?"

It was quiet in the car now as the sights and sounds of the expressway magnified. The rush of passing cars was making whooshing sounds like a windstorm against a screen door. The blurry stream of speeding headlights coming in the opposite direction was alarming. The beeps of horns as anxious drivers passed slower cars, added to the cacophony. As a large fully loaded semi-car-hauler, traveling over the 55-mph speed limit, spewing out grayish black diesel smoke from the twin-vertical exhaust stacks, sped passed them, Doris held her breath. She thought that for sure the truck was going to crash into them or one of the cars would fall on them. She white-knuckled the armrest on the door, took a deep breath, and tried to relax.

It was only fifteen or so streets and a few overpasses as they got nearer to the Livernois exit. They passed under the overpasses and both Mickey and Doris strained their necks close to the windows to see what was on the bridges.

A nanosecond was all it took!

Larry saw a body of a person leaping off the

overpass. That was all his mind registered before it went black and vacant. No time to hit the brakes! Doris saw and felt nothing. Her head produced a bulge in the laminated windshield with spiderweb cracks on both skull and windshield.

Larry would never polish his "Cat" again. His Simonize and Turtle Wax would sit idle on his garage auto-stuff shelf until they hardened into uselessness. His beloved "Cat" would be flattened by a monstrous machine that would encase his and Doris' traces of blood and flesh and Doris' patent leather pump shoe. Maybe one day the crushed metal and plastic and fabric and married human remains would be melted down and a new generation of Pontiac Catalinas would take life.

Doris and Larry's future ceased to exist. They would never feel the joy of Rosemary's future: if she finished college and became a lawyer, who she dated, and if she married and produced their grandchildren? They would never see Mickey's shyness fade and evolve into a strong resolve and lasting friendships. They would never see him grow into a fit and popular teenager. Only the future would see this. And they were no longer part of the future!

Mickey's consciousness went blank as his forehead hit the black, freshly polished, shiny vinyl of the back of the passenger seat where his mother had just been catapulted into the windshield. He didn't know in his unconscious state that his life had changed forever. His passion for banana splits from Jim Dandy's was extinguished forever. He would avoid passing the soda and ice cream shop on Livernois Avenue whenever he could. His closeness with his sister Rosemary would become even closer as they faced the future together. Closeness not only as his sister who had suffered the same loss, but as a surrogate mother. It would be difficult for both at first, but as the ugliness of the accident and their loss faded, they both became comfortable with their roles as a new and different family.

. . . only a nanosecond! Two lives changed forever along with others!

It took only five minutes for the police car to arrive from the McGraw 6th Precinct. Lookie loos and good Samaritans were stopped on the side of the expressway. Those trying to help realized there was nothing they could do. The split grille of the 64 Catalina was now split-in-two as the car met the corner of the bridge abutment and pushed the 421 V-8 and firewall and steering wheel into Larry's chest and lap. The two doors of the coupe had been sealed shut at impact. The good Samaritans attempting to help and looking in the front seat realized professional help was needed to recover the passengers.

The first two police officers to arrive were a seasoned veteran and a young officer who had recently transferred from the small town of Leelanau in Upper Michigan. They managed to weave their cruiser around the pile-up of cars leading up to the accident. They exited the car and the senior officer immediately started giving orders and taking charge of the scene.

"Get some flares out there and get those rubber-neckers back away from the vehicle."

The younger officer retrieved a box of flares from the trunk of the police car and proceeded to remove the caps and strike the flares and stick the wires of the flares into the expansion joints of the concrete pavement. The red halo, around the bright white flame from the flares, glowed eerily over the accident scene atmosphere. The strong hellish-acrid smell of sulphur added appropriately to the Devil's Night evil ambiance.

The senior officer walked slowly over to the vehicle, afraid of what he was about to see, based on the condition of the vehicle. He had been to many auto accidents in his career and he knew it would not be pretty. Auto accidents before the opening of the expressway tended to be mundane, but since the expressway afforded cars to drive at excessive speeds the accidents evolved into more deadly and grisly scenes.

After trying both doors and failing to even budge them, he peered into the passenger's side window and saw the driver pinned to the seat by the steering wheel and the firewall: compressing his chest and gushing all sorts of fluids into the clothing. The female he saw had her head implanted solidly into the windshield. He called the station and ordered the fire department rescue squad and an ambulance on the long shot there might be someone alive. He failed to see Mickey wedged between the seats on the floor over the drive-train hump.

"I called in for a rescue squad and an ambulance. Not sure if we'll need one. I tried the doors. They're sealed shut from the impact. Doesn't look good in there. Let's have a look around and see if there's anything we can retrieve from the accident," The senior officer told the rookie.

As they started to walk around the scene, the rookie saw what appeared to be a body lying up against the bridge support.

"Sergeant! Over here! Holy shit! There's a body here next to the bridge!"

They both walked toward the body and were both shocked to see that the body was headless. With stomachs reeling they moved with molasses like steps afraid of the next thing they would see. Surprising their expectations, there was no blood near the neck of the headless body. The sergeant approached, looked at the neck, touched the body with the toe of his brogan and realized what he was looking at.

"It's a dummy. Someone made a dummy. Probably for Devil's Night."

"What's Devil's Night?" the rookie asked.

"That's right. You're not from around here. Devil's Night here in Detroit is the night before Halloween when the kids roam around and do all sorts of pranks. Some harmless and some . . . not so harmless. I should have told you about it when we started shift."

The rookie shook his head vigorously and walked closer to the dummy. He stooped down and felt the arm of the dummy. He could hear the crinkling of the stiff paper that was stuffed into the red and black plaid shirt.

"Where's the head? Or maybe it didn't have one. Look around." As they looked around the scene, the rookie was distracted by movement on the overhead bridge. He looked up and saw the Styrofoam head still attached to the hangman's noose hanging from the railing.

"Up there Sarge. There's the head."

The sergeant strained his neck as he looked up and saw the old English 𝔇 and the evil clownish red lipstick grin staring down at him.

"Get up there and secure that area. Don't touch anything. Just make sure no one else touches anything and get all those people off the bridge until the State Police get here. I'll call in for backup."

The ambulance and fire rescue squad arrived as the rookie was clearing the bridge from bystanders and lookers. After trying the doors, as the police sergeant did, the rescue team realized that they needed help to pry the doors open. They worked in haste to rescue the occupants not knowing if they were alive or dead. It didn't matter. Their job was rescue. They brought out a 3-foot long crow bar, a 6-foot-long pry bar, and fire axes and began to pry the doors open (Jaws of Life started to be used in the late 1960's). When they finally opened the passenger side door, they cautiously pulled Doris away from the windshield and slid her off the seat and onto a waiting gurney. No sign of life was evident. As they pried open the driver's side door to extract Larry, they noticed Mickey crumpled on the floor in the back seat.

"Hey, guys, get over here. There's a kid in the back seat. See if you can get him out from the other side," One of the rescuers shouted.

Their trained eyes realized that trying to remove Mickey from the back seat with the front seat in the way would be difficult. They quickly used the crow bar to remove the seatback of the passenger seat. One of the rescuers reached in and saw that Mickey was still breathing but unconscious. He grabbed Mickey's shoulder, got his hand under his body and gently lifted and pulled Mickey out of the back seat. Mickey remained unconscious as he was lifted onto a gurney. The ride down to Detroit Receiving Hospital, the best trauma hospital in the state of Michigan, took only a few minutes.

After initial workup protocol checks for serious injury like broken bones or internal bleeding, Mickey was taken to one of the semi-private rooms for his recovery phase. He started to stir as one of the nurses in a sparkling white uniform with a matching white starched nurse's cap, was setting up an IV for dehydration.

"Where . . . am . . . I?" Mickey asked in a slow dry crackling voice. "Where are my mom and dad? What happened?"

The nurse looked sad and lovingly at Mickey. She knew his parents had been killed. She would have to be very careful in her response.

"You've been in a car accident Michael. We need to get you taken care of and get you better. Someone will be in shortly to explain everything." The nurse was hoping that Mickey wouldn't pursue asking about his parents.

"My name is Mickey. I don't like Michael. That's

what my mother calls me when she's angry with me. (He would never hear his mother call him Michael again) Can you call my sister Rosie so she can tell me what's going on?"

"They are contacting your sister right now and I'm sure she will be here shortly. You need to relax Mickey and get some rest. And then we can take care of all your questions."

Mickey started to feel some of the effects of the sedative in the IV and closed his eyes and slipped into another unconscious state.

Sergeant Douglas Emery from the Michigan State Police was put in charge of the investigation of the deadly car crash. Since the accident occurred on a federally funded highway, jurisdiction fell within the purview of the Michigan State Police as proposed by The Federal Highway Act of 1959.

After viewing the scene, the vehicle, and taking photographs with his Yashica 35 mm, he wandered over to backed-up vehicles close to the scene. An older man was leaning on a black Buick Roadmaster that was askew at the front of the line of vehicles. He was staring at the crash scene, with his head slightly bowed.

"Did you see the accident?" Sergeant Emery asked as he approached the man.

The man lifted his head showing teary eyes. Seeing a trooper's hat and the dark blue uniform shirt he responded. "I did, officer. It was terrible. All I saw was a slight blink of brake lights . . . so I hit my brakes as hard as I could, hoping I could avoid hitting him."

"Did you see anything else. There was a report that something was thrown off the overpass."

"No. Nothing. Just the brake lights and the car hitting the bridge. Do you know the condition of the people in the car? I saw there was a man and a woman taken in ambulances and a youngster. Do you know what happened to them?"

"Sorry, I don't." He didn't want to say anything about the fatalities from the accident to the distraught man. "I'm headed over to the hospital shortly to see what the outcome was. Are you okay?" Sergeant Emery asked as he looked into the man's sad eyes.

"Not really. It'll be a while to get this scene out of my head, but I guess I'll be okay. When can I get my car out of here? How long to open the expressway?"

"I'm not sure. It could be a while to take all the photos, take measurements, remove the car and clean up the debris off the road. Maybe they'll have all your cars turn around and go back to the last entrance to get off the road. I've seen that in the past when there's going to be a long shutdown. Good luck and thanks for the help."

After jotting down the man's name and phone number, Sergeant Emery laboriously hiked up the expressway embankment to the service drive where his patrol car was parked. He was familiar with the neighborhood, having grown up a few blocks away. His next stop was to the morgue where he knew the bodies of a man and a woman had been taken.

The familiar trip to the Wayne County Morgue was never a trip he wanted to take, but it was part of the job and he accepted the unpleasant role. The only thing worse would be telling the relatives of the death of their loved ones.

He made his way down to the autopsy room in the morgue and rang the doorbell on the side of the opaque windowed door. A familiar face greeted him with a serious look.

"Hello Sergeant. Here for the IDs. I found a wallet in his pants that will help you with that," the dark-skinned autopsy doctor offered in a sing-songy accent.

Sergeant Emery opened the imitation-leather dual-fold wallet. In the plastic window was a black and white wedding photo from years ago, with a young, beaming, perfect couple. He looked into the billfold section and saw a few singles, a five and one twenty-dollar bill. Also in that section were two school pictures: a smiling graduation picture of a strikingly beautiful coed, and a picture of a grinning chubby younger boy. He looked at the address on the driver's license and realized that the driver lived in the area, a neighborhood of mostly Polish Catholics, and they probably attended Saint Francis Church. His thought was to go to the rectory and see if he could get more information on the family before doing the death announcement to the next of kin. It might be easier having more personal information, he thought.

On his ride over to Saint Francis his mind was racing with what he had just witnessed at the scene of the accident and the pictures he found in the wallet. He couldn't remember the route he took as he parked on Wesson Street in front of Saint Francis of Assisi Catholic Church rectory.

Sergeant Emery walked up the cement steps to the leaded-glass door of the rectory. He rang the doorbell that sounded with an appropriate church-bell chime and waited for someone to answer.

Within a minute a stocky unshaven man in a v neck tee shirt and black pants answered the door.

"Good evening officer. Can I help you?"

"Good evening Father. Yes, you can.

"Come on in out of the cold." Father John said as he opened and held the door as Sergeant Emery entered. He followed Father John into a small sitting room off of the vestibule. Sergeant Emery removed his Smokey the Bear trooper's hat and took a seat on the overstuffed love seat and Father John took a seat in a matching chair.

"My name is Emery, Doug Emery. I'm a Michigan State Trooper. I was a parishioner here years ago, Father, when I was growing up, so I know the Church. I'm in charge of a fatal car accident investigation on the expressway and I need some information and maybe some help in the way of moral support. Do you have any parishioners here by the name of Lesko?"

"We do. There is more than one family by that name. Can you give me a first name?"

Sergeant Emery reached into his pocket and pulled out the wallet and removed the driver's license and handed it to Father John.

Father John reached for the license and stared at it for a moment. His face went from neutral to sad. "Yes, Larry and his family are parishioners here. I'm afraid to ask, but what is the situation?" Father John asked as he leaned over and handed the license back to Sergeant Emery. He placed his elbows on his knees and his face in his hands waiting for a response.

"I can tell you that both parents didn't make it. There was a horrific one-car crash on the expressway at the Wesson Street overpass. When I saw Mr. Lesko's license with the address, I guessed that he might be a parishioner here. The only good news – if you could call it that – is the young boy that was in the car in the rear seat, survived. He's at Receiving Hospital right now being treated. Can you tell me if there any other family members?"

Father John paused for a second to let the tragic news sink in before he answered.

"Yes. The boy is probably Mickey. He's around 13 years old. A very nice boy and an altar boy here at Saint Francis. There is also a girl by the name of Rosemary. She's around 17. I think she just graduated from high school and was thinking of going to U of D. They were both in my catechism classes and my preparation classes for First Holy Communion and Confirmation. What a tragedy. How can I help? Anything! Anything I can do to help!"

"You can help, Father. That's why I'm here. I have to inform the immediate family about the deaths . . . I guess that's Rosemary now! These things are never easy. I'm sure you've had your share of these dire situations in your line of work."

"I have. Both here at the Church and I was a chaplain serving in Germany during the War . . . so yes, I've had my share. I can go with you. And I know where they live. Give me a minute to put on my collar and tell the Pastor, Monsignor Gannas, where I'm going."

During the short ride over to the Lesko house Father John gave as much information as he could remember about the family. Impressing on him that they were a tight knit family with children that only brought joy to the family. Larry was a hard-working caring father and husband. Doris was also a loving wife and mother. The family were steady church-goers and participated in church activities on a regular basis. In short – they were the ideal, Polish, Catholic, American family. Now . . . that ideal family was shattered into bits on the I-94 expressway.

Rosemary had just finished a marathon gab session on the phone with her best friend Lorraine. Her mouth was dry from talking so she wandered downstairs into the kitchen at the rear of the house and peeked into the refrigerator. She grabbed a bottle of Faygo root beer, uncapped it and took a long swig. As she closed the refrigerator, she heard the doorbell ring.

"Who's that?" she said to herself.

She could see two figures on the front porch. As she opened the door, she saw Father John's Roman collar and a uniformed officer in the doorway. She had a look of surprise and doom on her face.

"Can we come in Rosemary. We need to talk to you," Father John said in as friendly a voice as he could conjure up.

She didn't answer. She just opened the door and waited for the two men to enter. They walked through the tiny vestibule into a large dining room. Father John pulled out one of the chairs and motioned for Rosemary to take a seat. She set down the Faygo pop on the table and sat down. She laced her fingers and rested them on the table that had a large crocheted-lace, overly starched, aging, white, tablecloth that her mother had made. Father John and Sergeant Emery took seats on the opposite side of the table.

"This is Sergeant Emery from the State Police, Rosemary. I'm afraid that we have some bad news." Rosemary's face, already with the look of dread, intensified even more. *Just do it*, he thought! "Your mother and father have been killed in an accident on the expressway. Mickey is in the hospital down at Receiving." Rosemary raised her hands to her mouth and shouted. "NO. NO! What are you saying? They just went out a little while ago and were going down to Jim Dandy's for some ice cream. This can't be true. NO. NO, NO!" The words faded into sobs with tears rolling down her face. Father John looked around for some Kleenex but didn't see any. He reached into his back pocket and pulled out a fresh, neatly folded hand-kerchief, that he always kept for such occasions, and offered it to Rosemary.

Rosemary was a dark-haired mixture of cute and beautiful. She wore her hair in a short cropped easy to care coiffure. She took the handkerchief and wiped her cheeks and dabbed her eyes.

Father John waited, along with Sergeant Emery, for the terrible news to start to sink in. They both knew that it would take a long time — for this shock to her life — to begin to ease. The realization that she would have to make major decisions in the near future and to be with her brother in the hospital put somewhat of an urgency in the situation. They waited and waited as Rosemary continued to sob. Then finally, Sergeant Emery spoke. "Rosemary, I know this is a very difficult thing to hear and both Father John and myself are here to help with anything you need. Are there any other family members we can contact?" Rosemary shook her head.

"It's important right now to get to the hospital and talk to Mickey. He needs you and he needs to know what's going on. I'm sure he's anxious."

"My Aunt, Anna, my mother's sister, lives on the next block. We should call her or go over there and tell her." Rosemary squeaked out between sobs and wipes with Father John's handkerchief.

Rosemary gave Father John the phone number. He called Aunt Anna and told her the story briefly without mentioning any of the deaths. He told her to meet them at Receiving Hospital.

Rosemary put on blue jeans and tennis shoes and grabbed a jacket and they all rode down to the hospital in the navy-blue Michigan State Police car.

They didn't talk about the accident on the way to the hospital. Rosemary's sobs were on the wane but would re-energize when she saw Mickey. Both Father John and Sergeant Emery, with their past experience in these matters knew that it was best for the families of the victims to ask for information rather than them offering up any. It seemed to be better and more calmly received in that manner.

They parked in the *Reserved for Official Cars* parking lot. Father John led the way, knowing from past Extreme Unction administrations, where to go. He asked at the first nurse's station for the room for Michael Lesko and was directed to the second floor. When they entered the room, Aunt Anna was already there, holding Mickey's hand with one hand and a crystal rosary in the other hand. Her eyes moistened with new tears as she saw Rosemary and a trooper and a priest.

Rosemary quickly raced to Aunt Anna's side and joined her in holding Mickey's other hand. Sergeant

Emery took the lead. He softly told Mickey and Aunt Anna what had happened and why they were there. Aunt Anna's sobs intensified. Mickey just stared at the uniformed trooper. His mind went back to the last thing he remembered – the whoosh of cars and then nothing.

Aunt Anna tried to ease the situation that Rosemary and Mickey were in, even though her heart was turning to syrup after receiving the news that her sister and brother-in-law had been killed.

"Rosemary, Mickey, my Dears, I am here. We will get through this together. I will work with Father John and you to make sure we have a holy, proper and memorable celebration for your parents." She consciously, or unconsciously, avoided the word 'funeral'.

Mickey still remained silent. Either from shock or from a concussion he may have suffered. Or maybe from both!

Sergeant Emery unbuttoned and reached into his heavily starched breast pocket and pulled out business cards which he handed to Father John, Rosemary, and Anna. "I'll be leaving now. Father, can you get a ride back with Miss Borovic and Rosemary?" Aunt Anna nodded.

"You can call me at any time if there's something you need or something you want to ask me. I'm sorry but the investigation (avoiding the words car accident) may take a while, but, as soon as I have any new information, I will pass it along. Just let me know who I should call first?" He looked from Rosemary to Aunt Anna to Father John.

"You can call me." Aunt Anna offered. "Is that okay with you, Rosemary?"

"Yes. Fine."

Mickey was still quiet. Blankly staring from face to face.

"Father, can I call you tomorrow morning to start the arrangements?" Anna asked.

"That would be great. After the Noon Mass is the best time. Tomorrow is Sunday and I have to say the Noon Mass. I can contact Jarzembowski's Funeral Parlor for you so they can start on the planning, if you want. Let me know. I'll wait for your call."

"Thank you, Father, please call them. And Rosemary, you can stay with me tonight or for however long you want or need to."

Rosemary nodded.

After the attending nurse came in and administered another mild sedative into Mickey's IV she asked, "Could you please leave and let him get some rest? You can return in the morning. And . . . he will probably be released on Monday, since tomorrow is Halloween and a Sunday with no releases on Sunday."

She didn't mention that Monday is All Saints Day. And that Tuesday was All Souls Day – Day of the Dead!

3

Clubhouse

The house was vacant with a hand-made battered, weathered, "for sale" sign on the front lawn. The owners had moved out over a year ago and the house remained empty. The boys' curiosity had led to an unlocked kitchen window at the rear of the house. They all shinnied up, entered and explored the house and found a room in the basement that was not visible from the outside. They called it their clubhouse and would meet there occasionally to smoke and talk and Georgie would steal a bottle, or two, of his father's beer. They would pass it around and take swigs and brag about imaginary girls they felt-up.

Georgie was the first to arrive at the vacant house. He cautiously made his way to the rear of the house, being careful not to be seen by anyone. He pushed up on the double-hung window and winced as the window replied with a loud creak. He shinnied up and into the house. He dropped onto the linoleum-floored kitchen and waited for the other four boys to arrive. He wandered through the house looking at the dust covered floors and smatterings of empty boxes and a few pieces of broken furniture, including an old Formica kitchen table. There was a wisp of light from the streetlight in front of the house that illuminated the dust blanket. As he inhaled the heavy, dusty smell, he wondered. *"How does all this dust get in here? Everything is shut tight. Oh well."* As his mind wandered, he heard the window repeat its screech and he went back to the kitchen. All the boys were in the house now.

"Okay guys, down to the clubhouse and keep it quiet," Georgie looked at all of them as his whispers echoed softly in the empty room.

They single-filed down the linoleum covered wooden steps into the basement and went directly into what was once an oversize pantry with handmade shelves on one wall holding an unimpressive array of canning jars. The room had no windows and was presenting a dank musty odor. Georgie snapped on a flashlight they kept there. He carefully placed the flat end of the flashlight on an upturned orange crate they had dragged from another part of the basement. The top of the crate had a mound of multi-colored wax that helped steady the flashlight upright. The light from the flashlight bounced off the walls and ceiling and onto the excited faces of all five boys.

Georgie, in his leader role was about to make an important quasi-adult decision. He thought carefully. It was deadly quiet!

"Here's the plan guys. We don't know what happened, except there was a car crash . . . I guess. No big deal. They probably have insurance and their cars will be fixed or they'll get new ones. Could be a good thing. We have to be careful about what we do now. We don't want to be blamed. So . . . let's do this." He reached inside the orange crate and pulled out a crumpled brown lunch bag. He emptied the bag onto the top of the crate next to the wax mound supporting the flashlight. It was a rainbow of colored dinner candles that the boys had contributed from forgotten candles they found in their mothers' hutches and kitchen drawers. They were lit on occasion to light their clubhouse when they sat around smoking and swigging on beer and bullshiting about girls.

"What we're going to do is give us an alibi. That's what we need . . . an alibi. We're going to go down to the corner at Steve's Drug Store and wait for a police car to pass by and we're going to start waxing the drug store windows. The cops will catch us and then we'll have an alibi taking us away from the accident scene. Any questions?"

Their frightened faces, with question marks written all over them, stared at Georgie. They were all trying to make sense out of . . . and understand his plan.

"Are you fuckin crazy Georgie? They might drag our sorry asses down to the police station and then what? They'll call our parents and then we're shit. Can't we just let it go and hope for the best?" Jimmy pleaded as the other three boys just listened.

"We could take a chance . . . but then maybe they'll try to nail us for the car crash. I'd sooner have an alibi. What do you guys think? Let's take a vote. Raise your hands if you like my idea. Majority wins."

The other three boys looked at each other and hesitated. Then Lenny slowly raised his hand and the other two, Stanley and Mark followed suit. They were either scared of being caught as the culprits of the accident or too scared to disagree with Georgie. It didn't matter — majority would rule.

"Okay that settles it. Everyone grab a candle and let's go." Jimmy reluctantly grabbed a candle. The others followed.

As they walked slowly, the two blocks to Steve's Drug Store, Georgie gave further instructions. He said that they would stand on the corner and wait until they saw a police cruiser, which were plentiful on this Devil's Night, and then start waxing the windows.

They didn't want to get caught by Steve before the police got there.

They didn't wait long. Within five minutes a black and white Detroit police car was spotted coming from Livernois Avenue down Buchanan Street toward Steve's Drug Store. They started to wax.

The police car pulled up to the curb emitting a short blast from the siren. The boys didn't run but looked at the car as two burly, seasoned, police officers exited the car and walked over to the boys. One of the police officers, with a blonde military brush cut and a pot belly, retrieved his billy club from the front seat. He wrapped the rawhide thong around his wrist and proceeded to slap the palm of his hand as he approached the boys.

"What's going on here boys? Trying to have a little fun? No one answered the rhetorical questions.

"Okay, line up against the window there," the officer said as he pointed his billy club at the store's side window.

"Here's what we're gonna do, my little devil pranksters. My partner here is going to go inside and tell Steve what's going on here." He motioned with a nod of his head to his junior partner to go inside.

"I'm going to take your names and phone numbers and send you on home. But . . . but you will return tomorrow with some window scraper blades and clean the shit of off these windows. If any of you don't show tomorrow then I'll contact your parents and maybe even charge you guys and your parents with a fine and a misdemeanor. How does that sound? Got it?"

They all nervously replied "Yes, officer." Except Georgie. He was smiling and taking pride in that his plan was working. They were caught more than a mile away from the expressway. How could they be involved?

4

Aftermath

Sergeant Emery spent the next week doing due diligence in the investigation of the accident. He went door to door at all of the closest houses that lined the service drives on both sides of I-94. No one saw the accident. The closest he came to an eye witness was the elderly man he interviewed at the scene. One of the householders heard the crash and called the police but never saw the crash. He searched the overpass for any clues left behind by whoever dropped the dummy off the bridge. There was little if any. The handrail that he had the forensic department examine only found partial prints. If there were any prints there, they were probably wiped clean by pedestrians sliding their hands along the rail as they crossed the bridge and gawked at the accident below.

The most significant clue he got was from the dummy. It was taken to the police station and disassembled, looking for clues. One of the pockets of the Wranglers had a receipt slip in the front pocket for a purchase of a garden rake from a local feed store. Sergeant Emery followed the lead and inquired from the store owner if he could ask his employees if they remember someone buying a garden rake recently. One of the clerks did remember, which led Sergeant Emery to the house that had the dummy on the porch. Trooper Emery was encouraged that he had found a clue leading to the accident. He talked to the man and woman and listened as they explained that they had built the dummy. He was satisfied they were not involved after they told him that the dummy had been stolen off their porch on Devil's Night. He could see that they were deeply impacted by the fact that their creation was directly involved in the death of two people from their neighborhood. The case went cold!

They all arrived the next morning as ordered by the police officer. Some had single edge safety razors for scrapping and some brought paring knives. Without any instructions they started to scrape the wax they applied the night before. Georgie still had a wry smile on his face, with the knowledge that this was his plan and it was working . . . so far.

Steve was irked by the scraping noise on his window and went outside to see what was going on. He was a short rotund man. His stomach stuck out from a white, much too small pharmacist's coat with his name embroidered in black over the breast pocket. He peeked around the corner and saw the boys hard at work. He went back inside and retrieved a bucket of water, a sponge and a squeegee. He went back outside and placed the bucket down without saying a word. He had a wry revengeful smile that he flashed at the boys as he went back inside.

They finished and waited for the police officer to arrive and verify their cleaning of the window. A police officer from the night before arrived shortly after they finished. He looked and nodded his head admirably at their crystal-clear masterpiece and told them good job and said they could go home now.

"Okay guys. Looks like our plan is working. We just have to lay low for a while until this thing blows over. By next week it will all be forgotten and we'll be in the clear. Let's split and we'll meet tonight when we go beggin. Got your costumes all picked out? The usual hobos, I guess, for all of us." Georgie said.

Without any further conversation they all left and went home.

It didn't take long for the news to spread throughout the neighborhood. Larry and Doris and Mickey were in a car accident on the freeway and Larry and Doris were killed. This type of horrific neighborhood news spread faster than any newspaper or radio could ever achieve. The five boys eventually heard of the deaths and all were shaken to different degrees. Some felt remorse, some felt fear and some felt both. The thing they had in common — except for Georgie — is they were all scared that it would only be a matter of time before they would all be found out.

When they met that night, nothing had to be said. It was all on their faces. And the usual fun-filled Halloween ritual of begging for candy by shouting out "Help the Poor" on porch steps was diminished significantly. The friendship that was starting to evolve into a lasting one was now melting like October snow on warm sidewalks.

The only thing they did discuss was, the word was out there would be a funeral on Friday and school would be suspended. They would all be attending the funeral with their parents — except for Georgie!

Jimmy tried to ease his mind and the other four with some words of caution. "Listen guys. This has got to stay with us. We can't talk about it with anyone. We can't talk about it with even the five of us. We have to forget about it and move on. Do you all agree? What else can we do?" They all looked at each other: some dry-eyed and some struggling to hold their tears back.

Lenny responded. "What if we turned ourselves in? We didn't mean any harm. It was just a prank that went wrong. They'll understand. Then we would have it off our chest and then we could move on. What do you guys think? Huh?"

"No way Lenny." Georgie snapped. We don't know what they will do. Do you want to go to prison? People died. I don't think they're going to slap us on the wrist and say okay it was just a prank. We have to do what Jimmy said. Keep our mouths shut no matter what . . . even amongst ourselves. And especially around Mickey!"

They shook their bowed heads and went their separate ways!

The twin-funerals that blended into one, were held the Friday after the accident. After release of the bodies from the morgue, they were taken to Jarzembowski Funeral Parlor for the traditional two day viewing prior to the funerals at a Requiem Mass at Saint Francis. The Mass was complete with a choir singing tear-producing hymns and the permeation of incense throughout the church. It was the first time that Saint Francis Church had celebrated a funeral Mass for two people at the same time.

Aunt Anna, Rosemary, and Mickey sat in the first pew next to the pall covered caskets that were sitting side by side in the wide intersection of the Church's nave and transverse aisles. The Church was standing room only with relatives, neighbors, friends and non-acquaintances just wanting to pay their respects for such tragic deaths. Aunt Anna held her black rosary throughout the Mass as she wiped away her tears. Rosemary held on to Aunt Anna's cold hand on one side of her and Mickey's warm sweaty hand on the other side. Mickey remained quiet and stared into the apse of the church with nothing registering.

The solemn funeral procession on its way to Saint Hedwig Cemetery, made an intentional turn onto 31st Street and slowed as it paid the traditional respectful custom and stopped in front of the Lesko residence. It would be Larry's and Doris' last visit to their beloved home. Rosemary and Aunt Anna looked out the window as the limousine stopped. Mickey stared at the back of the familiar vinyl seat-back and a shiver went through his body as his memory was jolted back to that day. He remained quiet.

It was a good day for a funeral (if there is such a thing?) The temperature was in the low forties with a light moisture falling, trying to make up its mind between snow or cold rain. It was a traditional Polish funeral. Father John prayed over Larry and Doris in the caskets that were sitting side by side next to open graves. He sprinkled holy water onto the caskets as the immediate family sat at the head of the caskets with heads bowed. The finale began that brought most to tears — the singing of the Polish funeral song *Witaj Krolowo Nieba (Hail Queen of Heaven)*. The older Polish knew the words and the meaning: the younger knew the song and the outcome. At the first word *Witaj*, the tears started anew and the sobs echoed across the flat grave-marker-covered hallowed grounds.

The ceremony ended with the participants taking flowers, that were brought from the funeral parlor, and placing them on the caskets. The immediate family sat with blank stares until it was their turn. The weather made up its mind as Rosemary and Anna placed a red and yellow rose on the caskets that contrasted with sparkling snow.

5

New Family

The day after the funeral, Aunt Anna, Anna Borovic, Doris' older sister, came over to see about Rosemary and Mickey. She was a middle-aged spinster. She had a traumatic loss of her betrothed in her early twenties. He was killed in battle while serving in the Army in Italy. That left an emotional scar, that remained through the years, shutting out any future relationships. She had bluish gray hair, usually worn in a bun with different colored ribbons holding her hair in place. She had a zoftig body and carried herself with a healthy posture.

Mickey and Rosemarie were in the kitchen finishing their breakfast of fried eggs and toast when she let herself in the front door.

"Good morning children. Finishing breakfast, I see. When you're done and have everything cleaned up, I'd like to go over some things with you that you may not have thought about. Okay?"

"Okay Aunt Anna." Rosemary replied. Mickey remained silent.

Rosemary was always the cleaner-upper after family meals and Mickey helped occasionally. Mickey's chores consisted of hauling ashes from the coal burning furnace in the basement and collecting the newspapers and bundling them to be sold to the sheeny man, who travelled the alleys and bought most anything of value. He was allowed to keep whatever meager change the newspapers brought. He was also given a dollar a week for carrying out his chores. Rosemary earned a modest amount from occasional babysitting and was given additional allowance whenever she needed it. That was the extent of their personal financial experience. Aunt Anna was about to enhance that experience on this first of many household finance meetings.

"Let's go in the dining room and sit at the big table. That would be more comfortable . . . and Rosie, get a pad of paper and a pencil to take some notes."

They sat at the dining room table. Rosemary felt the stiffly starched crocheted table cloth and remembered sitting across from Father John and the state trooper when they told her the dire news about her parents. She put her hands on her lap – trying to forget!

"I know this is sudden to be talking about money after what we've all been through, but we have to deal with it, so let's get it done and we can put it behind us. Rosemary, you have to go through your parents' papers looking for insurance policies, house mortgage payments, utility bills, tax bills, and any other official looking papers. I can help you with it if you want and Mickey, I think you should join your sister in looking through the papers. Like it or not you are now the man of the family." Mickey forced a small smile at Aunt Anna's comment.

"My mother paid all the bills. Dad just 'brought home the bacon' as my mother would say." This brought a bittersweet smile to all of their faces. "My mother was very efficient with the bills and the bill paying. She kept all of the paperwork and receipts here in the china cabinet drawer. I know she paid a lot of the bills with money-orders from Stokfisz's drug store and she kept all those receipts."

"One thing that I remember your mother telling me . . . and this is a good thing. I think she said that your father had a life insurance policy with The Knights of Columbus where he was a member. And better than that, she said he had a mortgage insurance policy that should pay off the mortgage. We'll have to find the paperwork on that – for sure! Rosemary was taking copious notes. Mickey sat beside her, across from Aunt Anna and peeked at the notepad as Rosemary wrote, showing a mild interest.

The next day Rosemary decided to start the search. She started in the most likely spot – the china cabinet that covered the wall between two bedrooms. It was the universal collection spot for not only the fine china for special occasions but also the linens and tablecloths, towels, candles, glassware and two drawers that were filled with bills and receipts and vital documents.

With Mickey's help they went through all of the papers, one by one, and checked off Rosemary's checklist as they found each item. They stacked different receipts: money order stubs, utility bills, tax notices, and miscellaneous. As Aunt Anna said, they found two insurance policies, one from Prudential for Doris and one for Larry from The Knights of Columbus. They also found the FHA mortgage insurance document. Rosemary grabbed the legal-sized, multi-page, stapled document and waived it at Mickey. "We got it Mickey. I think this means we don't have to worry about paying for the house or going to live with Aunt Anna." Mickey opened his arms and they smiled and hugged. This was the first emotion that Mickey had shown since that day!

Rosemary called Aunt Anna and told her what they had found and asked her to come over later or the next day to review the paperwork. Mickey was still sitting at the dining room table shuffling through the papers trying to understand all of them and showing a worried look.

"Mickey, let's have lunch and then we can talk about ourselves and what we're facing and how we can wade ourselves through all of this. I know you're hurting about losing Mom and Dad and so am I. But we have to face it and move on. That doesn't mean forgetting about them. That will never happen! We just have to carry on the way we think that they would want us to. Okay? Let's have lunch and then we can talk."

After a lunch of baloney sandwiches and Better Made potato chips, Rosemary started the conversation. "We'll need a car since Dad's Cat was totaled." Mickey pinched his throat to keep from sobbing at the word Cat. "I think we'll get some money from the insurance police to replace it. We can look around the neighborhood for someone selling a used one. There's always a clunker or two with for sale signs in driveways." Mickey nodded.

After reviewing all the paperwork and deciding to buy a car and working with Aunt Anna on all the details, Rosemary felt somewhat secure that their finances were in order and they would have minimal worry going forward. The question of how much Social

Security survivor's benefits they would get, would have to be looked into. Aunt Anna told the children they would qualify. It was just a question of how much and when they would receive the payments. Aunt Anna scheduled a meeting at the local Social Security office with her and Rosemary to fill out all the appropriate paperwork and present death certificates for both parents. Aunt Anna suggested to Rosemary, that once the Social Security payments were realized, she may have to put off college for a while and find a job. Another disappointment that Rosemary and Mickey would have to face along with all the rest that were pushed into their young lives.

It had been a few weeks and routines were getting established between Rosemary and Mickey. The one elephant in the room that was bothering both of them was their parent's belongings. It consisted of clothes, shoes, jewelry, tools, and a modest collections of coins, stamps, sports memorabilia, etc. Rosemary went into their parent's bedroom one morning and reluctantly peered into the modest sized closet. It was neatly separated with Larry clothes to one side and Doris's clothes on the other. Their shoes were neatly arranged on the floor with two pair sadly missing!

"Mickey, could you join me in here for a minute?"

Rosemary peeked her head out of the bedroom seeing Mickey reading a comic book at the dining room table.

"Sure. What do you need?" Mickey responded.

"It's Mom's and Dad's clothes and stuff. We have to go through it and donate it or keep whatever. I know it's going to be tough on both of us but it has to get done. The up-side, if there is an upside, is that it won't keep reminding us of the loss. Okay?"

"Yeah, I guess"

"I'm going to start with Mom's and keep what Aunt Anna might want. I know there isn't anything I would wear of Mom's so that part is easy. Sorry Mom." Rosemary looked up with her hands folded in prayer.

"I doubt if there's anything that I would keep of Dad's either. Sorry Dad." Mickey smiled and aped Rosemary's look upward and praying hands plea.

While Rosemary was sorting through and bagging the clothes Mickey wandered off to the garage to look at Larry's tools and car stuff. His memories of helping his dad work on the Cat came drifting back. He recalled his dad telling him how to set the points on the distributer using the proper gap and how to set gaps and change spark plugs and change the oil regularly. This recall seemed to light a spark in Mickey as he looked at the various assortments of car wax, rubbing compound, Larry's tool box, and the Comet cleanser that was used to keep the Cat's whitewalls pure white. He thought that these experiences would come in handy in keeping whatever car Rosemary would buy in working order. A smile of contentment lit up his face for the first time since the accident.

The sorting and bagging took only a few hours since there were little choices to be made. Rosemary said she would call Saint Vincent DePaul to donate the clothes after Aunt Anna looked them over

Mickey kept Larry's orange and blue Tiger's cap and his jacket with a large English on the chest that was still in a plastic cleaner's bag, ready for the next season. The season that would never come for Larry.

⚜

Mickey slept well after a few weeks. He pushed the loneliness of the absence of his father and mother out of his mind by thinking of one of the interests that he developed while working on cars with his dad. He thought about Rosie buying a used car that he could work on and contribute to the new family and repay her for her support in this difficult time. It worked most every night in allowing him to drift into a restful sleep.

Rosemary had a more difficult time falling asleep. When she did, it was usually short lived and she would wake in the middle of the night with nightmares as she struggled to fall back asleep. On one of those nights, she got up, slipped on her bathrobe and wandered into her mother's and father's bedroom. She wanted to smell their familiar smell in hopes of relaxing her and allowing her to get some rest. The bedding had not been changed since the funerals in hopes of keeping their presence, at least for a while.

She pulled back the *pierzyna*, a Polish quilt that her grandmother had made, and pulled back the sheet. She laid on her mother's side resting her head on her mother's pillow and inhaling what was left of her mother's scent. It worked and she fell asleep on her mother's tear moistened pillow. So, this became a ritual for her whenever the pangs of loss and sleep would not come. These smells could ease her into a pleasant dream filled sleep. The door to their parent's room remained open and the smells faded. As they did, Rosemary sprinkled their pillows with her father's Old Spice and her mother's Chanel no 5 – special gifts that Mickey and her had given to their mother and father on Mother's Day and Father's Day. The last special days that they had spent together!

6

Back to School

It was the Monday after the accident and the funerals. School was resuming. Four of the five boys were extremely nervous thinking about what they were a party to. Georgie saw the worried look on all of their faces and he was worried that if one of the other boys was questioned about that night, they might open up. The first thing he did was to tell the other boys to meet him at the clubhouse after school in the abandoned house. It wasn't a request — it was an order!

At Saint Francis Grade School, each grade had one room. Georgie had flunked one grade and was held back so he was a year older than all the other classmates in the eighth-grade classroom. He knew he had to get control of the boys otherwise they would crumble and tell someone about what had happened on that Devil's Night.

He rounded them up and gave them the order. "Listen you guys. I can see the look of worry on your faces and I'm not happy. We have to meet after school and discuss our situation. Head down to our clubhouse after class lets out and we'll talk."

The boys were nervous for the rest of the day, fidgeting in their seats and unable to concentrate on what Sister Angelica was trying to teach. They hurriedly filed out of class when she gave them their assignments for the day and they walked silently down to the clubhouse. Georgie lagging behind.

The basement clubhouse retained its dire ambiance of mold and dampness due to being closed up for a long time. Spider webs were inundating all the corners of the basement and had made their way into the clubhouse room. There was a collection of boxes and orange crates the boys had collected and were used for sitting on. They sat in silence and swatted away the cobwebs as they sat and waited for Georgie to talk. Georgie got there shortly after the boys and looked at them and paced a bit and scratched his chin.

"Okay guys. Here's the plan and you have to follow it to a "T" or else we're all in trouble. I don't know for sure but we have to assume that the cops or someone else, like Mickey's relatives, are going to know that we might have been around the neighborhood that night and we might be involved. Like I said, I don't know for sure but we have to be careful. Anybody have anything to say?"

They all looked at each other and then Jimmy said. "What do you suppose we do if someone questions us?"

"You have to make sure you don't tell no one – and I mean no one – that we were anywhere near Wesson Street and for sure nowhere near the expressway. If they ask, we tell them that we were hanging around the corner of Steve's Drug Store after we bought the bread at Kosta's. If you don't know what to say just say you don't remember. And – we have the excuse – that we were waxing windows. Remember? That's our way out. So, is everyone clear on what to do?"

They all shook their heads with hesitance and un-sureness and answered together. "Clear!"

They silently and carefully left the clubhouse and crawled out the back window of the house, careful that no one saw them. They never thought about un-locking the back door after they tried to open it from the outside and found it locked. The boys were just a little more relaxed now that Georgie told them what to say if someone questioned them. But there was that nervousness in the back of their minds, realizing what they had done and that someone might find out!

Lenny Solack was probably the most nervous and the most concerned of all of the boys. He walked home by himself after he split up from the rest of boys.

He wasn't as concerned about someone finding out, as he was of his conscious telling him that he should tell someone and get it over with and suffer the consequences. But who to tell? There was his mother who was mostly understanding in his infrequent minor troubles like poor report card marks or skipping school. His father was a bit less understanding so he wasn't an option. What about Father John in confession? But he convinced himself that what they did wasn't a sin — at least, not a mortal sin —maybe a venial sin. They didn't intend to hurt anyone. Maybe he was the person to tell? He certainly didn't want to tell the police. These troubling thoughts followed him all the way home until he was greeted by his mother as he entered the kitchen through the back door.

"Hi Lenny. Good day at school?"

"It was okay. I guess."

"You look a bit worried. Are you okay?'

"I'm fine. Just a little tired. I think I'll take a little nap before I start my homework."

Lenny laid on his bed with his face in the pillow and thoughts raced through his mind on what to do.

7

Investigation

Trooper Doug Emery had his share of auto accident investigations and most of them were routine. Observe the accident site, interview any witnesses, interview the surviving occupants, take photos and measurements of the scene. impound the vehicles, if necessary, fill out the accident report in detail, file it, and move on. But this auto collision was different, starting with the time he first came on the scene, until he met with Rosemary Lesko and told her of the death of her parents, and his meeting with Mickey and Aunt Anna at the hospital.

He decided that this accident or collision, or however it was classified, was different. The dummy scarecrow that was found at the scene added to the bizarreness and mystery of how the accident really happened. He felt an obligation to Mickey and Rosemary to give them at least some closure as to how, why, and who were involved in this tragedy. He decided to meet with his post commander the next morning.

After roll call and daily assignments, Trooper Emery approached his Commander, Commander Philip Ayolla, and asked him for a few minutes to discuss a matter. Commander Ayolla nodded and told him to follow him to his office. The office was in a corner of the squad room with venetian blind windows and a frosted glass door. Doug took a seat facing the neatly organized desk. Their relationship since Doug Emery joined the Michigan State Police was comfortable from the start. Doug respected the twenty plus years that Commander Ayolla had served on the force prior to his Command assignment.

"I have a favor to ask you Commander. I know you read my report on the tragic accident that killed the Lesko parents and put the younger son in the hospital. All things are pointing to some sort of prank or intentional act to cause the accident and the deaths. I don't have any outstanding assignments other than expressway patrol, so I was wondering if I could spend some time investigating further into this incident. I am convinced that someone, probably more than one, are responsible for this. I feel that we owe the surviving children and the rest of the family some answers so that they can at least know how and who did this. What do you think?"

Commander Ayolla scratched his chin and leaned back in his swivel chair with his fingers laced on his slight paunch. "I guess that's a worthy assignment. You're right. We do owe these people some answers and if someone is responsible for actually planning to have cars crash, then they need to be held responsible. What else do you need? And how long do you think it will take? Any idea?"

"Thanks Commander. I'd like the use of one of the cadets for a day or two. I'd like to start by looking into State Patrol reports and then Detroit Police Precinct reports to see if there were any arrests or reports or citations of any kind on the day it happened and see where that leads me. How does that sound and can I use one of the cadets?"

Commander Ayolla nodded. "You can have one of the cadets for a day or two. See the sergeant that's in charge of the cadets and tell him I said okay. Your plan sounds reasonable and I hope you can come up with something in a reasonable amount of time. Let me know on a daily basis the progress or any roadblocks we need to discuss. Okay?"

"Okay Commander and thanks again. I'll get right on it."

Doug Emery left the office, with a smile, and went immediately to the sergeant that had cadets working for him and told him the plan that was approved by the Commander.

Trooper Emery introduced himself to Cadet Jack Crocker, and explained to him the plan to research all Michigan State Police and Detroit Police reports for the night of Saturday October 30 of that year. They would start with their post and move on to the Detroit precinct that covered the area of the crash scene.

It was a laborious task, but a valuable teaching moment for Cadet Crocker as he read through every imaginable police report. Files of police reports were kept in file cabinets and filed by date. They weren't sorted by type of crime or ordinance violation so it was a matter of looking through page by page and reading the reports to see if they could in any way be related to the accident.

The first day of reading and sorting through the Michigan State Post files was fruitless. All that was uncovered were mostly minor traffic accidents and re-quests for assistance in domestic disputes.

The second day was even more work intense. The 6th precinct of the Detroit Police Department, located on McGraw avenue had the same sort of record keep-ing for their police reports. However, they were even more inclusive than the State Police reports. Once again, the reports were kept in file drawers by date and not separated by types of offense or crime. After they read through a drawer full of reports, with their eyes blearing from redundant reports of drunkenness, neighbor disturbances, domestic violence, minor traffic accidents, jay walking, dog attacks, loitering and littering – they finally had a hit.

Cadet Crocker found a report by Officer Kovac of five juveniles caught waxing windows at Steve's Drug Store in the general vicinity of the accident. The time, cross streets, and names and phone numbers of the teenagers involved were contained in the report. The time was suspiciously close to the time of the accident.

Cadet Crocker handed the report to Doug. He rubbed his eyes, sat back in his chair with his feet on an open desk drawer and slowly read the report and took notes as he read.

"I think you've got something here Jack. What I'm going to do is contact the reporting officer and see if it's something we should pursue. Thanks for your help and you can head back to your regular duties. If this report doesn't pan out, we may have to resume the search. I'll give your sergeant a good report on the help you gave me." Cadet Crocker thanked Doug and left the 6th precinct. Doug went to the day-watch sergeant and asked to see Officer Kovac.

Doug waited for Officer Kovac in a small 10 x12 foot interrogation room. It smelled from coffee, cigarette smoke and nervous sweat. There was a small table with a gold, tin, ash-encrusted ashtray on it and two worn, black, swivel-desk-chairs.

Officer Stanley Kovac was a twenty-plus year veteran of the Detroit Police force. He started with the usual rookie assignment of walking a beat, and moved on to patrol car duty, where he remained. He would never rise to the rank of sergeant and he was okay with that. He hated paperwork but enjoyed the daily patrol rides and the encounters with either victims and or suspects. Teaching rookies the ways of the streets in his own gruff way gave him pride and satisfaction in his role as a seasoned officer. His tall and barrel shaped physique and raspy voice instilled caution into any suspects that thought of challenging him.

"Officer Kovac, I'm Sergeant Emery, Michigan State Police. Can I call you Stan or Stanley? Which do you prefer? You can call me Doug."

"Stan is fine. My mother still calls me Stasiu (Staash-u), Polish for Stanley"

Doug gave a small smile and they both felt a little more relaxed after the introductions.

"I don't know if anyone has discussed the case of the deadly accident that happened on October 30th of this year but that's what I'm here about. I found a file in your offices that you and another officer, I forget his name, but you encountered a bunch of youngsters waxing a drug store's windows. This happened to be reasonably close to the time and area of the accident. Do you remember the boys and the incident?"

"I do. There were five of them. Four of them were scared shitless and the fifth one, who seemed to be the leader, had an arrogant smart-ass attitude about him. I don't remember any of their names . . . but the arrogant one seemed to be a bit older than the others. Their names should be in the report. Wait! I think his name was George or Georgie."

"Great. Yes, their names are in the report. What I plan to do is to bring them all in with their parents and question them – not interrogate – just to get a feel if they know anything about the accident. I'd like you to be available and maybe observe, or at least stand by, during the questioning. I can talk to your sergeant to make sure it's okay with him. What do you think?"

"Sounds like a plan. I would talk to that Georgie character last, after you see what the other kids say. That may give you an idea of what they were up to and he may tell you something entirely different. Wait . . . now that I think of it, there was a strange beginning to this story. As we drove down Buchanan Street, we observed the five of them on the street corner of the drug store and the strange thing was . . . that they probably saw us coming as they stood on the corner and they immediately went to waxing the windows. Weird! I would think that they wouldn't remain on the corner and would take off running if they were doing something crazy. It's as if they wanted to be caught. What do you think of that?"

"That is strange and we can look into that aspect when we question them. Good observation Stan. Thanks for that. That will give me something in my back pocket as we talk to them."

Doug opened the manilla folder with the police report that Officer Kovac and his partner had filled out and he read the boys names to Officer Kovac.

George Kolpacki

Jimmy Gorski

Lenny Solack

Stanley Kowalski

Mark Jackson

Officer Kovac nodded his head as Sergeant Emery read the names, addresses and phone numbers of the five boys.

"Okay, good. I'll have one of the cadets here contact the families and request the boys come in with at least one of their parents, preferably both parents. I'll let you and your sergeant know when the meetings will take place so you can be available. Thanks for your help Stan. It's been a pleasure and once again thanks for the heads up about how they were acting when you approached them.

"You're welcome, Doug. Glad I could help. I doubt

they had anything to do with the accident but you never know!"

Sergeant Emery contacted Cadet Crocker and asked if he could help with setting up the interviews. He gave him the list of the five boys and their phone numbers. He said to stagger the interviews about an hour apart and to make sure that he schedules the Georgie Kolpacki kid interview last.

"Officer Kovac suggested that Georgie was probably the leader, for lack of a better word, of the boys and it would be better to talk to him last to see if there were any major discrepancies in their stories. I think that was a pretty good suggestion. What do you think Jack?" Trooper Emery was trying to reinforce Cadet Crocker's role in the investigation. He recalled when he was a rookie and how important it was to be recognized for his contributions.

"Yes., I agree. It sounds like the right thing to do. You never know what might be revealed in talking to the boys?"

"Another thing Jack, make sure that they have at least one parent with them, preferably both. We might have working parents, so maybe we'll have to schedule for later in the day or evening. Get the parents schedule for all the boys first and then set it up once you know who's available at what times."

"Can do. Where do you want to do these interviews?"

"We'll use the conference room rather than the interrogation rooms except for Georgie. Schedule him for one of the interrogation rooms. My thinking is to put the four other boys at ease to see what they have to say. Then if there is anything nefarious going on we might want to scare Georgie a little in close quarters."

As Doug finished giving Cadet Crocker instructions, he thought of another thing that he had learned from a seasoned trooper when interviewing someone – especially suspects. It was the ten things to look for when talking to someone that might indicate they're holding back or outright lying.

"Jack, one more thing I just thought of. I want you to join me as an observer and I have a list of lying 'tells' that we can look for when we're talking to them. So, here they are and I'll write them down so you can have them fresh in your mind at the interviews.

Number one – truthful people usually use the pronoun "I". People being deceitful will sometimes avoid referring to themselves.

Number two – Truthful people usually speak of things in the past tense. Deceitful, usually refer to the present tense. As if they're rehearsing what to say in their mind presently. They'll pause frequently as they decide what answer to give so as not to get caught in a lie.

Number three — If they answer questions with questions, they're probably trying to avoid answering the question . . . like politicians do!

Number four — If they use a lot of words that ring of uncertainty like think, maybe, sort of, perhaps, might, guess, or anything vague.

Number five — Using mild oaths like 'I swear, cross my heart, honest to God, or on my honor.

Number six — Using euphemisms for harsh words like missing instead of stolen, bump instead of hit, borrowed instead of stole, etcetera.

Number seven — Alluding to something that happened without really saying they were there or took part in it.

Number eight — Lack of detail when telling a story. Truthful stories usually have a lot of detail.

There are two more I can't remember. In fact, I'm surprised that I remembered eight of them. As I said, I'll write them down for you. This is helping me getting familiar on what to look for and it'll give you an introductory class on interviewing."

"Wow! That's great Sergeant. I'm really looking forward to the interview now that I may have something to contribute."

Cadet Crocker got busy on the phones and set up

all the interviews for the next day. They would start at 4 p.m. and finish with Georgie at 8 p.m.

Lenny Solack was the first boy on the schedule. He arrived promptly at 4:00 p.m. with his mother and his father. Cadet Crocker escorted them into the conference room and introduced them to Sergeant Emery, who was sitting patiently at the conference table. He got up and shook hands with the Father, the Mother, and with Lenny. Lenny's father was a tall man with a healthy physique. His coal black hair was combed back and parted to one side. He was dressed in khaki pants and a blue work shirt with an oval Cadillac emblem sewed over one breast pocket and his name embroidered over the other breast pocket. Mrs. Solack was a petite attractive blonde woman dressed in a flowered summer dress and patent leather pumps.

"We brought you in to discuss a little matter of waxing windows on the night before Halloween. I think you call it Devil's Night. Is that right Lenny?"

"Yes sir. I mean officer. That's right." Lenny's voice wavered and cracked nervously as he answered the question.

Lenny's father interrupted. "You mean you brought us in here to discuss waxing windows. I don't think that's a major crime nowadays . . . especially for

Halloween. What's the real reason, officer?" Lenny's father said, showing signs of irritation in his voice.

"You're right Mr. Solack. It's a little more than that. We had another incident that occurred around the same time and we were wondering if the two are connected or if the boys can give us any clues as to what might have happened in the other incident."

Lenny squirmed in his chair as he heard the words "other incident." He knew what the other incident was.

"What's the other incident?" Mrs. Solack asked.

"I can't give you any detail right now. But, I will as soon as we know more about it. We don't want to muddy anything up for now until we have more facts. I hope you understand."

Both Mr. and Mrs. Solack nodded their heads slightly with a look of frustration.

"Lenny, I want you to tell me exactly what happened on the night that Officer Kovac stopped you and your friends for waxing the windows at Steve's Drug Store. Can you do that for me? Start with the time you met with your friends and take it from there. Okay?"

"Okay." Lenny answered nervously. He squirmed around in his chair again and looked at both his mother and his father and cleared his throat.

"We met in front of the old Radke house. The one that's empty. You know which one Mom, don't you?"

Mrs. Solack nodded.

Lenny looked at his mother and then his father and hesitated, as if to give himself more time to decide what he was going to say. He was thinking ahead of what happened that night and he was scared that he was going to slip up and *spill the beans*. He was afraid of getting caught in a lie but he was more afraid of what he and his friends had done that Devil's Night that killed two innocent people. Sergeant Emery waited patiently. After a few seconds and nods from his parents, Lenny continued.

"We were just walking around looking for something to do. We went to the bakery on Buchanan and shared a loaf of fresh bread. I forget what we did after that. I think we just walked around. Somehow, I guess, we wound up in front of the drug store and someone said let's wax the windows. That's it. The cops . . . er I mean the police officers came and took our names and said to come back the next day and clean off the windows. That's all I remember."

"Okay, Lenny that's good. Now tell me if you saw anything out of the ordinary. Did you see anyone doing anything crazy? Or did you see anyone that you didn't know from the neighborhood?"

"No sir. Can't think of anything." Lenny said in a quiet nervous voice, still trying to get comfortable in the heavy wooden chair.

"What streets did you walk down with your friends. Do you remember?"

"I swear, I don't remember, except for Buchanan where we got the bread. That's it. Nowhere else."

"Okay Lenny. If that's all you can remember you can leave now. Thank you, Mr. and Mrs. Solack for coming in with Lenny. We'll get back with you if there's anything else we need or if we have any updates we can share."

They shook hands. Trooper Emery felt a warm gentle shake from Mrs. Solack, a firm almost painful shake from Mr. Solack and a cold clammy weak shake from Lenny.

"Well Jack. What do you think about the interview? Any signs of deceit?"

"I did notice a few things. But maybe I was looking too hard. He was a bit nervous but that's to be expected. He did say "I swear" and he never referenced himself."

"Yeah, I saw the same things. Good catch. Another thing I noticed was that there was not a lot of detail. His answers were very short. Oh well, maybe there's something there and maybe not. We have to be careful not to read too much into what we saw and heard. Let's see what the other boys have to say and then make some conclusions."

The rest of the interviews with Jimmy Gorski, Stanley Kowalski, and Mark Jackson went pretty much the same as Lenny's. There were a few small tells, but nothing obvious from the rest of the boys, just the expected nervousness and looking at their parents for emotional help. Georgie Kolpacki was next. As planned, Trooper Emery had Georgie Kolpacki and his one parent, his mother, escorted to one of the interview rooms at the 6th Precinct Police Station. The room was small with an equally small viewing one-way mirror on one wall. There was a small wooden table with countless stress marks, carved initials with the profanity words scratched out and cigarette burns on the edges where cigarette butts were placed and forgotten and burned down. There were four chairs, two on each side of the table. Cadet Crocker escorted Georgie and his mother into the room and told them to take a seat.

Trooper Emery waited a while to sweat out Georgie and then entered the room and took a seat facing Georgie and his mother.

"I'm Trooper Emery and this is Cadet Crocker. Georgie and Mrs. Kolpacki, thank you for coming in today to speak with us. Where's Mr. Kolpacki?"

Mrs. Kolpacki was a slight woman dressed in a dark skirt and white blouse. Her graying brown hair was pulled back into a bun. "He couldn't make it.

He had to work." She said knowing it was a lie. Mr. Kolpacki refused to go to the police station with them and said he would deal with Georgie when they got home.

Georgie tipped the chair backward and leaned back with his laced fingers on his lap and a smug look on his face as he listened to the conversation. He smirked when he heard his mother tell Trooper Emery his father had to work.

"So, Georgie, I've talked to all of your friends and now I want to hear from you. We're interested in what happened on October 30th when you and the other boys were walking the streets."

Mrs. Kolpacki interrupted. "Could you tell us why were here? Is it because the boys did some waxing windows on Devil's Night? That seems a bit of a stretch to have us come down here for that," she said and tapped out a Pall Mall cigarette from a package, lit it, inhaled, and blew out the smoke over the table.

Trooper Emery waved the irritating smoke away. "Do you mind not blowing that smoke over here Mrs. Kolpacki? And, it's a little more than that. We're investigating another incident that happened that night and we're trying to see if the boys can give us any information that can help us in the other investigation. I can't give you any more than that but I would appreciate anything Georgie can tell us about that night., So

Georgie, tell me what you boys did that night. Start from the time you met up until the time you were approached by the police officer at the drug store."

Cadet Crocker was listening to every word as he sat on a chair in the corner of the room and took notes, just in case Trooper Emery might need them.

Georgie straightened up in his chair and brought his hands onto the table. He cleared his throat, maintaining his arrogant smirk.

"Well, we just met up on the corner of our block and started to walk around. You know, like guys usually do every summer night. No big deal. That's about it." The smirk continued. "What else do you want to know?"

"Tell me what streets you walked down and how you wound up at the corner of the drug store."

Georgie paused before giving his answer. "The guys were hungry so we went down to Kosta's and bought a loaf of bread. We walked and ate." Georgie was intentionally avoiding what streets they walked on. He knew that the police were fishing around to see if they were near the accident.

"Once again Georgie, what streets did you walk down? How about Wesson or Campbell or the expressway service street?" Trooper Emery was trying to keep from getting in Georgie's face. He knew Georgie was avoiding the question. He watched Georgie's face when he mentioned Wesson Street and the expressway. Georgie's face turned from a smirk to a frown.

Another pause! "Definitely not those streets! Why do you want to know the streets? I can't remember where they wanted to walk. I think it was down 32nd street or maybe Junction. I don't know, honest to God. I swear. I can't remember."

"Okay. We'll skip the streets you travelled for now. Tell me this Georgie. Why didn't you guys take off running when you saw the police car coming?"

Georgie scratched his chin and hesitated for a long minute. . . . . . . "They thought we would be caught anyway so we stayed there and hoped they wouldn't notice that they put some soap on the windows. I guess."

Georgie was enjoying the word game he was playing with the trooper. Any apprehension he had coming in, faded as he skillfully avoided anything that might put any suspicion on what they did that Devil's Night.

As clever as Georgie thought he was being – Trooper Emery was picking up on all the signs. Even Cadet Crocker, as he listened to the back and forth, was picking up on some of the tells that Trooper Emery clued him in on. One of the most striking to Cadet Crocker and Trooper Emery, even before the conversation began, was Georgie's walk and attitude and arrogant nature. Strutting into the interrogation room with a smug look on his face, Georgie thought, *you're not going to get anything out of me. I'm too fucking smart.*

Trooper Emery had enough of what he wanted to know for now. There was little more that he could do. He would have to think about what he heard and decide what, if anything, he could do unless more information came to light about the accident and exactly where the boys were at the time of the accident. Were they near there, or witnessed, or actually are the ones who threw or hung the dummy over the expressway bridge railing? This was a question that would linger for a while.

Trooper Doug Emery arranged a meeting with Cadet Jack Crocker and his Commander, Phil Ayolla the next day.

"You asked for updates Commander, so here's what we got from the search for clues. We found an incident of five boys waxing a drug store's windows on the night of, and close to the fatal accident. We brought them in for questioning to see if they could shed any light on what happened. We stayed away from hard interrogating . . . just interviews. They brought their parents with them so as not to step on any parental rights. It went pretty smooth with the help of Cadet

Crocker here."

"So, what did you find out . . . if anything, from your interviews?" Commander Ayolla interrupted.

"We didn't get much. We felt that they were holding back somewhat, but it was hard to tell exactly how much they were holding back. Chime in any time, Jack. You were there. What was your impression?"

"I agree that we felt they may be holding back somewhat. But with the natural feeling of nervousness, being questioned by police, it was hard to tell. And I'm new at this so I don't know if I have a lot more to offer."

"Another thing Commander, I think the first boy we interviewed, Lenny Solack, seemed exceptionally nervous and I think he wanted to tell us a lot more than he did. He kept looking at his parents. As if he was looking for their approval to let loose with the whole story. You agree Jack?"

"I do. I think that was a great way to put it. That he was looking for approval."

"The main thing we observed was from the obvious leader of the group. He's about a year older and has a real 'kiss my ass' attitude. As if he's smarter than us, and I got the feeling, he probably got to the other boys and told them to keep their mouths shut. Using our list of tells when questioning suspects, I think we hit on six or seven of them real solid. He definitely knows something about what went on that Devil's Night and how much they might have been involved."

"Sounds interesting and I'm glad you were giving Cadet some schooling on lying tells. I'm sure he'll be able to use them in his future career." Commander Ayolla smiled a warm smile toward Cadet Crocker. "So now what? Is that the end of it? What plans, if any, are you thinking of?" Commander Ayolla said with his elbows on his desk and leaning forward, getting closer to Emery and Crocker.

"I think we let them stew for a few weeks. Then I would like to call Lenny Solack back in, with his parents of course, and question him again. Maybe he'll soften up."

"Doug, I would approach his parents. Whichever you think he is close to and kind of give them a heads up before you talk to him. Tell her or him that you think that Lenny, is that his name; knows something about the crash and you need her or his help in getting to the bottom of it. Gaining their confidence by telling them what you're investigating could be very helpful in getting their son to open up." Commander Ayolla offered with a proud smile feeling happy to be of some help.

"I like that. And I felt it was the mother that he was closer to. He seemed to look at her more often and sat next to her side rather that his father's side. How about you Jack? Let's do that. If that doesn't work, then I think we'll have to put the screws to that smartass Georgie kid."

Doug and Jack left the Commander's office with smiles, knowing that they had a plan to move forward and that their interviews were not for naught.

8

Lenny

After a night of sleep and waking, sleep and waking, Lenny carried the burden into the next morning. He walked to school still thinking on what he was going to do to ease his conscience. He knew he would have to face Mickey and this increased his anxiety. He would try to keep his distance from the other boys – especially Georgie. Facing Mickey would be hard enough without being reminded again by Georgie to keep quiet.

The classroom was in the usual chaos before Sister Angelica entered the room. The spitballs fired back and forth, rubber bands used to launch tightly folded paper wads, and pieces of chalk thrown at the clean blackboard. As soon as Sister Angelica entered the room, she didn't have to say anything except "Good morning class" and all fell silent. The usual first two classes of arithmetic and social studies filled up the morning until noon recess.

Most students brought their lunches in grease-stained reused paper bags and the school supplied pint size bottles of warm white and mostly chocolate milk. A few of the students that lived within a block or two went home for lunch.

Lenny started his lunch and curiosity got the best of him as he turned his head to see if Mickey was in his desk at the rear of the classroom. He saw Mickey weakly biting on his baloney sandwich and staring blankly at the empty inkwell.

After hurried lunches and finishing their warm milks, most all of the students raced onto the playground that was conveniently located just outside the school's rear entrance door.

Lenny waited for all the students to leave. There was only him and Mickey. He walked nervously up to Mickey and looked down at Mickey who was still staring at his half-eaten sandwich and untouched milk.

"You want to go out to the playground and play catch or something?" Lenny said, waiting for an answer. He thought this effort might help or at the very least break the ice on what might be a path to some comfort.

Mickey looked up at Lenny, still with a blank stare on his face and nodded almost imperceptibly. Lenny waved his hand and said, "Let's go or you can finish your lunch. I'll wait."

"No. That's okay. I'm not hungry."

They walked out the back door of the school, across a narrow delivery-driveway and onto the playground. There was the daily replay of activity on the playground. Some students on swings with the boys keeping an eye on the girls in skirts hoping to catch a glimpse of thigh. Others were on the teeter-totters and some of the boys were playing catch. The day was the beginning of an Indian summer day with temperatures quickly climbing into the 80's. A Good Humor ice cream tricycle cart was parked just outside the playground fence with a line of students with lunch money clutched tightly in their fists, hoping that the toasted almond ice cream bars or Creamsicle wouldn't run out.

"You want to play catch or something. I think they have mitts and some softballs in the rec building and it looks like it's open." Lenny asked.

"Naw. I'm not much in the mood. Let's just sit on the bleachers till recess is over."

They climbed to the top of the bleachers, avoiding a smattering of students on the lower benches that were finishing their lunches.

Lenny forced the next bit of conversation. "How are you doing Mickey? I'm sorry about your parents." As the words squeezed past his lips, the ugly memories of his role in Mickey's sadness gripped his throat.

"I'm okay, I guess. I miss my mom and my dad,

but mostly my dad." Mickey said with a slight waver in his voice and his finger touching a tear in the corner of his eye.

Lenny had to think before he said anything more to remind Mickey of the sadness he was suffering. "How about we do something after school, after we finish our homework or chores or whatever. You wanna do that?" Lenny was thinking of ways to mend what they had done and that it was his fault that Mickey was going through all of this. And the thought slammed into his brain that this was not just a moment on the bleachers with him trying to ease some of Mickey's pain . . . this was a forever thing. This was not going to go away. How was he going to deal with the permanence of what they had caused?

Mickey nodded and said, "Yeah sure we can play catch or something. I used to play catch with my dad, so it might be nice to do that again. Thanks. Just come over when you want. I got mitts and baseballs or softballs." Mickey got up from the bleacher seat and Lenny followed and they trudged back into the hot stuffy classroom for another round of boring subjects: history, reading, and . . . religion!

Lenny finished his homework of studying the meaning of the seven sacraments for Religion class, finished his chores of straightening up his bedroom and he hesitantly thought about meeting with Mickey. Once a boy that he and the other boys shied away from and treated badly, was now a boy Lenny was nervous to face. He grabbed his mitt and slowly walked over the half block to Mickey's house. Each step pounding into his head that awful night. As he approached Mickey's house, he saw Mickey sitting on the front porch and casually tossing up a weathered baseball with frayed red stitching into an equally weathered mitt. Mickey's dog Perro was sitting at Mickey's side with his head resting on the porch.

When Lenny reached the front walk leading up to the porch, Perro raised his head and sprinted toward Lenny. Lenny bent over and reached down to pet Perro and was startled as he heard Perro growl, show his teeth and lunge at Lenny's outstretched hand. Lenny quickly withdrew his hand and stood up with a frightened look on his face.

Perro was a short, overweight, aged, chihuahua-mix. He hadn't moved this fast in months. As Lenny pulled his hand back, he felt Perro's teeth as they scraped the skin on his hand, just up from his little finger. Mickey jumped off of the porch and grabbed Perro and carried him up to the front door and dropped him inside and shut the door. Perro was still growling and fighting to be let loose.

"What the heck is wrong with him? He never barked or growled at me before. I didn't do anything to him. I was just going to pet him like I always do," Lenny asked with fear in his voice.

"I don't know what got into him. He never growls or even barks at anyone — not even strangers. Let me see your hand, Lenny."

Lenny shook his hand and presented it to Mickey. There was a smear of blood from the tooth that scratched his skin. "You need a bandage? I can get one in the house."

"Naw. I'll be okay, Lenny said as he wiped his hand in his pants. "Let's just play some catch. Forget about it."

They spread out on the sidewalk and began to throw the baseball back and forth. Lenny was trying to forget about what had just happened with Mickey's dog Perro. He had heard anecdotes that dog's have a keen awareness of fear. *They can smell fear. They attack when they smell fear because now — they're afraid! Did Perro smell that I was afraid of meeting with Mickey because of what I knew? Is Mickey now going to know that something is going on with me and the other guys? Is he going to start questioning me?* Lenny's mind was racing and he lost track of the game of catch and he missed a catch and the baseball glanced off the top of the webbing of his glove and hit him in the forehead.

"Okay. That's enough. I keep thinking about your dog and I lost my concentration. Let's sit on the porch and take a rest," Lenny said as he panted.

They sat next to each other on the porch and Mickey looked at Lenny sideways and saw the sweat on his forehead and the red mark where the baseball hit him. "Are you okay Lenny? I'm a bit confused by your sudden friendliness. I guess you were just being kind after what happened to my parents. And this thing with Perro and you not catching the easy lob I threw. What's going on Lenny?"

Lenny could feel the anxiety building up even more now that Mickey was questioning his actions. Maybe he shouldn't have tried to get so friendly. Maybe this opened the door to Mickey finding out about what really happened.

"You're right. I was just feeling a little sorry about what happened to your mom and dad . . . I guess. And Perro got me a little upset when he nipped me. I'm okay. Are you okay?"

Mickey, even without knowing all of the tells that Trooper Emery had instructed Cadet Crocker on, could feel that Lenny was lying or holding something back. It gave him an uneasy feeling. "Thanks for the thoughts about my parents. I wish I knew more about what happened. You guys were out that night. I was supposed to go with you, but my dad wanted me to go for ice cream. He was a little afraid I might get into trouble with you guys."

Mickey stood up and faced Lenny. He looked at Lenny directly in the eyes and asked him. "What did you guys do on Devil's Night? Did you guys see something? I've got a feeling that you know something Lenny, and you want to tell me something. That's why you've been so nice to me. I won't say anything to the other guys — especially Georgie. I don't care too much for Georgie. So, tell me, is there anything you can tell me?"

Lenny could feel Mickey's stare burning into his eyes. He shook his head and tried to avoid looking directly at Mickey. "There's nothing Mickey. We just walked around that night and got caught waxing Steve's windows. I was just trying to be nice. I'm going to be going now. Sorry again about your parents." Lenny turned and left without waiting for a reply from Mickey.

The tells in Lenny's voice were even more concerning as Mickey watched Lenny walk away. Now, he knew there was something else bothering Lenny. But what was it?

Mickey went inside. Missing his mother's voice and his father's after-shave smell. He petted Perro who was now quiet and laying in his favorite spot under the dining room table.

"What's with you and Lenny? I didn't know you were such close friends. And I heard Perro barking and saw you put him back in the house. "What's going on," Rosemary asked Mickey as he sat down at the dining room table next to Perro. He kicked off his shoes and rubbed his feet over Perro's back, a favorite routine they both enjoyed.

"I don't know what's with Perro barking at Lenny and he took a small nip at Lenny's hand and drew some blood, but Lenny said he's okay. I need to tell you something Rosie, and I'm not sure what it all means. Do you have a little time before you head for work?"

"I do have some time. Working part-time at the bank as a junior teller for a while is working out so far, until we can get our feet on the ground and see what our finances will be and maybe then I can start college, just a few night classes to start. So, tell me what's bothering you, Mickey?"

"It started at school today. Lenny asked me to join him on the playground at lunch time. Him or any of the other guys, never done that. I was surprised. I thought he was feeling sorry for me because of Mom and Dad. Then he asked to come over after school to play catch . . . another surprise. But when Perro attacked him, which he's never done before with anyone, I began to wonder what's going on. Do you think Perro can sense something in Lenny that we can't see?

"What do you mean Mickey?"

"I mean does he sense some fear in Lenny or something else. It's just so strange. And I also asked Lenny about that night. I asked him if he and the other guys that I was supposed to go out with that night, had seen anything. He really got nervous when I asked him that. I really think that he knows something and that he wanted to tell me something. What should I do?"

"Wow! That is strange. I would say this. Why don't you continue to friend around with Lenny if he wants? Don't push him. Just act friendly and maybe over time if you get closer, he may tell you what's bothering him. I sure hope he and the other boys are not involved in any way in Mom and Dad's death. I do like most of those boys – except for Georgie. I don't trust him. Anything else before I get ready for work?"

"No, I think that's it and I'll take your advice about getting along with Lenny and see what happens. Thanks Rosie and have fun at work," Mickey said with a devilish smile and Rosie returned the devilish smile.

Lenny walked slowly home with his mitt tucked under his arm. He stared at the scab that formed where Perro had nipped him. As he went inside, he was greeted by his mother.

"Hi Lenny. Playing catch, I see. Oh! What's that on your hand?'

"It's nothing. I just scratched it on the fence over by Mickey's."

"How is Mickey? Is he doing okay since losing his parents? It's got to be tough on him and Rosie. You tell them that if they need any help, like a ride some-where, to let us know. We would be glad to help them. I can't imagine what that feels like to lose both of your parents."

Lenny didn't need any reminder of what he and the other boys had caused. His thoughts went back to Perro and Perro's attack on him. "I'll tell Mickey. Thanks Mom. I'm going to take a little nap before Dad gets home and we eat."

"Okay. You do that. We're having spaghetti for dinner. Yours and your father's favorite. I'll wake you when he gets home."

Lenny laid face down on his bed and the anxiety continued!

The next day at school Lenny continued his warming up to Mickey. He approached Sister Angelica before class the next day and asked her if it would be okay if he moved his seat next to the empty desk next to Mickey in the last row. He wanted to sit next to Mickey and maybe give him some support . . . another attempt to ease his conscience.

"That's a great thought Lenny. How kind of you. I just don't want any chattering back and forth during class. I'm sure Mickey would welcome some companionship in these trying times for him, Sister Angelica said as she placed her hands on Lenny's shoulders.

Lenny felt a little uncomfortable with a nun's hands on his shoulders and quickly moved away as he thanked her.

Lenny collected his notebook, pencils and some textbooks and a catechism and walked back to Mickey's desk where Mickey was already seated. He looked up at Lenny with a question mark on his face. "What's going on? Why are you moving?"

"I asked Sister if it would be okay to move back here and she said okay. I didn't like sitting up at the front of the class anyway. You good with that?"

"Yeah sure. Welcome to the back of the class."

Georgie was the last to enter the class, as usual, just before Sister Angelica arrived. When he saw Lenny sitting at the rear of the classroom next to Mickey, he gave Lenny a scowl and an emphatic nod of his head. Lenny got the message that Georgie wasn't happy with his move. He didn't care. He was feeling more animosity toward Georgie as his guilt and sorriness increased. He was feeling there was a leveling of the field in being kinder to Mickey and a growing dislike if not hatred, for the leader that pooh-poohed the deaths of Mickey's parents.

At the lunch recess Georgie quickly went back to where Lenny and Mickey were sitting and he pointed his finger at Lenny. "I want to see you on the playground as soon as you're done eating and make it quick. We've got stuff to talk about."

Lenny could feel the anger in Georgie's voice and could see the look of fright on Mickey's face. He knew what was coming and he was going to face it with all his resolve.

As soon as Lenny exited the rear door of the school on his way to the playground he was stopped just outside the door. Georgie grabbed him by the arm and swiveled his body so that they were face to face. Georgie was slightly taller so Lenny had to look upward to see the evil in Georgie's eyes.

"What the fuck are you doing, getting shmoozie with Mickey? I'm telling you right now Lenny, you better not be telling him about that night. If you do and I find out I'm going to kick your skinny ass. And if we wind up going to reform school, we'll be in the same place and I will make your life hell – just like Devil's Night. Got it?" Georgie said and punched Lenny in the chest.

Lenny got nervous and perturbed as he listened. "I

got it Georgie. I'm just trying to be friendly. So don't worry. And I'm not afraid of you. You're just a big bully and your day will come. There are a lot of guys tougher than you think you are. You push around us younger guys but we're not going to be under your thumb forever. Just be careful on who you threaten."

Lenny's resolve in telling-off Georgie surprised even himself, let alone Georgie. He felt relieved and satisfied for himself in what he had just told Georgie. He hadn't felt this comfortable since Devil's Night. This was telling him that he was on the right track and doing the right things.

Georgie couldn't believe that Lenny stood up to him and he had to renew his control and machismo. "Big talk for a little guy. Just remember that I can still kick your ass, so keep your mouth shut when it comes to Mickey." Georgie punched Lenny again in the chest and turned and left before Lenny could get in any parting shots.

Lenny smiled!

9

Georgie

Georgie wandered home after school and his encounter with Lenny. He was feeling rejected and pissed off that Lenny had stood up to him. He would have to keep an eye on Lenny and he would wait for his time to even the score.

His house was located one block away from the other boys. It was pushed back to the rear of the lot. Being pushed back made it even more obvious rather than hidden. The front yard had not seen a blade of grass since the Kolpacki's had moved there years ago. A lonely, naked apple tree sat in the middle of the weed infested front yard. The house was a clapboard bungalow in desperate need of a coat of paint, maybe even two coats. Georgie took the one step onto the tiny porch and opened the screen door that signaled anyone's entering with an irritating squeak. A torn corner of the screen allowed entry to any inquisitive insect.

The entrance was directly into the kitchen area.

His mother was sitting at the grey Formica table with signs of rust on all four legs. She was sipping an amber liquid out of a tea cup, that certainly was not tea. There was not a tea pot in sight. Georgie said, "Hey Mom."

She looked up from a crossword puzzle she was working on. A daily routine of tea cup booze, cigarettes and crossword puzzles. She nodded at Georgie, put down the stubby pencil and picked up the already lit cigarette from the overflowing amber glass ashtray and took a deep drag, letting out the inhaled smoke through her mouth and nose.

"What are you up to today? You need to collect the garbage and get it out in the alley. It's starting to stink around here."

"Yeah, I'll get it later. I'm tired. Where's Dad? I thought he would be home from work by now. What's for dinner?"

"You know your father. He's probably at the bar as usual. He'll come home grab a sandwich and head back to the bar. You're on your own for dinner. There's lunchmeat in the fridge."

Georgie winced and headed to his bedroom. *She's right*, he thought, *it does stink in here.*

His bedroom was a small 8 X 10-foot room with a telephone booth size closet covered with a dirty grey muslin drape hanging on a curtain rod. He grabbed a Batman comic, laid on his crumpled damp bed and started to leaf through the pages, attempting to get his mind off his situation. Just as he was getting into the story of Batman and Robin fighting The Penguin, he heard the usual argument erupting in the kitchen. Dad was home!

It was nothing new. It was the usual back and forth; her drinking booze out of a tea cup, the house a filthy mess, his living at the bar and barely keeping up with the bills, not to mention she was embarrassed to see or talk to any of the neighbors because of the unsightliness of the house and yard. The argument ended as scripted. He changed from his work uniform into blue jeans and a denim shirt, washed his face, and without saying a word, left the house, slamming the already fragile screen door. He would show up early next morning after the bar closed. He would sleep it off and head to work to his boring assembly-line work at Cadillac Assembly.

Georgie's feelings of weakness from Lenny's confrontation and his reminder of his dire situation at home had him thinking. He envied what the other boys had. They had loving and caring parents. Dads that would coach and play catch with them and take them to Detroit Tigers ballgames. Mothers that would keep the houses clean and neat and smelling nice and have a home cooked dinner every night. And when there wasn't a home cooked meal, the families would go out to eat, maybe on a Friday to have a fish fry at one of the local bars. He had none of this. His strong control over these friends was his way of dealing with his longing to be like them. As long as he could control them, he could feel like he was better than them and their families. But in his mind, he knew that he and his so-called family was nothing like theirs. Now that Lenny challenged him, he would have to take that challenge and turn it on Lenny. He would watch Lenny like a frog waiting for an unsuspecting fly, especially in school when he was around Mickey. At the slightest indication of Lenny telling Mickey anything about Devil's Night – He would strike!

The following weeks at Saint Francis Grade School, Georgie spent stalking both Lenny and Mickey. He had the occasional meetings with Mark, Stanley and Jimmy just to make sure they were keeping their mouths shut. He was closest to Jimmy but that friendship seemed to be fading as Georgie became more paranoid. Lenny and Mickey got used to the stalking and took it in stride to the point of throwing Georgie's paranoia back in his face.

The more Georgie saw the friendship strengthening between Lenny and Mickey the more he felt he was losing control of the situation. His paranoia was telling him that it was only a matter of time before Lenny would tell Mickey what had happened – if he hadn't told him already? He followed them home almost daily. He observed their chatter and smiles and playing catch and stopping at the candy store for treats after school. His dire situation at home only hardened his resolve that he had to do something to stop this friendship. A friendship that he wished he had. His role of leader and quasi-friendship that was there last Halloween had all but disappeared. He would confront Lenny the next time he caught him alone.

Two days later Georgie noticed that Mickey was not in school. His desk next to Lenny's sat vacant. This was his chance. All during the day, through all the classes his mind was racing on what he had to do to keep Lenny in check. Sister Angelica had noticed Georgie's mind wandering and not paying attention to what was going on in the class. She knew that Georgie was not what you would call a participating student in any of her classes. He was not one to raise his hand to answer a question. He was simply putting in his time waiting for the final bell to signal the end of classes. She called on him specifically for this reason; to get his attention and maybe get him engaged . . . just a little.

"Georgie, what is the third sacrament we receive as Catholics? Can you tell the class?"

Georgie lifted his head slightly and his mind exited his thoughts of Lenny and said, "I'm not sure. I think it's matrimony." Georgie said with a smirk.

The class let out a deafening roar of laughter. Sister Angelica shook her head and shooshed the class with her finger up to her lips. "It's the sacrament of Eucharist, Georgie. You might want to get your head straight and pay attention to the class. I'm giving you, and the rest of the class an assignment to study the sacraments – in order and correct spelling – for tomorrow's class. I will be calling on you to recite the sacraments."

Most of the class moaned and Georgie fashioned a smirk directed at Sister Angelica. He resumed his thoughts of confronting Lenny after class. The bell rang and Sister Angelica waved her hand signaling it was okay to leave. Georgie remained seated until he saw Lenny get up from his desk. He followed him out of the door, down the waxed wood hallway and out the front door.

Lenny walked alone. He thought about Mickey and how close they had become. He still struggled with his knowledge that he played a part in the loss of Mickey's parents. But as their friendship grew, the guilt faded. There were still the occasional uncomfortable moments when Mickey would want to talk about that night and his terror when he woke up in the hospital bed. Lenny would try to change the subject or would ask questions about how he and Rosemary were getting along. Mickey would oblige and fill Lenny in on Rosemary's and his life and Aunt Anna's help and how things were going. This usually changed the subject enough for Lenny to feel comfortable again.

Georgie quickened his pace and moved directly behind Lenny and shouted in Lenny's ear "Boo!"

Lenny quickly turned and was face to face with Georgie. "What do you want, Georgie? Leave me alone. Go find someone else to harass."

"I like harassing you and Mickey, your new asshole buddy. I warned you not to get too chummy with him, and I see you're not listening."

"I don't take orders from you anymore Georgie. Those days are over. Go find someone else to boss around. Even Mark and Jimmy and Stan are staying away from you." Lenny said as he looked up into Georgie's face. He was still a bit shorter than Georgie but was catching up.

"Well, I don't think they're over and I'm going to prove it." Georgie grabbed Lenny by his shirt-front at the neck and tightened his fist. He swung with all his might landing his fist directly into the side of Lenny's face. Lenny waivered for a minute and then fell on his back onto the sidewalk, striking his head onto the rough cement. A group of girls were walking home on the same route and witnessed the punch. They didn't want to get involved and just kept walking. Lenny reached up and felt the side of his face and could feel the warmth and the soreness already seeping in. Just then Georgie thought he would give Lenny another thing to think about. He drew back his foot and kicked as hard as he could into Lenny's rib cage. Lenny let out a yell and tears streamed down his face.

"Just a little warning Lenny that if you think you can cross me and get away with it, you got another think coming. And that goes for Mickey also. And one more thing, if you tell anyone I hit you, I've got a couple more tricks up my sleeve."

Lenny groaned and didn't respond. Georgie let out a *hmph* and walked away with a gloating look. *That should convince him*, he thought as he walked away.

Lenny got up slowly and looked around. He saw some girls from across the street staring at him. One of them shouted "You okay Lenny?"

"I'm fine. Just a little bruise." He felt the rush of blood to his face, not from the punch but the embarrassment blood rushing in. He got up, looked at his clothes and picked up the few books he was carrying.

As he walked slowly home, he was thinking of what to say when his mother and father would certainly ask "what happened to you?" As he passed Steve's Drug Store, he stopped and peered into the glass that was still relatively clean from the job he and his friends had done on Halloween day. It showed a slight puffiness at the corner of his eye but didn't show any discoloration — yet! *Maybe they won't notice*, he thought.

He was wrong. As soon as he stepped in the door and his mother went to greet him, she threw up her praying hands to her mouth. "Oh my God Lenny! What happened to you? You're getting a black eye. Were you in a fight?" She continued to hold her fingers to her lips.

Lenny forced a smile. "It's nothing Mom. We were playing flag football on the playground at lunchtime and someone forgot and thought it was tackle. I had the football, so they tackled me, and someone's elbow caught my eye. Oops! I'm okay. Just stings a little."

His mother went to the freezer and found a frozen package of Bird's Eye peas. "Here Lenny take these and lay down and keep them on your eye. It'll keep the swelling down."

Lenny grabbed the frozen peas and went immediately into the bathroom. He hesitated to look at his face in the mirror. He held the cold package up to his eye. It felt soothing until the coldness grabbed onto his skin. He slowly slid the package down his cheek and looked. It was shocking to see his eye socket swollen and his skin starting to turn an ugly shade of purple. His eyelid was swelling and starting to close his field of vision. He headed for his bedroom and took his mother's advice and laid on his bed with the frozen, now thawing, package of peas on his eye. His thoughts raced to Georgie and Mickey and how was he going to fix this whole mess. Continued bullying by Georgie was not an option. He drifted off to sleep shortly after he saw his mother peek in on him and softly close the bedroom door.

Georgie returned home with a satisfying grin on his face. He felt he had regained some of his power with the boys he hung out with when he took care of Lenny. He would wait and see if the beating was enough to retain that power. That power waned a bit when he entered the dire surroundings of his house. It was the usual sight of his mother at the kitchen table sipping on her daily cup of favorite amber liquid and the soon to be entrance of his father and the argument that would follow. He grabbed a piece of baloney and sniffed it. Grabbed two pieces of stale Wonder bread and slapped a sandwich together after a brief hello to his mother in light of the fact that there would be no dinner for that evening – as usual.

He finished most of the sandwich and threw the crust into the overflowing waste basket next to the sink. "Time to empty that, Georgie. It's stinking up the kitchen."

"Yeah. I'll get it later. I got things to do."

No reply from his mother as he left the house. He wandered down to the corner where there was usually someone he knew hanging out. He pulled out a crumpled package of Lucky Strike that he had stolen from his father's drawer. He tapped out a cigarette and lit it with his signature flipping of his chrome plated Zippo.

Jimmy Gorski was standing alone on the corner in front of the corner pool hall. He was smoking a cigarette with his leg bent and his foot planted against the brick wall of the building.

"What's up Jimmy?" Georgie asked as he approached.

"Not much. How about you?"

"I just kicked Lenny Solack's ass. Gave him a real shiner." Georgie said with a grin spread across his face.

"Wha'd, you do that for? Lenny's a good kid. One of us."

"He was getting a little too close to that Mickey kid . . . and I'm afraid he's going to spill the beans on what happened at the expressway and blame us for that little accident. So, I had to give him a message on what might happen to him if he has any thought about telling Mickey what we did. Got it?"

"Got it. I forgot all about that little prank. Why would you think Lenny would ever tell anyone about that night? After all, he was there with us."

"I saw him getting too friendly with Mickey and you know when you get too close to someone you start to tell them all your secrets. If he talks, we're all in trouble. And that goes for you and Mark and Stan. That just gave me a thought. I want you and Stan and Mark to meet me at the clubhouse tonight to discuss our little problem that Lenny might create. Okay?"

"Okay. . . I guess. What time?"

"Run over to their houses and tell them after supper to meet us there. I'll be waiting." Jimmy nodded and dropped his cigarette butt and squished it with his foot and started his way up the block to alert Mark and Stan about the meeting tonight.

After supper that evening, Jimmy, Stan and Mark met and made their way to the clubhouse in the empty Radke house. They entered through their usual entrance of the rear kitchen window. The spiders had re-established their domain with new cobwebs. The mustiness had increased along with the dust covering all of the surfaces. Georgie was waiting for them, seated on an orange crate. He had lit a candle that was giving his face and the surrounding walls sinister shadows.

"Where you guys been. I've been waiting quite a while."

"We had to finish dinner Georgie. What's the hurry and why did you call us here."

Mark replied with an arrogance that Georgie hadn't seen before.

"I need to talk to you guys about Lenny and his friendship with Mickey. I already told Jimmy that I'm a bit worried about Lenny spilling the beans about our little prank. And . . . I gave Lenny a little tune-up to remind him about not telling anyone."

"What for Georgie? Lenny's a good kid and one of us." Mark repeated what Jimmy had already told Georgie.

"Just making sure. I want you guys to keep an eye on him and Mickey to make sure we're safe. I don't want to be going to no reform school and I don't think you guys would want to be going either. Remember we'll be starting high school next year."

"So, you want us to snoop on Lenny and Mickey. I mostly forgot about that night and chalked it up to something we did in the past that didn't turn out so good. So why try to stir it up again?" Stan questioned Georgie.

Georgie was getting an uneasy feeling. In the past, none of the boys, except for Jimmy — once in a while — would ever challenge him. What he said would be it! Now he was feeling the boys were showing signs of resistance and independence. He had to try to regain that hold on them.

"I'm not trying to drag it up again. I'm just being cautious. Just being careful." Georgie said as he looked at the faces covered with flickering shadows from the candle. He was getting an eerie feeling that his hold on them was melting like the wax flowing down the side of the candle.

"Okay Georgie. You said your piece. We're gonna leave now. We'll be careful. And you do the same. You need to let go of this because you may be stoking a fire that's not there and you're going to get Lenny really pissed and he may talk just to get even with you. Have you ever thought of that Georgie Boy?" Jimmy said as he leaned over and stared into Georgie's eyes. Georgie hated being called GEORGIE BOY.

Georgie had never been challenged like this by any of the boys and it was eating into his resolve. Maybe Jimmy had a point about stirring up Lenny. But he didn't care. His paranoia was overwhelming any common sense he had. His anger and jealousness of the other boys' lives was creating an anger in his soul that might lead to unforeseen consequences! There was no more conversation. Jimmy, Stan and Mark turned and made their way through the spiderwebs and out the back window. Georgie remained seated on the orange crate with his head in his hands. The meeting did not go as he had planned. He was losing the control he had over the boys and he had to counter it with some other action. But what could he do? He would have to think long and hard to come up with his next plan.

The next day in school was traumatic for Lenny. Fellow students gathered around him and stared at his black eye, now turning a rainbow of yellow, purple and red. He tried to brush off the attention and told them it's nothing, that he just had an accident. The girls that had witnessed the attack by Georgie knew the real story. There were no secrets in school. Both rumors, untruths and truth always erupted like wild fire. Even Sister Angelica noticed the hubbub around Lenny and asked him what happened. Once again, he told her it was nothing, he just had an accident. Georgie was taking pleasure in the fact that he was the cause of all the attention. He listened to all the chatter, just waiting for Lenny to say he was the culprit. Lenny cautiously avoided that scenario until after school.

Now that Mickey was back in class after a day off, he walked with Lenny on their way home.

"Okay Lenny, what's the story. Did Georgie really do this to you?"

"Yeah, he did. He thinks that you and I are getting too chummy. Actually, he's losing control, or has lost control of the guys he hung around with like Jimmy, Mark, Stan and myself. It's just his way of bullying to show that he's tougher than everyone else. His day will come."

"Why don't we do something about it? There's two of us. We could show him what for." Mickey replied.

"Nah. I don't want to do that. It might make things worse. And I guess I'm a little afraid even with both of us ganging up on him that we could take care of him. I know he is pretty tough. Let's just leave it and try to ignore him. He'll fade away." Lenny was hoping.

Mickey was feeling that he wanted to do something. He had a good feeling as his friendship with Lenny was growing. He never had a close friend. He only had contact with the other boys when they needed something from him. He wanted to keep this relationship and didn't want Georgie to destroy it. His thoughts went back to when Perro attacked Lenny, thinking that Perro sensed some fear in Lenny. And now this. He was starting to think that there was more to the story and he had to find out what it was.

"Lenny, I really enjoy hanging out with you but something is bothering me and I think bothering you.

Is Georgie holding something against you and me?"

"I'm not sure what you're getting at, Mickey. There's nothing. Georgie is just a bully that needs control. I think he's also jealous of us guys that have decent homes and he lives in the shithole with his mom and dad . . . who are both drunks. Let's leave it at that and let's play catch or checkers or something tonight after dinner or just hang out. Okay?" Lenny was desperately trying to change the subject and avoid telling Mickey any more than he had to – for now.

"Okay. If you say so. But, if there's anything you want to talk about to get off your chest, let me have it. I can handle most anything after what Rosie and I have been through."

At hearing these words Lenny felt the tension building up inside him and the uncomfortable feeling of remorse for what he had done. It was close to the first fears he had about facing Mickey. He also thought about Perro and that Perro probably sensed his fear, uneasiness, and the guilt he was trying to hide.

Nothing more was said. Lenny relaxed and they continued walking home. Now talking about baseball and the weather getting cold and snow would soon be falling and winter fun and the holidays of Thanksgiving and Christmas would be there soon enough.

The rest of the school year up to Christmas break went relatively smooth. There friendship continued.

Georgie kept up his stalking and harassing but even that started to fade as they approached the end of the year. Lenny was hoping that was the end of it. Next year would be a new year. Things would return to normal with Mickey, his new friend. And, he was looking forward to going to high school. The one thing that slipped his mind was that when he was hanging out with Georgie and Jimmy and Stan and Mark, they all agreed to go to the same high school. After all, they were all close friends. At least at that time they all thought they were close friends and their friendship would last forever. But now — reality set in. Mark, Stan and Jimmy had Devil's Night in the back of their minds. Georgie, Lenny and Mickey had that night gnawing at them all too often.

When Lenny thought about starting high school and Georgie being there to constantly remind him, he got depressed. He was struggling with the secret he was holding from his now close friend Mickey. He felt that if he wanted to keep that friendship and at the same time ease his conscience, he would have to tell Mickey the truth. Tell him that he was partially responsible for the death of Mickey's parents. But not just yet. He had to strengthen his resolve and mold in his mind exactly how and what he would tell Mickey. That might take him a while and maybe even, into the beginning of high school.

10

Rosemary, Anna, Norman

Rosemary was settling in with her and Mickey's new life. Aunt Anna was becoming a new mother figure. After she helped Rosemary figuring out all of the finances, the insurance, Social Security payments, and purchasing a new used car, she started to help Rosemary with the household chores. Rosemary had helped her mother with the cleaning and laundry and groceries on rare occasions, but she never paid much attention to the details.

Aunt Anna took her grocery shopping and taught her, first of all, to make a list, and to keep a running list whenever she ran out of something. Look for the bargains. Buy a large size, if it made more sense and saved money in the long run. And of course — never grocery shop when hungry. After a few visits to the local A&P grocery store, Rosemary got the hang of it and started to enjoy the weekly or bi-weekly trips. She even encouraged Mickey to help her at times when the grocery lists grew or it was close to holidays and the grocery load would be greater.

Laundry and keeping the house neat and clean was easier than the details of grocery shopping. Using the right soap and fabric softener, and separating colors from whites and delicates was about all there was to laundry — except for the sorting, ironing, folding and hanging. House cleaning chores of: dusting, mopping, bathrooms, kitchen, and seasonal cleaning were split up between Rosie and Mickey, with Rosie getting the bulk of the chores. Mickey gladly chipped in where needed as long as he didn't get too much of the 'womanly chores.'

Cooking was the biggest challenge for both Rosie and Aunt Anna. Rosie had not spent a lot of time cooking with her mother. She didn't know the difference between a teaspoon (tsp) abbreviation and a tablespoon abbreviation (TBSP) or that 3 tsp equals 1 TBSP. Cooking experience would come in time after she did a little cooking using either her mother's recipes she found in a kitchen drawer or from recipes that Aunt Anna had copied and given her.

One of the hard and memorable lessons she learned regarding teaspoons and tablespoons was on her first attempt to make meatloaf and mashed potatoes. The recipe called for a teaspoon of salt and a teaspoon of pepper. Rosie read the recipe as tablespoons instead of teaspoons. The final product looked amazing as she removed it from the oven. She was proud of herself. Mickey helped her with setting the table for her and Aunt Anna and himself. He helped peeling and mashing the potatoes. They all sat down for the inaugural dinner.

Rosemary sliced the meatloaf into perfectly-even slabs and dished them out onto the three fine china dinner plates. Everyone helped themselves to the mashed potatoes, and the green bean casserole that Aunt Anna contributed. Mickey was the first to bite into the meatloaf and the potatoes. His mouth was watering.

Almost immediately his hungry smiling face turned to a wince as he leaned back. Aunt Anna took her first bites and aped Mickey's reaction. Rosemary looked on and knew immediately she had done something wrong.

"I'm afraid Rosie that you may have mixed up the teaspoons and tablespoons when it came to the salt and pepper." She said with a slight lilt in her voice. "But it's not really that bad. The overall taste is excellent. You'll learn as you go. It took me and your mother a while to learn how to cook. Even Julia Child took some training to become a master at French cuisine."

After Mickey got over the shock of the original taste of too much salt and pepper he dug in voraciously and enjoyed the rest of the meal. Rosemary and Aunt

Anna had a good laugh as they watched Mickey devour the salty, peppery meatloaf . . . and went for seconds. It would be a laughable topic of conversation for many years as Rosie became an excellent cook.

Anna had longed for a married life and motherly role before her fiancé was killed in battle in the Second World War. That dream faded as the tragedy sunk in. She worked for many years as a saleslady at Federal Department Store on Michigan Avenue. She was frugal with her money and purchased a house close to her sister Doris and her family. There were times where she envied her sister and her family as she thought of what she had lost so many years ago. It was not a spiteful envy. She loved her sister and her husband Larry and their children Rosemary and Mickey.

The awful tragedy of losing her sister and brother-in-law brought back her heartache from her long-ago loss. It was cutting a new facet into her life. She didn't think of it consciously but it was affording her that motherly role that was blown up in a battlefield in Europe. She was becoming a mother to Rosie and Mickey and she was enjoying it despite the road it took to get to this new role. She took pleasure in helping Rosie with the household chores and at times, helping Mickey with homework.

This motherly spark that was lighting up her life had also lit up another emotional part of her soul. Could she kindle a new relationship at this stage in her life? Consciously or unconsciously, she began to pay more attention to her dress and her hair and her makeup. It did not go unnoticed by Rosemary.

"Aunt Anna, I love what you've done with your hair. It makes you look so much younger. Not that you didn't look young before." Rosie quickly added so as not to offend.

"Yes. Thank you, Rosie. I figured it was time for a change. I was getting tired of tying up my hair in a bow everyday so I went to Nellie's for a wash and dye and a set. Glad you like."

Anna's spinster persona was wearing off. Along with her hair style change and using a little more makeup, other than just a pat of powder on her cheeks, she delved into a new, younger wardrobe of clothes — getting away from the matronly navy-blue suits and gray dresses. Working at Federal's afforded her a daily look-around for any new piece of clothing that looked younger, more colorful, maybe even with a hint of cleavage and . . . she could also use her employee discount. Her life was evolving just as Rosemary and Mickey's lives were evolving. All in different directions!

With her new look and outlook on life she began to notice more and more the male shoppers that infrequently shopped at Federal's. For the most part . . . women did all the shopping. Men would only shop out of necessity, not as a pleasurable pastime as women often did. As she watched the men that shopped there, she soon figured out that any of the men shopping there were either widowers, single, or desperate and shopping for a gift for their wives or girlfriends.

One man, in particular, came into her radar as she noticed him on a routine basis shopping for clothes or kitchen items. She deduced that he was probably a single man by the items he was buying. She never saw him buy any female clothes, perfumes, jewelry and this was a signal that maybe . . . just maybe.

He was a man in his fifties, as was Anna. He was trim and fit and always dressed neat and casual – never a necktie. His hair was black with flecks of red. But the most striking feature were his green eyes and his handsome prominent nose. Anna decided that she would take the step that had evaded her for all these many years. The next time she would see him she would take a chance at getting friendly and see where that would go . . . if anywhere?

It was barely a week after she decided in her mind to get friendly that she saw him with some clothes draped over his arm and walking aimlessly around the kitchen appliance and gadgets department. Anna walked quickly over to that department, hoping to intercept him before another saleslady got to him first.

"Hello, can I help you with something? Anna said and looked up into his friendly green eyes.

"As a matter of fact, you can help me. I'm looking for a new toaster. Mine went kerflooey on me the other day."

Anna was trying to concentrate on the job in hand of helping him and not getting too involved with his looks. "Let's walk over here and see what we've got."

He followed Anna closely and she could feel his presence. "There's quite an assortment here. I can recommend this two-slicer Toast-rite brand. I have one myself. Unless of course you've got a large family and need a four slicer?" Anna said touching the toaster and waiting for an answer.

"Nope, no family. Just me. I'll take your recommendation and take that Toast-rite. And these clothes I picked up"

"Okay. Follow me over to my register. I'll grab a toaster here under the counter."

Once again, she felt his presence as he closely followed her to the cash register. She took the clothes he had draped over his arm and the toaster, looked at the price tags and totaled them up on the register. He handed her four 20-dollar bills and waited for the change. He was watching her with fascination as she methodically went through her steps. She placed the clothes in one shopping bag and tied twine around the toaster box and fashioned a small handle so he could carry it easily.

"Wow, you've got it all covered even a little handle for me to carry the toaster. Thank you so much. You make shopping easy. I hate to shop but I don't have any other choice. No wife to pawn it off on." He smiled . . . now he was waiting for a response.

Anna thought deeply as he remarked that there was no wife. She decided to take the cue. *Was this a flirt he was sending my way and what should I answer to keep this conversation going?* she thought.

"Oh, glad I could help. Can't believe you're single and that no one has grabbed you yet." She was wondering if she went too far?

"The right one hasn't come along yet, I guess, or if they did, I missed the train. By the way, what is your name?" He asked as he immediately noticed the name tag on her lapel. "Whoops, didn't see your name tag, Anna."

"And what is your name now that you know mine?"

"It's Norman, Norman Aringa, Call me Norm or Norman, Anna."

"Italiano huh. I can see that in your face now that you gave me your name."

"You mean my big nose?' Anna blushed. "Well, thanks for everything Anna and I'll see you on my next shopping trip. Soon I hope."

"Me too. See you Mr. Aringa, ah . . . Norm."

"Will do, Anna. *Ciao*." Norman said with a smile.

She watched as he turned and walked away. She had a good feeling she didn't say too much and embarrass herself and she felt that he was taking some interest. The following days were spent daydreaming and fantasizing about what might turn into a date. A date she had unknowingly been waiting for – for all these years. It was time to move on from her heartache of so many years ago. Even Rosemary and Mickey noticed the change in Aunt Anna.

"Looking pretty spiffy lately Aunt Anna. Someone special you're getting all dolled up for at work?" Rosemary commented one day as she caught Anna straightening up the seams on her nylons.

"You never know who might come along?" Anna answered with a mischievous smile.

Norman Aringa owned and operated a popular bar on Michigan Avenue called Nifty Norman's. It was in the shadow of Cadillac Assembly on Scotten Avenue which afforded his bar a steady flow of Cadillac hourly and supervisory workers. As an added source of income, he was the central drop off point for all the numbers games in the immediate neighborhood. Bets of nickels, dimes and quarters up to hundred-dollars would pay off at 500-to-1 odds. The player would pick three numbers and the pickup man or woman would write down the name, the numbers and the amount of the bet. The three numbers would come out on race day at The Detroit Race Course, based on daily receipt numbers. One win of $125.00 for a quarter bet would hook any unsuspecting better. Norman could pull in a hefty sum in a week after he paid off the main policy house called "Big Four Mutual." This steady flow of colorful characters gave the bar a compelling ambiance; with factory workers rubbing elbows and sharing drinks with 'made-men' and low-level criminals and single men and women looking for a night out and maybe a date. If you wanted to find someone to carry out a dangerous and or unlawful deed: there was a parade of 'fixer' candidates at Nifty Norman's. Norman also knew whose palms to grease. Part of his planned overhead was taking care of the local police from the precinct commander down to the beat cop that would make regular stops on Fridays for a freebie fish fry.

Norman, just the same as Anna, was thinking about and fantasizing about his meeting and chatting with Anna. He had dated his share of women over the years given his good looks, the owner of a successful and exciting business, his contact with a plethora of characters and his command of the art of conversation. He had help with the bartending, but he enjoyed the back and forth behind the bar so he would roll up his sleeves, bartender style, on a regular basis to keep his bartending skills honed.

It had been a couple of weeks since their first meeting. Anna was waiting on a customer when she saw Norman enter the store. He looked her way, saw that she was busy and gave her a nod and a small wave. She returned the nod and continued to finish the sale process.

He wandered around the immediate area until he saw that she was through with the customer. Anna finished the sale and saw him coming here way. A nervous rush came over her and she could feel her heart speed up a bit.

"Hello Norm. Doing one of your favorite pastimes . . . shopping?"

"Not really. I'm all caught up on my shopping except for the groceries, which I hate even more. The reason I came here was really to see you. I've been wondering since our meeting if it would be possible for us to have a dinner together?"

Anna hesitated, just a bit as her heartbeat took

another jump up. "That would be great. I was thinking the same thing after our meeting. Of course, I had to wait for you to make the move. Women are so hand-cuffed when it comes to this sort of thing. Oh well, maybe things will change in the future and women will take more initiative. So, of course. I would be happy to have dinner with you."

"What are your work hours? I was thinking Saturday early evening. I could meet you here or pick you up at your house. I assume you live somewhere nearby."

"I work five days a week, eight hours a day. This Saturday I only work half a day. So, it would be great to meet you here. I get off at 5. Will that work?"

"Perfect. Do you have any preference in restaurants?"

"Not really. I don't eat out that often. You make the choice. Surprise me."

"Okay. Will do. See you Saturday at 5."

As he left, Anna was overcome with a warm friendly feeling. What she hoped for, for the past two weeks had come to pass. She would be on pins and needles for the next few days waiting for Saturday. It would be a time of thinking, planning a wardrobe, a hair appointment, telling Rosemary and Mickey the good news, and waiting!

Saturday at 4:45 Norman came into the store, found Anna and told her he would be outside when she's ready. He was lucky enough to find a parking space on Michigan Avenue right in front of the entrance to Federal's.

As she came out, he got out of his car and rushed around to open the door for her. He took a swift glance at her shapely legs, as she hiked up her flowered dress, and slid them in and over. He gently closed the door.

He had decided to take her to an upscale, but family-friendly Italian restaurant called Stromboli's. He was a frequent diner there and knew the staff and the owner. He had made reservations and asked for a table off to the side away from the kitchen din and the main aisle traffic.

Once again, he got lucky with parking spaces and found one in the restaurant parking lot not too far from the entrance. As they got seated and the waiter brought over water and breadsticks, they both started to relax. Norm started the conversation with some innocuous chit chat. They shared their family situations, both being single, Anna's job, and Norman told her about his bar — but not all of it. Anna stayed away from her tragedy of losing a sister and brother-in-law. She felt it was not the right time to talk about tragedy. She didn't want to spoil what was a special night so far. They both felt that the details of their lives would be shared later if their relationship continued.

The rest of the evening went smoothly. They shared a bottle of Chianti with their Italian meals. The conversation was not forced and moved back and forth at a comfortable pace.

Norman parked in her driveway, opened her door and walked her up the front steps. No kisses or pecks on the cheek, just a friendly hand-hold and an agreement to meet again. Anna closed the door leaned against the closed door and smiled to herself. A broad life changing smile that had been bottled up inside her for a long time. Sleep would come easy that evening.

11

Georgie's New Friends, Perro

Georgie's sociopathic tendencies peeked into his life in his pre-teens. His family life with alcoholic and abusive parents was the perfect brew to feed his damaged psyche. Most likely one or both of his parents passed on the gene that led to his antisocial, deceptive and manipulative behavior.

The only discipline he got from his father was a whipping with a belt or a punch to his chest. His mother would throw in the occasional slap across the face that seemed to hurt even more than his father's punches. This confusing discipline taught Georgie that it was okay to bully to get what you wanted. His control by threat over Lenny, Jimmy, Mark and Stanley suited him well . . . as long as it lasted!

Georgie's control that he once had over Lenny, Jimmy, Mark and Stanley had all but faded into the past. His sense of power at school was also fading.

Students no longer feared him. The beating he gave Lenny was the turning point that turned his classmates totally against him. Lenny was well liked and now that Lenny had become close with Mickey, the class helped blend this union. Most of the class had felt sorry for Mickey after the loss of his parents. That sympathy gradually turned to empathy and friendliness and a sense of togetherness. As if they felt what Mickey felt – all except Georgie. He felt nothing and even took pleasure in the sorrow he was partly responsible for.

As this friendship increased, Georgie's hold on some of his classmates waned. He could feel it everyday as he went to class. Once there was the power and the control he felt. Now, all he could see was Lenny and Mickey and their friendly interaction with all of their classmates. What was once a warm, overpowering feeling as he stalked Lenny and Mickey had turned into a feeling of spitefulness. He boiled inside. He could not let this continue. He would have to turn the tide and get his power back. Lenny and Mickey were the cause of this and they would be his targets.

The loss of power that he felt had even drifted into his walk home after school. He had to walk alone past Mickey's house on his way home from school. There had never been anything that caused him concern on this walk which was usually with a few friends. On his last lonely walk past Mickey's house, Mickey and

Lenny were sitting on the front porch, side by side, and petting Perro sitting between them. As Lenny and Mickey became closer and Lenny's fears and guilt about the accident waned, so did Perro's aggression toward Lenny. The fact that he would carry animal crackers in his pocket and give one or two to Perro when he came to see Mickey, didn't hurt either.

Both Mickey and Lenny raised their heads and stopped their petting and conversation as they saw Georgie approaching. They didn't say anything. Just stared.

When Georgie was directly in front of Mickey's porch Perro leaped off the porch, growling and barking and headed directly for Georgie. He nipped at Georgie's ankles and continued to growl and show his teeth. Lenny could only think of that same action before he became friendly with Perro. The thought entered his mind, *He's feeling Georgie's fear and guilt.*

As Perro held on to Georgie's pantleg, continuing to growl, Georgie brought his other leg backward and with all his might kicked Perro in the ribs. Perro let go of Georgie's pantleg as he tumbled sideways and let out a terrifying whine that softened into a whimper.

"Get that fuckin dog off me Mickey. The next time he attacks me will be his last. You hear me?"

Mickey didn't respond. He jumped off the porch, ran and picked up Perro and tried to calm him down as he petted him and took him in the house.

Lenny responded to Georgie as Mickey came back and joined him on the porch. "He's picked up on your fear Georgie. Got something you're afraid of? Where's all your friends Georgie Boy?" Lenny said with a huge grin on his face. Georgie just bowed his head and continued to walk toward home. He mumbled as he walked. "You'll get yours too Lenny. I'm not through with you guys and that fucking mutt of yours.

Lenny and Mickey look at each other and smiled. They were united. Georgie was alone.

Georgie thought long and hard on what he needed to do. Since he saw his control almost gone and the realization that this would continue into high school since most of his classmates, including himself, would be moving on to the same high school. Something had to change!

His plan started with changing things at home. He started by taking out the garbage on a regular basis without being told. He was keeping his bedroom somewhat neat and orderly and he volunteered to help his mother with the rare housekeeping chores. She was surprised, but she knew Georgie, and she knew he must have ulterior motives.

She was right. Georgie approached her one day

after he had run a chore for her, getting her weekly supply of cigarettes from the pool room on the corner of their block. He kept a pack for himself. She didn't notice as he put the carton in an overhead cupboard in the kitchen.

"Mom, I have a favor too ask." Georgie politely asked his mother as she sat at the kitchen table sipping on the ever-present tea cup and nibbling on a burnt piece of toast.

"What is it, Georgie?" I knew you wanted something with all the help you've been showing around here."

"I changed my mind about going to St. Andrew where most of the class is going. I need to get away from those losers. I wand to go to Chadsey, the public high school and I need you to help me register and cancel the St. Andrew thing. It will also save you the $50 bucks tuition fee. The public school doesn't have a tuition. What do you say? Huh?" Georgie said and looked at his mother with as much as a warm smile as he could muster.

She took a sip and a deep drag, lifted her head and blew the smoke up into the air. "I don't know. I'll have to talk to your father. If I can ever catch him sober?" She paused and thought. "Oh well, never mind. I guess I'm okay with it. I can use those $50 bucks. Just give me the phone numbers I need to call."

Georgie smiled and bent over and forced a light hug on his mother's shoulders, smelling the booze and cigarette smoke.

Georgie's plan was working so far. He would get away from the cold shoulders and stares he was feeling in his last days in grade school. He was moving on. Moving on, but not forgetting. Not forgetting that Lenny and Mickey were the reason for this change. They were the ones responsible for his change of plans. He thought that maybe that was a good thing. He could carry out his plan of revenge and at the same time he would distance himself from the targets.

The next plan was to get chummy with some of the "greaser" students at Chadsey. New friends that could help him on his road to revenge. A few weeks into classes it was easy to see who those students were. The usual signs of the misfits were evident. There were the jock groups, the cheerleader groups, the brainiacs and then there were the outsiders. Georgie was glad he had grown his hair a little longer, combed it in a DA (duck's ass) and wore his leather motorcycle jacket to school. His Levi's and motorcycle boots completed the greaser ensemble.

The greaser sub group that showed the most anti-social and controlling persona was a group of three

— Ali Khan, Chico Kowalski, and Jimmy Zaffino. The names were fitting to their rebellious nature.

Ali Khan stood out by the mere rarity of someone from the Middle East in the middle of a Polish neighborhood. His features were hard to miss. A sallow complexion and coal black glistening hair contrasted with the lighter-skinned European majority in high school. His uncle was a Pakistani diplomat that helped get his father and their family into the United States on a temporary visa. His uniqueness helped him making friends with the outsiders in the neighborhood and high school.

One of those friends was Chico Kowalski. Another up-and-coming delinquent candidate. He also had a unique heritage for someone in the mostly Polish environs. His mother was Mexican and his father was Polish, which made for a mix that led to the Chico Kowalski moniker. His given name was Francisco. His mother started calling him Chico (small boy or child in Spanish) when he was a toddler. It stuck. Francisco liked it and wore it with a rebellious proudness. His tallness from his father and his Spanish features from his mother accentuated the Chico Kowalski persona.

Jimmy Zaffino rounded out the trio. His Italian heritage instilled in him a taste for the glamour of the criminal life. His father, and most of his uncles traveled in the lower tier of organized crime. Never making the "made man" status, they made their livings with low-level robberies, extortion, drugs and gambling. And – any unwanted opportunities the "made men" wanted to throw their way. Jimmy's father never bragged about or even talked about his way of making a living, but it was obvious to Jimmy and the rest of the family how anyone could make a living without ever going to work. Jimmy liked that idea and this gave him the impetus to start early and get friendly with boys of the same ilk.

Georgie made his move subtlety. He saw the three potential friends regularly hanging out at Bill's Luncheonette on the corner across from the school where they could smoke without any interference from the teachers or counselors. He wandered over there on a few occasions, offered up some of his mother's or father's stolen cigarettes and gradually started conversations on how school sucked, sexual comments directed at the girls that dared to walk by, and plans for the after-school shenanigans.

Gradually, his presence became part of the group. He taught them how he used his flipping of his Zippo to open and light their cigarettes and they in turn started to include him into their plans. Most of the days after school were just walking around the neighborhood and looking for mischief. Since the clubhouse in the empty Radke house had been abandoned after Georgie and his previous gang had disbanded, Georgie thought he might invite his new friends into the clubhouse.

It was a place to sit around and talk and smoke and Georgie ingratiated the bond even more when he brought bottles of beer from home. He was becoming part of the gang of outsiders.

"So . . . you guys like the digs? No one ever comes around here and we can sit and drink and bullshit without anyone bothering us."

"Yeah. Pretty neat Georgie Boy. I like." Chico commented and Georgie winced at the Georgie Boy name but kept quiet. It was what Lenny called him to piss him off. "Were you and some other guys using this before? And what if they tell someone about this hideaway?"

"Not to worry. The guys that were with me before have moved on. They got too squirrelly and I ditched them. They were afraid of getting caught. So, we got this place to ourselves as long as it stays vacant."

Ali, Chico and Jimmy listened to Georgie, as they swigged on the beer Georgie brought, and continued to smoke the cigarettes Georgie brought. Georgie gladly contributed to strengthen his place with them. His one worry now was if he stopped contributing would they still include him in their activities. Over the next two weeks he gradually weaned them off the bumming of cigarettes by failing to offer any when he tapped one out of a pack. On a couple of occasions when they decided to meet at the clubhouse, he didn't bring any beer. Chico and Jimmy took turns with beer they pilfered from home. Ali Khan couldn't contribute since his household, being Muslim, banned any alcohol.

Georgie was pleasantly surprised when his part of the trio, now quartet, still seemed to be solid. He felt welcome and part of the gang. His plan was working. He decided that he would start to reveal his secret: Devil's Night and the consequences of that night and what he planned for revenge on Mickey and Lenny!

They spent most of their days after school and evenings walking around looking for trouble. Since they didn't have any allowances to speak of, they looked for other sources of income. Petty shoplifting from the local candy stores and drug stores was becoming routine. Some of the store owners were catching on and kept an open eye out whenever any of them entered their stores or in some cases, kicked them out and told them their presence was not welcome. And when they got really desperate, they would strong arm the vulnerable students for their lunch money — or even

more desperate they would wander into other neigh-
borhoods where they weren't known and rob paper-
boys on collection days.

They also spent time standing on the corner of
the pool hall, smoking and talking and thinking about
ways to get a few dollars. When they couldn't steal
any beer from home, they would stand in front of
Chorian's beer store and look for a likely candidate
to buy beer for them. Jimmy saw one of his father's
friends walking up to the store, so Jimmy approached
him.

"Hey Tony. You know me, I'm Angelo's kid. How
about you buy us some beer. We'll kick in and buy a
jumbo for you." Jimmy said.

"Hey, Jimmy. I don't want to get in trouble with
your old man. He'd kick my ass." Tony thought for a
minute. "Okay. Just this once. Give me the cash."

Jimmy reached in his pocket and pulled out a
small fold of dollar bills and peeled off some and
handed them to Tony. Tony went in and bought three
quart-size Stroh's jumbos. He exited and told Jimmy
and the rest of them to follow him around the corner. He didn't want anyone seeing him buying beer for
teenagers.

They took the two jumbos in a brown paper bag
and headed back to the clubhouse. They took turns
swigging on the jumbos and passing them around.

They were all feeling a little more than high and full of liquid courage, Georgie had a thought.

"Hey guys. Let's take a walk down the block. I want to show you the fucking dog that's been giving me a hard time and I may have to do something about it. Okay? You wanna?"

They all looked at Georgie in the candle lit clubhouse and shrugged their shoulders.

"Yeah, okay. We got nothing else to do. You can show us that doggie bitch that's giving you a hard time." Chico laughed.

They made their way out of the basement clubhouse, up the stairs and out the kitchen back door. Georgie's new friends figured out that the door was much more convenient to enter the house than the window. They followed Georgie out onto the street, staggering toward Mickey's house.

Right on cue, as they approached Mickey's house, they could hear Perro barking behind the screen door.

"That little bitch of Mickey's barks every time I walk buy here. He even took a nip at my ankle once. I'm gonna take care of him one of these days. Maybe give him a little treat." Georgie said with a smirk on his face.

"Is Mickey the kid that had his old man and old lady killed in a crash on the Xway last year?" Ali Khan asked as they continued to walk and Perro's barking stopped.

"Yeah. He's the one. His old man ran his front end into one of the bridge pillars. Must have been drunk," Georgie laughed and slapped his hands together simulating a crash.

"That's not the story that was going around. The story was that someone threw something off the bridge, like a dummy or something that caused the accident. In fact, I think they were looking at someone from the neighborhood . . . like you Georgie. What's the story?" Jimmy asked.

"Yeah, I guess. The flatfoots questioned me and Mark and Jimmy and Lenny but they didn't have anything on us. And that brings us to this problem with Mickey and his dog and him getting friendly with Lenny. He was one of the guys that was with us when we threw that dummy over the bridge."

They all looked at Georgie with mouths agape.

"You mean you really did cause that accident that killed those people?" Chico asked with a look of disbelief on his face.

"Hey. It was just a little prank that went a little wrong. We were hanging that Halloween dummy over the bridge and the rope broke. Mickey's old man should have been paying attention to the road and he wouldn't have run his junk into the bridge. And another thing . . . Lenny getting chummy with Mickey has me a little worried that he'll tell Mickey what happened and who was there and maybe even go to the police. I had to give him a little tune up to show him I mean business and if he goes to the cops, I'll tune him up again, maybe even a little more than a tune up. So back to that pesky dog. I'm gonna come up with a little treat for him. You guys want to join me next week?"

They all looked at each other, back and forth and then Jimmy answered. "I'm not real fond of dogs either. My old man had a pit bull that I think he was using in some dog fight gambling. Anyway, that bitch took a nip at me and I had to go to the doc and get checked for rabies. So, I'm all in. I hate dogs."

The other two remained silent. Not giving their opinions. They didn't want to appear that they were soft on dogs.

Georgie returned to an empty house. As usual, his father was at the bar and his mother was probably joining him. He began searching the house for what he needed to satisfy his taste for revenge. He started in the kitchen and went through all the cupboards. There was a lot of wincing from the smells emanating from the seldom opened doors. He continued his search into the basement. He hadn't been in the basement for a long time. The dim hanging bulb gave the cobwebs and surroundings an eerie feeling. As he looked around and thought to himself, *our clubhouse is cleaner than this shithouse.*

He hurriedly went around the basement, waving away the spider webs as he went. He was getting frustrated and thinking that what he was looking for had been thrown away or hidden where it would be hard to find. One more place to look. He went outside and made his way to the garage. Another one of the seldom used areas and just as dirty and disgusting as the basement. With all the dead mice, rats, and birds it smelled more like a burial vault than a garage. He took a flashlight with him since the burned-out bulb on the lone light fixture hadn't been changed, nor would it be changed. He swept the light from the flashlight across the walls and over to makeshift shelves that his father had cobbled together in his pre-alcoholic years. All the contents were covered with grime and dust. There were dried-up paint cans, motor oil cans, used rags, mouse droppings, dead insects, and a handful of rusty tools. He picked up a rusty screwdriver and moved around the paint cans to see if there was anything behind them and "voila", there it was – a bottle of Cowley's Rat Poison. He gently lifted it with his thumb and forefinger, scared of what was inside. He looked at the fading-red skull and crossbones and the words "CAUTION – POISON – CONTAINS ARSENIC" and he grinned back at the skeleton skull.

The next move was to find something to put it in. He went into the kitchen, carefully holding the bottle with a reasonably clean rag he found in the garage. He opened the Kelvinator refrigerator and peered around the shelves littered with sticky crumbs of food and an ice encrusted freezer door, begging to be defrosted. He opened one of the vegetable drawers and found what might work. It was a few hot dogs wrapped in brown butcher paper. He unfolded the paper and lifted out one with his index finger and thumb. He looked at it and saw a little green around the end of the hot dog. *Can't hurt*, he laughed to himself. He threw the rest of the hot dogs into the garbage pail and took the greenish one over to the sink. He took a paring knife from the drawer and carefully slit a small slice into the hot dog skin. Once again being careful, he opened the bottle of rat poison and tipped it carefully toward the slit, until he saw small drops absorbed into the meat of the hot dog. When he thought it was enough, he wrapped the hot dog in the brown butcher paper with some writing on it and took both the rat poison and the hot dog and hid them on the shelf where he found the bottle of poison.

Mission accomplished. He was now ready for the next step.

Perro was a puppy when Mickey and Rosemary picked him out of a litter at the Detroit Humane Society Kennels on the Detroit Riverfront. He was the runt of the litter and being a Chihuahua- mix made him even more of a runt. He was loved from the very moment they brought him home and showed him off to their friends and neighbors. There was no fighting on who would take care of the feeding and cleaning up after for Perro. Rosemary and Mickey gladly took turns. The joy and love he showed them only reinforced their wanting to take care of him. He kept his puppy cuteness into a fully grown dog.

Mickey would spend hour upon hour playing with Perro in the back yard. With help from his dad, they fashioned a pretty decent doghouse and set it in the back of the yard near the alley. Perro would sit in the doghouse on hot days to escape the sun. Mickey made sure there was always fresh water and fresh straw on the wood floor, especially in the winter months. Perro was brought in nightly and would sleep in the living room on one of Larry's old Army blankets. His time spent with the family inside was usually on someone's lap, frequently Mickey's or Rosemary's, but occasionally Larry's or Doris's.

Those backyard times together were usually spent with Mickey throwing a yellow tennis ball and Perro fetching it and bringing it back to Mickey.

His small limited size mouth presented a problem with grasping the ball but after many days and attempts he finally mastered picking up the ball with his teeth. Over a couple of summers, the tennis ball transformed from a fuzzy yellow ball to a bald, greyish shiny ball. Mickey and Perro became the best of friends. He was Mickey's substitute for a best friend in the days before Lenny and he connected. Now Mickey had two best friends, one two-legged and one four-legged.

Georgie joined Chico, Ali and Jimmy who were smoking and talking in front of the pool hall, where they were not legally old enough to shoot pool. Steve, the owner, would allow them on occasion, when business was slow, to play a few games.

"What are you guys up to?" Georgie asked as he walked up to the group.

"Not much." Jimmy answered. "Why you got something in mind?'

"As a matter of fact, I do." Georgie answered as he pulled out a tightly wrapped package from his leather jacket.

"What the fuck is that, Georgie? It smells like shit." Ali said holding his nose.

"It's my little treat for that bitch of Mickey's that

took a nip at me. You guys wanna come along just for the fun of it, when I drop it in his yard?"

"Sure, why not?" Chico answered. "Nothing else to do."

All three finished their cigarettes, flicked them into the street and followed Georgie down the block toward Mickey's house.

"Here's the plan guys. Jimmy, you come with me. You're the one not too fond of bitches. Chico, you and Ali walk slowly in front of the house and if you see anything going on in front of the house give us a loud whistle. Jimmy and I will go through the alley and drop the little treat for Rover by his doghouse. I've been walking up and down the alley over the last week and he's usually in his dog house until late, before he goes inside. Got it?"

"Got it," they all nodded and replied.

Georgie was smiling to himself as he and Jimmy walked through the alley toward Mickey's back yard. His plan was working and his power was returning as he saw how easily the other three boys responded to his instructions. He was looking forward to getting revenge on the dog that tried to bite him and barked at him every time he passed Mickey's house. More important to him was showing Mickey and Lenny who was in charge. He knew that they would suspect him, but that was okay. He wanted them to know it was him and at the same time they would have no way of proving it. So he thought!

As suspected, Perro started barking as soon as he detected Georgie approaching. Georgie had to act fast before Mickey or someone else came out and caught them in the act. He pulled the rancid, poison laced hot dog out of his pocket, quickly unwrapped it, being careful not to touch it, and holding it by the brown paper he reached over the chain link fence and tossed it toward a fast-approaching Perro! He crumpled the paper and threw it in the yard — not noticing something written on the paper.

Perro stopped, sniffed the hot dog and started to chew at one of the ends. The barking stopped and Georgie and Jimmy with their elbows on the fence, smiled as they saw Perro devour the hot dog. It didn't take long before Perro rolled over on his side and began to convulse. At the sight of vomit and pink foam oozing out of Perro's mouth, Georgie slapped Jimmy on the back with a grin on his face. "Let's go Jimmy. I think the deed is done. That bitch won't be bothering me — or anyone else."

The wind had picked up and a stream of cold air rushed down the alley. They hurriedly walked back down the alley to meet up with Chico and Ali.

Mickey noticed it was getting dark earlier and he had forgot to bring Perro in. He grabbed a flashlight from the kitchen drawer and went out into the back yard. He called out "Perro, Perro, time to come in. Getting cold out here, boy. Come on. Hurry up. I'm getting cold." He swept the flashlight beam across the yard expecting Perro to run up and follow him into the warm house. The yard was silent except for the whistling wind. He walked slowly toward Perro's dog house. His shadow from the full moon following him as he continued to sweep the flashlight and call out to Perro.

As he neared the dog house, he was startled by what he saw. Perro was laying on his side, not moving, eyes with a blank stare and a soupy pool of vomit, pinkish foam and blood encircling his wide-open mouth. Flies had begun to gather. Mickey gasped and knelt down beside Perro and petted his side. It was cold and still. "No, no, Oh, Perro." The warm tears began to roll down his cold face.

He was still kneeling beside Perro when Rosemary came out to see what was going on. She heard Mickey yelling and crying. "Mickey, what's going . . . she paused when she saw the awful sight of Perro laying still and Mickey softly petting his side. She turned and ran into the house. Perro's comfort blanket was in its usual place in the living room. She gathered it up and put it to her face to smell Perro's doggy smell. The smell caused her tears to start flowing. As she walked slowly out to Mickey, she thought that she would have to be strong for Mickey. Even though it was a heavy loss for her, she knew it was devastating for Mickey.

Rosemary knelt next to Mickey and put her hand on his shoulder. She could feel the sobbing reverberate through his body. "What happened Mickey. He wasn't sick. Let's wrap him up in this to keep him safe from whatever until we decide what to do. We can cremate him or bury him in the back yard here. It's up to you Mickey. He was your dog more than anyone else's."

Mickey looked up at Rosemary with tears leaving a trail down his cheeks and his hand on Perro's side. "That bastard Georgie did this, Rosie. I know he did. Perro would always bark at him and actually nipped him. Georgie is a piece of shit that would do this. Look at what Mickey threw up. It looks like a piece of hot dog. We never fed him hot dogs. That fucker poisoned him. I know it."

Rosemary didn't argue. She looked at the disgusting vomit at Perro's head and did see what looked like a piece of a hot dog. *Should I go to the police with this?* she thought. She would wait until tomorrow to decide on that.

The shooed off some of the flies that were already gathering to lay their eggs, and carefully wrapped Perro in Larry's OD (Olive Drab) Army blanket.

Mickey carried him into the house with Rosemary walking close behind.

They met in the kitchen, after a sleepless night for both of them. Rosemary made coffee for herself and poured a glass of orange juice for Mickey. Neither felt like eating just yet.

"Mickey, have you thought about what you want to do with Perro? I know it's tough but we have to make a decision right away. We can't leave him on the porch. He's going to start to smell and the bugs will take over."

"Yeah, I know. I've just been thinking about Georgie and getting even. You're right. Let's take him to the vet and have them get him cremated. Then we can decide what to do with his ashes." Mickey said and wiped a tear away with the sleeve of his tee shirt.

They got Perro's ashes back in two days. They were contained in a Mason jar with the name PERRO written on a piece of masking tape stuck onto the side of the jar. *Pretty tacky*, Rosemary thought but didn't say anything to Mickey.

"I think I want to visit Mom and Dad's grave and maybe do something with the ashes there. Can you drive us over Rosie? Or do you have to work?"

"No, I'm good. I don't work until this afternoon. We can go to Saint Hedwig's Cemetery. We should be going anyway. We'll get some flowers on the way and you grab a trowel and some rags and we'll clean off the gravestones."

Rosemary laid a pot of golden mums between the headstones and they both knelt at the foot of the gravesites with their own silent prayers. Rosemary got up and waited for Mickey to get up.

"I think what I want to do Rosie, is to bury Perro's ashes here between the graves. Do you think that would be okay? We won't get in any trouble, will we?"

"I think that's a great idea. Let's just dig a little hole between the headstones and sprinkle in the ashes. I don't see a problem."

Mickey smiled, grabbed the hand trowel and started to dig. He sprinkled the ashes carefully into the hole and pushed the dirt on top of the ashes with his hands and smoothed it over so it wouldn't be obvious that someone was digging at a grave site. He stood up, looked down and with a slight crack in his prepubescent voice he said. "Goodbye old friend. I'm going to miss you."

On their silent ride back home, Rosemary had a

surprise for Mickey.

"Mickey, look in my purse. There's a poem in there that you might take some comfort in."

Mickey picked up Rosemary's purse from the car floor, snapped open the clasp and found a multi-colored folded piece of paper. He unfolded it and saw a poem entitled "Rainbow Bridge". He started to silently read.

> *There is a bridge connecting Heaven and Earth*
> *It's called the Rainbow Bridge because of its many*
> *Colors. Just this side of the Rainbow Bridge there*
> *Is a land of hills, meadows and valleys with*
> *Lush green grass.*
>
> *When a beloved pet dies, he goes to this place*
> *Where there is food and water and warm spring weather.*
>
> *The old and frail animals are young again.*
> *Those who are maimed are made whole again. . . . .*

Mickey continued to read and Rosemary could feel a smile breaking out and replacing the tears on Mickey's face. She wasn't sure when she first had the idea to show Mickey the poem. She didn't want to bring more sorrow into his young life. The smile told her she did the right thing. The poem was one that she had discussed in her literature class in high school and it gave her deep thoughts about the meaning of heaven and is it real? And if it's real, does that mean its real for our pets who become so much a part of our family? Mickey asked that very question.

"Rosie, do you really think that Perro is in Heaven?"

"Why not? If Mom and Dad are in Heaven, why not Perro? I think its possible we'll see him again one day along with Mom and Dad. How about you? You believe it's possible?"

"Yeah, I guess so. It's good to think that way." The rest of the ride home was with similar thoughts going through both of their souls.

The following day after the visit to the cemetery and leaving Perro's ashes at his parent's gravesite, Mickey decided to go in the backyard and clean out Perro's house. October weather was rearing its ugly head. The wind was howling. Leaves were blowing in small eddies and the threat of colder weather was evident in the bite of the air. Mickey looked around the yard as if Perro was still there and he would come running up to him. That thought quickly faded as he saw the stain and remnants of vomit on the patch of dying grass in front of the dog house.

Mickey knelt down at the entrance and reached inside and scooped out all of the straw. He could still smell the mixture of the smell from the straw along with Perro's familiar smell. He was cried-out, so no tears came. He bundled up the straw with both hands and carried it over to the fence and threw it into the alley. The wind caught it and distributed it along the alleyway. The last of Perro was fading into the wind.

As Mickey turned to get out of the cold and back into a warm house, he noticed a wadded-up piece of brown paper caught under a corner of the dog house. For whatever reason, he stooped down and picked it up. He unfolded it and stared at it and hot blood rushed into his face as he read the faded pencil markings on the paper . . . **Kolpacki!**

He folded it back over and walked into the house and shouted "Rosie, I need you. Where are you?"

Rosemary rushed into the kitchen where Mickey was standing and looking at the piece of paper. "What's the matter Mickey? You scared the shit out of me yelling like that."

"Look at this Rosie. I found it in the yard when I went to clean out Perro's straw from his house. I told you that bastard Georgie did this and here's the proof."

Rosemary took the paper, unfolded it and looked at the writing. "Why do you think this is tied to Georgie. It's just a piece of paper that blew into the yard with the Kolpacki's name on it."

"I know. But he probably brought that hot dog over in that paper. I'm sure of it. Can't we take it to the police or something?"

"I don't know if they would do anything about it. To them it's just a dog. I know to us Perro was part of the family. Its not like losing Mom and Dad but it still hurts. Listen Mickey, here's what I'll do. I'll take the paper and talk to Aunt Anna and see what she thinks and if she agrees, I'll take it to the police. Maybe give it to that Trooper Emery that we talked to after the accident. Will that work for you Mickey?"

"Yeah. Thanks Rosie." Rosemary opened her arms and Mickey took the cue and they gave each other a warm hug.

Aunt Anna made one of her weekly visits to Rosemary and Mickey. She had been visiting two to three times a week but now that her and Norman were seeing more and more of each other, her time visiting the children lessened.

"How are you doing Rosie? And Mickey, how is he doing? Sorry I haven't been visiting as much. I got a lot going on I'll tell you about."

Anna proceeded to tell Rosemary about her meeting Norman at Federal's Department Store and that they had been dating at least weekly, sometimes more. "Things were getting serious," she told Rosemary with a broad smile on her face.

"In fact, I am going to his bar, Nifty Norman's, this weekend to see what that looks like. I'm all excited and nervous also."

"So glad to hear all of that Aunt Anna. You deserve a nice man to have in your life. I hope for the best. Now as far as Mickey and Me, we've had a bit of a sad week. We tried to reach you but you were working or with your new friend. Not to worry. We handled it okay. Perro is gone! We think someone poisoned him. We cremated him and put his ashes near Mom and Dad." Rosemary dabbed a tear from the corner of her eye. "Mickey is devastated, as I am. Let me ask you a question Aunt Anna. Mickey thinks that Perro was poisoned by Georgie Kolpacki as a way of revenge because Perro was barking at him and took a nip at his leg. He found a piece of butcher paper with the name Kolpacki on it and he thinks Georgie poisoned a hot dog and fed it to Perro. My question to you is should we go to the police with this story? Mickey thinks we should. I'm not so sure they would do anything about a dog being poisoned – even if it is true. What do you think?"

"Oh Rosie, I'm so sorry. Perro was such a cute and friendly dog. I can't imagine him trying to bite anyone. Georgie must have done something to him. Dogs are smart and they can sense a lot of things in humans, like fear or hatred or even love. I know the Kolpacki family down the street. The Mother and Father are both drunks and it's not a very good household — no discipline and all that. So maybe he would do something like that to get back at Perro. As far as the police, I'm not so sure either, if they would do anything. Let me do this Rosie. I will talk to Norman about it. He says he has a lot of policemen customers, so maybe he can ask around and see if makes sense to go to the police. I'll let you know." Anna opened her arms and Rosie came forward and they hugged.

"Thank you, Aunt Anna. I'll tell Mickey that you're going to follow up with some police. He'll be glad to hear that."

12

Nifty Norman's

Norman picked up Anna Saturday evening. Anna was losing the nervous side of her anxiety but keeping the pleasant excitement in their dates. Since this was a new adventure for her, some of the nervousness returned along with the excited feeling. She knew she would be meeting a lot of his customers, that in most cases were his friends. She worried about making a good impression and not embarrassing herself or worse . . . embarrassing Norman.

Nifty Norman's was not far from her house. On the way there they made small talk and she tried to relax. Norman parked at the rear of the bar in front of the sign on the wall of the bar that said "Private Parking – Violators will be towed." It was next to the rear entrance of the bar and had a cartoon drawing of a tow truck. Norman said they should walk around to the front of the bar to make their entrance; so as not to look like they sneaked in and were hiding their new relationship.

The front door was a heavy, dark, oak-stained door with a multi-colored, beveled, oval glass insert, worthy of a church window. There was a small vestibule and a heavy metal door that was kept open and only locked when the bar was closed.

Anna entered the dimly lit interior as Norman held the door. Coming in from the sunlight blinded her for a second. She was overwhelmed by what she saw. It was not your typical neighborhood bar. Anna could not remember ever being in a bar so this was a double shock to her system. Her first visit to a bar and now dating the owner of that bar.

They walked hand-in-hand along the aisle running alongside the classic wood bar. Anna noticed the mirrored back wall behind the bar with glass shelves holding all varieties of liquor, from bar whiskey to single malt scotch in crystal decanters. Hellos and brief handshakes and stares at Norman's partner followed them to the rear of the bar where there was one empty booth . . . obviously Norman's private booth. Norman held Anna's hand as she gracefully slid into one side of the booth and he slid into the other side.

"What can I get for you and the lady, Boss?" an attractive petite waitress asked as she stared at Anna.

"Hi Doris. This is my friend Anna. What can Doris get for you? I'll have Macallan . . . neat."

Anna nodded to Doris and hesitated. She never even

thought about ordering a drink. She quickly thought of something she heard on a TV show that sounded benign. "I'll have a rum and Coke."

While they were waiting for the drinks to come, Anna surveyed the bar. She saw couples occupying booths all along the wall away from the bar. The bar stools were mostly occupied with a variety of characters: single and married middle-aged women dressed to the nines, young men leaning their elbows on the bar-rail talking to the women in hopes of making a score, and a smattering of the men with Roman noses looking as if they were cut out of a Jimmy Cagney movie. There were also a few men standing, wearing suit jackets that were hiding bulges on their belt line, either legal or illegal.

"This is the main bar and as you can see it's pretty busy. I've got a great crew here so I don't have to worry. Some have been with me since I opened up a while back, about ten years . . . I guess. There's a back room with a pool table, shuffleboard table and a jukebox we can visit after a few drinks." Norman nodded toward the back of the room. Anna could hear a soft Sinatra tune wafting in from the back room.

The drinks came and they both sipped as customers came by and Norman introduced them to Anna. "I'll never remember all their names. I'm overwhelmed. You sure have a lot of friends, customers. Must give you a warm feeling."

"Yes., It sure does. I can tell you that anything that I might need done as a favor or whatever, I can find in this mixture of humanity. Some legal and some . . . not so much." Norman grinned and raised his glass to Anna to toast. She responded in-like manner with a smile and a clink of their glasses.

"That brings me to a question I have. My niece and nephew had their dog die last week and they think it was one of the local teenagers that poisoned the dog. They were wondering if they should report it to the police or just forget about it. Do you have some police customers here that might know what to do, Norman?"

"I certainly do. And one or two are detectives so they might know what to do or not to do. Not now, but next week when it's a little quieter around here I can ask around. Will that work Anna?"

"Yes, fine. No hurry."

"I see two open stools at the bar. Let's go over there. I want you to meet my main bartender, Lanny . . . aka Big Tuna. This guy is the absolute best bartender in the state and you'll see why."

Anna followed Norman over to the empty barstools. She had never sat on a barstool so she was careful as she placed her backside on the stool, put one foot on the stool foot-rail and tried to gently slide on. She did it — but wasn't too sure if it came off as ladylike.

Norman introduced Anna to Lanny and she could see why he acquired the nickname Big Tuna. He had a folded apron tied around what had been his waist, but now was a well-rounded pot belly. As Anna talked to him and their small talk went back and forth, she could see why he was such a good bartender. He was friendly and he listened and talked with a friendly smile that never seemed to wane.

The following Wednesday Norman picked up Anna after she got off work and asked her if she would like to grab a bite to eat at the bar and he said he had someone who could answer the question about the dog poisoning.

Anna was pleased that Norman had taken her request seriously about Perro and his poisoning. "Wow! That was fast. Who are we going to talk to?"

"You'll see. It's one of my acquaintances that has helped me in the past. We'll have a burger or whatever you'd like from the limited menu. Friday is our big meal day. Fish fries on Friday in this Catholic neighborhood are a real boon to my business. The cops from the neighborhood and even from out of the neighborhood love the FREE fish fries and it helps when I need a favor.

They parked Norman's shiny black El Dorado in his spot at the rear of the bar and this time they entered through the back door. Anna felt honored as some of the customers that she met on her first visit, remembered her name as they greeted both her and Norman. They walked into the back room where there were four customers playing pool and two other customers playing on the table shuffleboard. "Rags to Riches" by Tony Bennet was softly playing on the juke box. Nods to Norman and Anna were given as they took a seat at one of the tables spread throughout the room.

"I'm going to go up to the bar and order something for us. No wait staff this early in the evening. What'll it be? I think they have burgers or hot dogs, Reuben sandwiches but no fish until Friday. And to drink?"

"I'll have a Reuben and just a Coke."

She watched as Norman walked out of the room and over to the bar. She felt a bit uncomfortable, sitting by herself and tried to look interested in the pool game. When one of the players scratched on his bank-shot to sink the eight ball, he let out an, "Oh Fuck". Anna was a bit shocked. She tried to act as if she didn't hear it, moving her head away from the pool game and looking out toward the bar. Anna looked surprised as the player walked over to her. He was a middle-aged man with a broad-shouldered physique and a slight paunch that was emphasized by his yellow golf shirt. His hair was jet black with streaks of grey at the temple.

The pool player, realizing what he had done, and knowing that this was Norman's friend immediately apologized to Anna.

"I am so sorry if you heard my crude language. I forgot that you were here. Please accept my apologies. Sorry I don't know your name?"

"It's Anna and not to worry. Not that I haven't heard it before. No need to apologize."

Anna tried to brush it off.

As they were talking Norman returned with Anna's Coke and his bottle of Stroh's beer. "I see you two have met. Great. Anna, this is Anthony – don't call me Tony or Ant, and he is the contact I told you about that can help us with that dog thing. Anthony smiled. Anna smiled.

"I told Anthony about your little dilemma with the dog poisoning. What was his name?"

"Perro. That's Spanish for dog and he's a Chihuahua . . . so why not Perro?"

"Clever. Before we go any further, a little background on Anthony here. He spent twenty years with the Detroit Police Department. From beat cop up to homicide detective. He retired and is now a security person, if you will, for people in the neighborhood that need personal protection. We'll leave it at that."

"Yeah, leave it at that, Norm." Anthony said with

his elbows leaning on the table and his fingers laced.

"Okay Anthony. Tell Anna here what you think she should do." Norman said as he nodded his head over toward Anna.

"First of all, Anna, happy to meet you. Sorry about my language a minute ago. Norm always did have excellent taste in women and I must say Anna, you are one of the best looking,"

"Enough with the schmoozing, Anthony. Get to the info."

"Okay. So, with my past experience in the police, I know for a fact that they would do very little to follow-up on a dog poisoning. They might come out and make a report but that would be it. They have more important things to do. So, no I would not report it to the police. It would be a waste of time." Anna nodded her head as she listened to Anthony's explanation of police protocol.

"Here's what I would recommend. It's strictly up to you and Norm, I guess. If this kid is harassing you or your family and you think he poisoned your dog, then I could pay him a visit and put the fear of God in him. Nothing serious, just send him a message. You can think about it and discuss it with Norm and Norm, you know where to find me. I'm here most days, but busy bodyguarding in the evenings and nights."

"It's not my dog. Perro belongs . . . I mean

belonged, to my niece and nephew. The kid that they think poisoned Perro lives in the neighborhood and they found some evidence in the way of some paper with the family name on it. I sure don't want to hurt anyone but as far as putting the fear of God in him, as you said, I want to talk to my niece and nephew first. What do you think Norman?" Anna said.

Norman shrugged his shoulders. "You're right. You should talk to Mickey and Rosie and let them in on the decision. I can be with you when you tell them the options if you want."

"Okay, good. I'll do that and Norm will let you know what we decide, Anthony. Thank you for your information and offer to help." Anna said as Anthony got up and extended his hand to her. She shook it and Anthony went back to shooting pool.

When they were done eating, Norman asked Anna, "Would you like to visit my bachelor pad up-stairs? No etchings to show you just watch a movie or listen to some music and discuss what you are going to tell the kids about what Anthony said," Norman said with a snicker.

"I'd be happy to see your place."

There was a door in the corner at the back of the room that led up to Norman's apartment. He pulled out a key on a key ring and unlocked the door. The stairs, lit by a bulb at the top off the stairs provided a well-lit staircase. Norman had a tough time following Anna up the stairs and trying to keep his eyes above her waste ... to no avail.

Norman's apartment consisted of a large living room with a small dinette at one end and comfortable looking sofa and easy chairs at the other. There was a television next to a record-player on a bookcase filled with LPs, hardcover books, and stacks of magazines. A full-size bathroom with a shower head over the clawfoot tub, a pedestal sink, a generous sized bedroom, and a small kitchen completed the apartment.

Norman, without asking, went into the kitchen and brought out a chilled bottle of Chianti and two long-stemmed wine glasses. Showing off his sommelier knowledge, he held the glasses upside-down with the stems between his fingers on one hand and the bottle in the other hand. He nodded his head as he presented the bottle and glasses to Anna. "You want a glass? Or two?"

"Yes, that would be great. A wind down from all that Anthony told us."

Norman set the glasses on a large oak coffee table and poured two half-glasses of the Chianti. He gave one to Anna and presented a toast to her. "Here's to our meeting and the pleasant times we're spending together."

Anna reached up with her glass and smiled, tapped her glass on Norman's, smiled and nodded her head as she took a sip.

The evening was comfortable for both of them. Norman put a Vic Damone album on his Victrola and turned it on low.

Anna had not had her breasts felt in more years than she cared to remember. The rush she got was overwhelming. Norman knew from talking to Anna over the previous weeks that she had not dated for a long time. She had told him of the love she lost so many years ago. She never told him about any recent affairs, so he assumed that their relationship was almost as it was her first. Keeping all that in mind, along with her shyness, he was determined to take it slow and not ruin what was turning out to be something that he wanted to continue and develop into something he never had with all his previous relationships . . . a meaningful long-lasting relationship!

The soft touch of her breast and his hand on her nyloned thigh was all that they needed for this first encounter. Thinking about their future encounters would be exciting in itself and worth waiting for – for both of them!

Anna arranged for Norman to meet with her and Mickey and Rosemary the next week. Norman would pick her up and they would go to Mickey and Rosie's house.

Rosie answered the door and invited Aunt Anna and Norman in. Introductions were made and they sat down at the dining room table to discuss the matter of dealing with Georgie and the poisoning of Perro.

"Mickey, can you take me outside and show me where it happened and show me the paper you found in the yard?" Norman asked.

"Yeah, sure. Follow me." Mickey got up and Norman followed him through the kitchen and out the back door.

Mickey pointed to the dog house and the spot where he found Perro. There was still a stain on the fall grass and some dried and dying grass from the aftermath of the poisoning. Mickey reached in his back pocket and handed the piece of brown butcher paper to Norman.

"This is the paper I found next to the dog house. You can see the name on the paper and I think that Georgie used it to carry a poisoned hot dog over here."

They both looked around for a while, then went back inside where Anna and Rosie were waiting.

"Did Anna tell you what my friend suggested

about giving that kid Georgie a bit of a scare to keep him away from you?"

"She did. Mickey, they want one of Norman's friends to give Georgie a message to keep him away from us. He said that going to the police would not do much good. They would file a report and that would be it. What do you think? Do you want him to give Georgie a scare?" Rosie asked Mickey.

Mickey scratched his chin as he thought. "I don't know. Knowing Georgie and his hate for me and Lenny since we became friends, might give him more reason to harass us. Let's just wait and if he does anything else then we can go with that. Okay?"

"Okay Mickey. I agree. Let's just let it go for now and wait and see," Rosie answered.

Rosie offered drinks, coffee, pop and a beer for Norman and they sat around the table and got to know each other. Rosie could see the light in Aunt Anna's eyes when she looked at Norman and could also see that Norman was definitely interested in Aunt Anna by his very interest in her family. After a while, Norman said he had to get back to the bar and asked Anna if she wanted a ride home. She said she would walk back home, that she wanted to spend some time with Mickey and Rosie.

"Well kids, what do you think? You like?"

"Wow, Aunt Anna. Looks like a good catch. Tall

dark and handsome and owner of a bar. I'm impressed. How about you Mickey? You like him?"

"Yeah, he seems like a cool guy," Mickey answered.

"Is everything going good for you two, except for losing Perro?"

"Pretty good. Mickey made some friends in high school and I'm busy with working at the bank and probably start night school in January. Thanks for asking."

They talked some more about school and work and Aunt Anna's new boyfriend and Aunt Anna promised to keep in touch and told them to let her know if there were any problems.

13

Devil's Night II

It had been one year since the crash that killed Mickey and Rosemary's parents, Larry and Doris. Mickey had gone over to Lenny's house where they decided to stay in and play checkers or chess and watch a scary movie on TV, rather than Devil's Night pranking. Rosemary had the night off from work and declined an invitation from her girlfriends to spend the night with them. They knew it was the anniversary of Rosie's parents' death and they wanted to keep her company. She decided to spend the night in wonderful thoughts of her parents. The hurtful aching of their loss was waning a bit and she felt things were going as good as could be expected. Mickey was doing good with his new friend Lenny. Aunt Anna was doing great with her new boyfriend, Norman. It was an unexpected relationship that Rosemary never would have guessed. She knew her mother would be so happy for her sister Anna, that everyone had thought of as an old maid-spinster, but now was in a meaningful relationship and who knew where it was going? Since Anna had transformed herself, she was looking more and more like her sister Doris. Rosemary and Mickey were unconsciously feeling their mother's presence in Aunt Anna. It was a wonderful change in Aunt Anna's life that made Rosemary warm inside when she thought about Aunt Anna, her mother's sister.

The night was warm, especially for October 30th. Rosemary decided to sit on the front porch steps and make sure there was no mischief going on – on this Devil's Night. The night was eerily quiet as well as warm with a slight breeze shuffling the fallen leaves around. Deep in her thoughts about this anniversary, she caught a figure walking alone down the sidewalk toward her. As the figure got closer, she recognized who it was. It was Georgie! She kept her eye on him as he got closer. When he was directly in front of her house, he swiveled his head toward her. She could see an evil grin on his face.

"Where's your bitch dog, Rosie, you bitch. I see he's no where around to take a nip at me."

"We know you poisoned him, Georgie. And if you have any other thoughts in mind about getting at me or Mickey, you've got another thought coming. Just keep walking before I call someone to take care of your sorry ass." Rosemary said, as she stood up with her arms akimbo and walked down the steps toward Georgie.

"Have a nice Devil's Night, Rosie. Like you did a year ago," Georgie yelled back at her and continued to walk.

As he picked up his pace, he thought he heard a growl coming from the shadows that covered the sidewalk behind him. He turned his head and could see the shadowy-dark black and brown figure of a Dobermann Pinscher blending into the bushes. His ears were raised pointing straight up and his mouth was open showing his sparkling white teeth lit up by the moonlight. The growling continued as it got closer to Georgie. Georgie's heart started beating faster and a cold sweat broke out on his forehead. He walked faster and the Dobermann stayed on his heals, growling and drooling. Georgie walked even faster as his heart beat faster. He broke into a trot and then a run and the beast kept pace.

Georgie had walked this route most of his life, back and forth to school and around the neighborhood. He knew every crack and uneven sidewalk. As his fear of being attacked by this dog increased, he lost track of where he was. The two-inch-high uneven cement sidewalk pad that he would normally skip over, caught the toe of his boot and he tumbled forward skidding on his palms. He turned to see where the dog was. Nothing! There was no dog! All he could see were the moonlight shadows of the trees and bushes smeared on the sidewalk. He pushed himself up, starred at his skinned palms and once again looked around for the dog that was chasing him. He thought that Rosemary was behind all of this. He was breathing hard and fast as he walked back to the Lesko house. Rosemary was not on the porch. He went up to the front door and rapped heavily with his knuckles on the door and shouted for Rosemary to open the door.

"I know you sent that dog after me, you bitch," Georgie shouted at the closed door. He turned, looked at his bleeding palms again, wiped them in his Levi's and swiveled his head in both directions, looking for the dog that followed him. He thought. *Was that a real dog? I saw him. I heard him. I smelled him. Am I imagining things? He just disappeared. What the fuck is going on. It must be they got another dog to hassle me. I'll fix her ass. For Sure!*

Rosemary heard Georgie screaming on the front porch. She went to the door and peered out. She saw Georgie going down the steps and talking to himself. *What dog is he talking about?* she thought. "You're crazy Georgie. And keep away from our house and me and Mickey. Like I said, I'll have someone take care of you if you continue to harass us." Rosemary shouted back at Georgie as he faded – alone – into the shadows.

Georgie continued home with the spectre of the Dobermann Pinscher fresh in his head. As usual, his parents were out at one of the local bars and he was left to fend for himself. He gobbled down a stale do-nut with orange sprinkles on it and opened the fridge door. There were twelve bottles of E&B beer on the bottom shelf. He grabbed a paper sack and carefully put four bottles in the bag — one for each of his new friends and himself.

They had agreed to meet at the Radke house and clubhouse to discuss their plans for Devil's Night. Ali, Chico, and Jimmy were already there when Georgie arrived and entered through the back door. He care-fully tiptoed across the kitchen and down the base-ment steps. They were smoking and sitting around an upturned orange crate with three different colored candles burning and flickering from a draft seeping under the door. Georgie could smell the wax and see the candle light flickering under the closed door. He rapped lightly on the door and whispered, "I've come to kill you and cut off your heads and put them on the fence posts."

All three of the boys jumped to their feet when they heard Georgie trying to scare them.

"You asshole," Chico said as Georgie opened the door that let out a small squeak, adding to the eeriness.

"Where you been? We've been waiting for you for over an hour."

"Had a little scare of my own. That Rosie bitch got a new dog and he was chasing me and then I went home to get the beer.

"Just a little scare, guys. I come bearing gifts." Georgie said, as he passed out one beer to each of the three. He pulled out a bottle opener on a key chain and they passed it around and opened the warm shaken beer bottles. All four bottles erupted over onto the floor as the boys tried to catch the foam with their mouths.

"So, what's the plan guys? You do know it's Devil's Night. We need something scary to do. I'm sick of the waxing and trash cans and bags of shit lit on fire on porches. You guys think of anything?" Georgie asked, swiveling his head to each of the boys seated on orange crates. He was unconsciously thinking of the same request to his previous friends exactly one year ago.

"The last time you dreamed up a scare you caused an accident that killed some people, Georgie! We don't need any more police shit — especially if they're looking at you for the accident. We heard Mickey and Lenny are asshole buddies now and know what happened, so let's stay away from any of your dangerous shit, Georgie," Jimmy cautioned.

"Okay, Okay. No dangerous shit. So, you guys

come up with something and I'll go along."

"Hey, how about we go down to the railroad tracks down on Hammond and see if Boxcar Bertha is there. She can give us all a blow job. You guys got money? I think she'll do the whole crew for ten bucks. You in?" Chico asked.

They all searched around in their pockets and came up with a total of thirteen dollars and 75 cents.

"I'll go along with you guys but I don't want that skank touchin my dick. I'll keep guard." Georgie said in an attempt to be part of the gang but afraid of how he might react - or not react – to a female touching him. He had never been with a girl except for the occasional titty-grope, which never excited him. He was afraid of embarrassing himself if he couldn't get excited in an act of fellatio.

"I've got a better idea. Not tonight but in the near future. I would like to get that Rosie bitch here in the clubhouse and we could all have a little fun with her. What do you guys say to that huh?"

"You're crazy Georgie. How would you get her down here? 'Please Rosie, come down to our leetle clubhouse. All the guys want to play house with you and fuck your socks off.' Is that how you're going to do it, Georgie?"

Ali, Chico, and Jimmy all let out a laugh. "I'll figure something out. I just want to teach that bitch a lesson for scaring me with that dog."

"Okay Georgie. You do that and let us know when you have a plan. Now let's go see Bertha." Chico said as he grabbed his crotch and waved his hands to follow him out of the clubhouse room and up the stairs.

Halloween Day. Rosemary had spent a restless night thinking about her encounter with Georgie and the strange shouting at her about a non-existent dog. That was strange and a bit worrisome. She also thought about her parents and how she missed them and about Mickey. Mickey had stayed overnight at Lenny's house so she didn't have to worry about him getting into any trouble on Devil's Night. She was having her first cup of coffee and thinking that Mickey should be home shortly. She tightened the waist tie around her powder blue chenille bathrobe and decided to retrieve the newspaper from the front porch. As she approached the front door, the door suddenly opened. It gave her a start, thinking about the events last evening. It was Mickey, holding *The Detroit Times* newspaper.

"Sorry Rosie. Did I scare you? You look like you saw a ghost."

"You did startle me a bit. Had a bad night thinking about Mom and Dad and another encounter with Georgie. I'll tell you about it when you get settled and we have some breakfast. Hope you had a better night."

Mickey quickly took his duffle bag with pajamas and some of his games and threw them on his bed and joined Rosemary in the kitchen for breakfast. An overnight rain was continuing and was intensifying as they cooked and sat down to eat.

"Listen Mickey. I don't know what to do after we got that offer from Aunt Anna and her new boyfriend. Georgie walked by last night and made some crude remarks to me and some remarks about Mom and Dad's death and also about Perro. He also was a little loopy or maybe he was drinking with his friends. He yelled at me for some dog he saw. I never saw a dog. He threatened me and I'm a little scared. I'm thinking about calling Aunt Anna and have that guy they know give him a little scare before he does something else. You didn't happen to see him last night, did you?"

"I didn't. We stayed in and played checkers and watched a Sir Graves vampire movie. So, what do you want to do? I'm all for giving him a scare. I just want him to leave us alone. I'm enjoying my new friendship with Lenny and I don't want him to spoil it. Lenny was a bit secretive when we first started hanging out, but lately he's been a lot more open. I think he knows more about Mom and Dad's accident and I think it has to do with Georgie."

"Okay, I'll contact Aunt Anna later and tell her we need to talk. Are you going begging tonight? What are you dressing up as?"

"I'm not going. Lenny is coming over here and we'll help you pass out candy. I hope you remembered to get some Tootsie Rolls or Mary Janes or whatever. We can sit on the porch with you. Anyway, it looks like it's going to rain or even pour tonight."

"Oh . . . Great. I've got the candy. I just need to keep you and Lenny away from eating it all before the kids get here. If it's a slow night you'll have a lot to divvy-up. Porch light on around 6, so have Lenny come over for dinner before that. I've got some dogs and mac and cheese for dinner."

Mickey was right. The pouring rain ruined the trick or treat night. Only a few tricksters in make-shift garbage bag raincoats braved the weather. Lenny and Mickey would have more than enough Squirrels, Mary Janes, Dum Dum's, and Tootsie Rolls to share. Georgie and his friends were nowhere to be seen.

Rosemary called Aunt Anna and asked her to have Norman come over to discuss the action to take on the Kolpacki kid.

Norman came to Mickey and Rosemary's house

without Anna. She was working that day and she had told Norman that Rosemary would be expecting him. Mickey had a Catholic school off-day on this November 1st, All Saints Day. He was spending his time with Lenny.

Rosemary invited Norman in and he took a seat at the dining room table across from Rosemary. He was smartly dressed in an open collar hunter-green silk shirt. The green in the shirt brought out his green eyes and caught Rosemary's attention. She was trying not to stare but she was thinking what a handsome man Aunt Anna had latched on to. She quickly got to the subject at hand.

"That kid Georgie was harassing me the other day and he was acting a bit crazy . . . seeing imaginary dogs. He brought up my parent's death and the poisoning of our dog Perro. I'm a bit scared that he might take it further and try to hurt Mickey or me. So can you help us out as we discussed before?"

"I think I can. I'll contact a guy that has done some work for me and I can have him send a message to this kid so he won't bother either you or your brother. And, I will make sure no one gets hurt — just a not-so-friendly message to back off. Will that work for you?"

"It will. I'll give you all the physical details that I can about Georgie and where he lives and hangs out at. I don't know the names of the boys he hangs out with but maybe Mickey can help with that."

The ball was rolling. Mickey called Norman later that day and told him the names: Chico, Ali, and Jimmy. He told Norman they mostly hung-out after dinner and evenings on the corner where Steve's pool hall was located.

Norman picked up Anna later that day when she got off from work.

"I talked to the kids and got all the information I need as far as who the Georgie kid is and what he looks like and his friends. Rosie and Mickey are sure that they want to go through with this and Rosie told me that he was harassing her and talking about her parent's deaths and the death of their dog. She said he was acting a bit strange and was talking about a dog that was chasing him and Rosie said she didn't see any dog. This kid might be a bit delusional and paranoid or even sociopathic and that's not good. He could take this further and try to hurt one of them. I just wanted to update you and see what you think about sending a message to this Georgie."

"If that's what they want and this kid is acting dangerous then I'm all for it. Do what you have to do with your friend Anthony. But as we said before . . . nothing physical. Okay?"

"Okay ma'am, at your service." Norman smiled and gently grabbed Anna's shoulders, brought her to him, and gave her a mild hug. He felt good about help-ing Anna and her family. Being a loner for a good part of his life made this family bonding so much more rewarding.

Georgie, Ali, Jimmy, and Chico were standing in front of Steve's pool hall, smoking, swearing and laughing about their encounter with Boxcar Bertha on Devil's Night. Anthony walked slowly, led by his Dobermann on a short leash. Chico was the first to notice. "Holy shit. Look at that dog. I wouldn't want to mess with him."

Georgie looked where Chico pointed and cringed. He unconsciously moved behind the other three boys in an attempt to hide himself. As Chico said, *he didn't want to mess with that dog* – as he thought of his ghostly encounter two nights ago.

Anthony continued to walk slowly toward the group with a wry smile. The Dobermann, with a shiny silver spiked collar around his neck, was lead-ing him and Anthony was straining to keep up a walking pace. The smile turned to a frown as he got nearer. "Which one of you is Georgie?" He asked and quickly noticed Georgie hiding behind the other three boys. The dog sniffed at the three standing in front of Georgie. When he approached Georgie, his ears raised and pointed sharply up. He barred his teeth and a deep growl seeped out of his mouth.

Chico raised his hand with his thumb pointing behind him. "That's him. Why? What do you need?"

Georgie peeked around Jimmy's shoulder without moving and looked at Anthony. "Who the fuck are you and what do you want me for?"

Anthony let out a little guffaw at the brashness of Georgie – especially with his growling Dobermann at his side.

"Never mind who I am. I just want you to meet my friend here. Looks like he's not very fond of you Georgie. His name is Lucifer. And Lucifer has a little message for you. You need to stay away from the Lesko house and Rosemary and Mickey. If Lucifer sees you around that house or people, I will take off this leash and let him have at you. Do you understand? This is the only warning I'm going to give you . . . so make sure it sinks in. And you guys, make sure you tell your friend that I mean business. I'm used to dealing with punks like you and quite frankly . . . I enjoy it!"

Anthony didn't wait for a reply. He could see the fear in all of their eyes, even though the message was given directly to Georgie. He turned, tugged at Lucifer's leash and slowly walked away, smiling to himself. *I think I scared the shit out of all of them.* He thought.

"What the hell was all that about, Georgie? That dog was pretty scary, especially when he got close to you. And that guy . . . he was also scary. He looked like some kind of hood with connections, like one of my dad's goombahs. I wouldn't want to mess with either of them," Jimmy said.

Georgie was feeling both fear from another encounter with a Dobermann and more than the fear . . . was the anger. The anger that had been building up in him since that fateful Devil's Night. And his miserable life, as he compared it to the other boys. Even his new friends were better off than he was. If he could convince them to help him get his revenge then that's what he would do. He would bring them down to his level. He was beginning to feel the power he had with his old friends: Jimmy, Lenny, Mark, and Stanley. Now he would have to convince his new friends to help him with his revenge on Rosie, Mickey and Lenny.

"It's that damn Rosie. I told you she threatened me the other night – Devil's Night – when I walked past her house. And maybe that was the dog I saw. I don't know. But I'll tell you this, she's not going to scare me with some goon she hired. And that bitch Dobermann, I'll poison it like I got rid of Mickey's dog. I'm thinking of what I told you guys before. We can grab her and take her down to the clubhouse and have a little fun with her. Maybe that'll teach her not to fuck with me or us. What do you guys think?" Georgie was bringing them into his world adding "us" to his plan.

They all shrugged their shoulders and Ali said. "I know that Rosie. She's got a pretty hot ass. I wouldn't mind getting a taste of that. Would be better than the blow jobs we got the other night from Bertha. Count me in. Just come up with a plan."

Jimmy shook his head. "You guys are crazy. As I said, that guy looked like one of my dad's goombahs and I don't think I want to fuck with him. You'll have to come up with a pretty good plan Georgie to cover our asses otherwise count me out."

"I'm with Jimmy. Unless you come up with a good plan Georgie, count me out," Chico said.

"I will. You'll see."

Georgie thought about what he had started to plan in the way of revenge on Rosie for the threat she made with the man and the dog. The obsession was hardening the more he thought about it and the more he saw the Dobermann in his head. His parents were sound asleep or passed out from a night of drinking. He could hear them snoring in unison as he entered the kitchen. He grabbed a hunk of welfare cheese from the refrigerator and went to his room to think about what he needed to do to convince his friends to help him in his act of revenge.

He laid on his unmade bed with the smell of body odors and damp moldiness and pushed his brain with a dozen different schemes. Nothing was registering. He had to have something foolproof. Something to convince his friends to grab Rosie and do his dirty deed.

After a while, of trying to come up with a plan, he grew tired and fell asleep with his clothes on and dreamt of packs of Dobermanns chasing him through the neighborhood, nipping at his heels. The faster he ran the faster the dogs ran. There was no escaping. He ran out of the neighborhood and could not find his way back. The chase was relentless and went on and on until he finally woke up in a cold sweat. The sun was breaking through his dust-covered flimsy-curtained windows. The snoring in the next room was still there. He washed his face with cold water, smelled his armpits, put on a different tee shirt, ate two pieces of toast and went out to walk around and clear his mind of the nightmare of Dobermanns. It cleared as he remembered that he still needed a plan for his revenge.

Then it came to him. The plan he had devised when he wanted to have an alibi on that Devil's Night and the dummy hanging from the bridge had worked. Why not a similar plan to produce the perfect alibi. Since he was still struggling about whether he could perform with a girl, especially Rosie, he thought that having the other three boys taking care of her while he provided an alibi for them might just work. He started to work out the details in his head. He knew that Rosie worked at the local bank and that she often worked late. He had seen her walking home regularly from the bus stop. It would be easy to grab her and force her into their clubhouse in the Radke house, since she had to pass it on her way home. Solved!

Now for an alibi. Not solved!

He began thinking out loud as he walked down the street, heading to Steve's pool hall. *"Maybe if we convinced Steve to let us play some pool in the rear of the hall, we could establish an alibi? And then, the guys would leave and grab Rosie while I stand outside the pool hall and keep watch. Steve did let us play sometimes when business was slow and even though we weren't eighteen yet. That could work. I have to think about that some more. Not quite sure that's doable?"*

As he walked and thought he realized he was in front of Steve's pool hall. He walked in and saw Steve sitting on a stool behind the cigar case reading *The Detroit Free Press.*

"Hey Steve. How's it going? How's business?"

"Little slow right now. What do you want, Georgie? Ciggies for your old lady?"

"Nope. Not today. I was just wondering if me and the boys could come in some evening and shoot a little

8-ball. You know, like we did a couple times before. I know we're not eighteen. We wouldn't cause any problem. What do you say?"

"I don't know. Maybe. Thursdays are kinda slow. Maybe. I'd have to charge you double the rack rate . . . 50 cents. You'd have to play on that last table, back by the rear door. Come in Thursday and I'll see how it's going. Thursdays are my slow night, so maybe I can let you guys play. No swearing or spitting on the floor and once again you'd have pay double the rack rate."

"Okay Steve. Thanks. See you Thursday."

Georgie walked out of Steve's and had a huge smile on his face. He would have to meet with the other three and tell him his plans. Another thought came into his head. *Steve said they would have to play at the table in the rear of the pool hall — near the rear door! That could work just fine. A couple guys could sneak out and take care of business and we would have the perfect alibi. PERFECT!*

14

The Gales of November

Rosemary thought she was smart; she wore a winter coat that day. WJR radio weather said that winter would shortly be rearing its ugly head with freezing rain and wind. She decided to take the bus instead of driving. When she started out for work that afternoon the weather was cool and calm. October was stretching a bit into November. While she was at work, the first gale of November flipped the page from October to November's wind and freezing rain. As she stepped down from the bus at the bus stop on the corner of 31st and Buchanan she felt the cold immediately wending its way into her coat sleeves. She quickly hooked her purse strap over her shoulder, zipped up her coat as far as it would go and put her hands in her pockets. She was glad that she only had a block and a half to fight the wind and rain before she reached her warm house. She wished she had taken her Michigan State woolen hat and woolen gloves with her, but at least she had a woolen scarf that she put over her head, knotted it around her neck and tucked the trailing ends into her coat.

Georgie told Ali, Jimmy, and Chico to meet him at Steve's Pool Hall that evening. Before going in, he told them of his plan to grab Rosie and get her into the clubhouse. He said Steve gave them the okay to shoot some 8-ball at the rear of the hall. He told them that he had been stalking Rosemary on her daily routine coming home from work, usually on the bus. And if everything went as planned, they would be able to pull it off.

"Okay guys, here's the plan. I'm going to go in and see if Steve is still okay with us shooting pool at the last table near the rear door. The bus usually is on time and arrives at the bus stop around 8:15. She gets off the bus and walks right past the Radke house. Two of you . . . Ali and Chico, will be waiting next to the hardware store side-wall, next to the house. When you see her coming, you grab her and drag her ass to the rear of the house. If the door is locked, one of you will climb in the window and open the kitchen door. I tried it the last time we were there. There's a key on the inside that unlocks it. You drag her in the basement and have your way with her. Any questions?"

Chico and Ali smiled and rubbed their palms

together. "Sounds like a plan Georgie. I'm already getting a boner," Ali said as he rubbed his crotch. "What about you guys? What are you going to be doing? Why aren't you going Georgie? I thought this was your revenge plan?"

"It is my plan and she'll know I was part of it. But, she won't be able to ID me. She knows my voice and she doesn't know you guys. And Jimmy here, is afraid of that dog and the hood that looks like one of his dad's goombahs." Georgie said trying to justify all of his actions because of his fear of non-performance with Rosie!

"We're going to stay here and continue to play pool. You'll sneak out the back door and me and Jimmy will continue to play pool just like you were still here. Steve usually sits his ass on that stool behind the front counter most of the night so he won't even know you're gone. When you guys are done with having some fun with that Rosie bitch, you return here as if nothing happened."

"What do we do when we're done with her, Georgie? Just leave her there?"

"I don't know. I guess you guys just have to figure it out as you go. Did you guys remember to bring your ski masks? Don't want her to ID anyone. She'll probably think it was me anyway. But we've got the perfect alibi. Right?"

They all forced a smile and nodded nervously.

Georgie walked boldly into the pool hall where Steve was sitting on his stool as Georgie predicted. "Hi Steve. I've got a couple three guys with me. Is it okay to play some 8-ball on that back table? As we discussed?"

"Yeah, okay. But like I said. no spitting on the floor, no swearing, no butts on the floor, no cigarette burns on the tables . . . and double the rack rate . . . 50 cents."

"Okay good. Here's three bucks for six games. And thanks again Steve. We'll behave."

Georgie walked to the door and waved in the other three. They nodded to Steve as they entered and walked to the back of the hall. Steve nodded back and went back to reading *The Detroit Free Press,* spread out on the glass counter/humidor. They walked past a snooker table in the middle of the lined-up tables. It was the only other table being used.

"Rack em, Jimmy. I'll keep an eye on the clock, and when it's 8 o'clock I'll tell you guys and you can hike over to the hardware store and wait for her."

Jimmy gathered the balls from all the pockets and racked a tight rack as the other three grabbed house-cues from the rack on the wall next to the locked-up Balabushka cue sticks. He signaled Georgie to 'break'. Georgie made a low numbered ball on breaking the rack and continued to shoot making another low ball.

"We've got lows. And Chico and Ali, you got highs." Georgie said loud enough for the other players on the snooker table to hear. He wanted to reinforce their alibi that four of them were playing pool at that time.

Georgie kept an eye on the minute hand of the Cylkowski Funeral Parlor wall clock. The minutes were slow to pass. . . then the minute hand hit 8. "Okay guys time to go and be quiet with the door. Me and Jimmy will stand in front of the door to shield your exit," Georgie said in a hushed voice.

Chico and Ali took the cue and carefully exited the rear door and held the door pushed by the wind, and eased it closed. They were both wearing Levi jackets and the cold wind easily pushed through the denim material and quickly chilled their arms and chests. They trotted across the street anxious to get on the side of the hardware store wall to protect them from the wind. They could hear and see the wind slapping a few lonely stubborn wet leaves against the limbs of an oak tree in front of the Radke house.

Georgie was right. At exactly 8:15 Rosemary carefully stepped down from the high step of the bus exit onto the curb. Ali and Chico were taking turns with their head peeking around the corner of the building waiting for the DDOT bus. Chico signaled Ali. "She's here. Get ready. Pull down your mask."

Rosemary hunched over, in an attempt to keep

in her body heat, with her hands in her pockets she quicky crossed the street and made her way to the front of the hardware building on her way to her waiting warm house.

With the wind whistling and the leaves in violent eddies around her feet, she didn't hear or see the two until they were on either side of her, each grabbing an arm. "Just keep walking where we point you and listen to what we say and you won't get hurt," Chico loudly whispered into her ear making sure she heard him.

She looked at each of them and seeing their faces covered with black woolen ski masks she knew instantly she was in trouble.

"I have some money in my purse. You can have it all. Let me show you. You don't have to hurt me. Please, take the money and go. Please!" Rosemary pleaded as her nose started to drip from the bitter cold.

"We don't want your money, just do as you're told and you won't get hurt." Ali repeated with his slight middle-eastern accent. They both increased their grip on her arms and pushed her toward the rear of the Radke house.

"Get in and get the door. I'll hold her here till you open it," Chico said, careful not to use Ali's name.

Ali shimmied up and through the kitchen window

and went directly to the kitchen door. There was a skeleton key in the door lock. He twisted it and heard the lock grind and he pulled on the door that was stuck after being unused for a while. It finally opened with a loud creak. Ali stuck his head out and motioned to Chico to bring her in.

Rosemary was still pleading as Chico pushed her toward the open kitchen door. *What is happening? This is not Georgie. I would know him and his shitty voice but I know he's behind it somehow.* She thought as she felt a hand squeezing harder on her arm. She had forgot about the cold weather that remained cold in the house except without the wind and the rain.

She was led down the steps into the equally cold and damp cellar. Ali went into the clubhouse room and brought out a flashlight and two candles. There was an old worn oak kitchen table on the far end of the basement. Ali took the two candles, lit them, dripped some wax onto a peach crate and placed the candles onto the liquid wax and waited for it to set and support the candles. He motioned with the flashlight for Chico to bring her over to the table.

She tried to resist but he was much stronger than she was. She felt the futility as she continued to resist him. She was realizing what was coming next and it frightened her even more. The core of her body was shivering violently not only from the cold and dampness but from the fear of what was happening to her

Realizing they hadn't planned on restraints, Ali looked around the almost vacant basement. There was nothing. He swept the light beam around and around until he noticed that there were string-type cords hanging down from two overhead bulb fixtures. He walked over to one and yanked on the cord. The bulb didn't light. The power was off. He yanked harder and the cord came loose from the fixture. He walked over to the other light fixture and did the same.

"Get her over here at the table. We'll tie her wrists to the table."

Chico pushed her to the table until her hips were touching the edge of the table. He grabbed the strap of her purse and yanked it from her shoulder and threw to the cement floor. He reached around and unzipped her coat and forced it off her shoulders and threw it under the table. He pushed her forward so that she was bent over the table. Chico grabbed one of her wrists and pulled it toward the corner of the table top. He tied one end of a cord to her wrist and forced it until he could tie the other end to the table leg. She struggled but to no avail. Her head was forced sideways onto the table. She felt the heat from the candles and she could see brown-skinned arms tying her wrists to the table. She felt she should scream but who would hear her?

The physical pain was bad enough, but when they ripped off her underwear all emotions surged into her head: fear, anger, shame, confusion and terror. They took their turns and laughed as they finished their disgusting dirty deeds. Rosemary's mind collapsed into unconsciousness to protect her fragile psyche at the moment when all the emotions swarmed into one large feeling of terror.

She revived as Chico was untying one of her wrists. As her wrist was set free, she could only think of one thing. She raised her hand and with all her might she lunged her fingernails into the side of his neck and scraped her nails with all the energy she had left in her.

Chico let out a scream. "You bitch. We were going to free you, now you can free yourself. Let's go Ali. Leave this bitch," Chico said as he wiped the blood from his neck under the balaclava. They turned and left. She heard the name Ali!

Rosemary waited until she heard the footsteps overhead fade. With the one free hand she reached over and tried to untie the knot in the light cord on her other wrist. It was too tight and she was too weak. She moved the tied wrist back and forth, back and forth, and after what seemed like hours, she was able to squeeze her hand through the stretched cord. She stood up and rubbed her wrist vigorously to get the blood flowing again. She looked down to where her coat and purse lay under the table. Her ripped and soiled panties, that the attackers used to wipe themselves, lay on the floor under the table. She put on her coat. Her scarf was still tied loosely around her neck. She picked up her purse that now had a broken strap and tucked it under her arm.

In their haste they forgot about the candles and the flashlight sitting on the upturned orange crate. She walked over, and as she did, one candle flickered out. The other candle was still bouncing evil shadows on the basement walls. Her mind clicked into careful mode and she picked up the flashlight with her scarf, thinking that fingerprints might be on the flashlight tube. She carefully picked up her disgustingly stained panties and carefully folded over the worst of it and placed them in her jacket pocket.

The wind and the rain continued outside as she left by the kitchen door. She left the door open. The cold rain pelting her face actually felt good; as if it were washing away the evil that was consuming her. The pain between her legs was sharp and she could feel the cold mixing with the wetness as she made her way home.

Mickey was asleep when she entered into the warmth of the house. She didn't wake him. She called

Aunt Anna and asked her to come over and bring Norman with her if he was available.

They rushed out the back door without saying a word. They ran across the street to the back of the pool hall. The door was still unlocked. Their hearts were beating with the excitement that they felt that was now turning from physical and mental euphoria to fear of what they had just done.

Georgie and Jimmy were still shooting pool as planned. Ali and Chico grabbed the cues they left leaning against the wall and attempted to resume the façade of their alibi.

"How did it go guys? Did you enjoy? Did she enjoy?" Georgie laughed.

"It went as planned. We left her there to free herself. I'm scared Georgie. She scratched the hell out of my neck." Chico said as he pulled down his shirt collar to reveal a scabbed scratch that was showing red around the entire scratch.

"That's nothing. Look what you got for it. A great piece of ass and helped me with my payback for that bitch."

"I'm not so sure Georgie. If this comes down on me and Ali, we're all gonna pay. Not just us two. Remember we're all in this. Chico said as he leaned on his cue stick and nervously rubbed cue stick chalk on the tip of his cue.

"Don't worry. We got your back and I'm sure she's not going to say anything. She'll be too afraid and she doesn't even know who you are. And I wasn't there. And we have the perfect alibi. So, calm down and let's finish this game. You guys can break," Georgie said as he peered up from setting up a new rack.

Aunt Anna answered the phone on the fifth ring. Rosemary was still shaking from the cold and the terror.

"Aunt Anna, could you come over and bring Norman with you if he's available. I had a terrible thing happen to me and I need your help. Okay?"

"Of course. I'll be right over. Norman is working at the bar. I'll call him and see if he can meet us at your house."

Rosemary hung up the phone and sat down and started to think of what had just happened to her. The shivering from the cold and the assault were starting to die down. But the trauma was increasing. She would have to tell Aunt Anna and maybe Norman of the awful thing that just happened to her. She was also thinking that she would also have to tell Mickey and that would be even harder to do. After all he was just a young boy and probably not wise to the female sexuality.

Aunt Anna rapped on the front door. Rosemary locked it after she had entered. Something that she never did in the past. She opened the door and Anna could see that Rosemary was visibly upset. Her eyes were red and tears were streaming down her cheeks.

"Oh my God Rosie! What is it? What happened?" Anna said as she grabbed Rosemary's shoulders and brought her into a firm warm hug.

"Just sit down Aunt Anna, and I'll tell you the best I can what happened." She thought the best thing to start this difficult conversation was to start with the most horrible words she could conger up. "I was raped!"

Anna gasped and she walked over to Rosemary and leaned over her and gave her another hug: hoping to absorb some of the hurt she could see pouring out of Rosemary's body. She waited a few minutes for Rosemary to calm down and then she asked her to give her the whole story.

Rosemary didn't want to relive the whole assault again but she had no choice. She would have to tell her everything from the time she stepped off the bus until they left and she freed herself and came home.

Anna listened to every word with intensity and horrific images going through her head as Rosemary described in detail what the two had done to her.

"The best thing we can do Rosie is to get you to a hospital and to get the police involved. I called Norman and he was working. I'll call him again and have him come over before we call the police. He has a lot of friends in the Police Department and he might have some other thoughts on how to handle this. Okay?"

"Okay Aunt Anna. I'd like to take a shower and get this filth off of me."

"You can't do that just now Rosie. Let them examine you first at the hospital. I think that's best." Rosemary shook her head.

Norman arrived a short while after Anna told Rosemary to wait.

"What's going on?" Norman said as he saw Anna and Rosemary sitting at the dining room table with red and watery eyes.

"It's Rosie. She was raped by a couple of hoods. We think it has something to do with that Georgie kid. But she doesn't think he was one of the attackers. I told her to wait from taking a shower in case the police want to collect any evidence. You agree?"

"Oh Rosie. I am so sorry. If you asked me here for advice, I can give you that. If you asked me here for comfort, I can try to give you that. If you asked me here to take on revenge for you, I can certainly do that." Norman offered as he looked at both Rosie and Anna.

"We certainly need all of that Norm," Anna answered.

"Okay. The first thing we need to do is call the police and tell them what happened and let them do their due diligence. They'll know exactly what to do to find out who did this and I'll make sure they're brought to justice. I'll call, if you want me to and have them come here. They'll want to question you here as soon as possible while things are fresh in your mind. I know it won't be easy Rosie, but your aunt and I will be here to support you in every way we can."

Rosie looked up at Norman and over to her aunt. "I'm so glad I have the both of you to help me through this. As I think about it, all I want to do is catch those bastards and make them pay. If you can help me with that then I'm okay with whatever I have to do. I don't care what it is. I'm over the embarrassment phase, except for telling Mickey. He's asleep and I didn't want to wake him until I talked to both of you. Can you help me Aunt Anna when I tell him?"

"Of course, Rosie. Do you want to wake him now or wait till morning?"

"Let's call the police first. Will you do that Norman? And then we'll wake Mickey and explain what's going on."

Norman called the 6th Precinct and talked to the desk sergeant on duty and explained the situation.

Both Rosie and Aunt Anna went into Mickey's room to wake him and give him the awful news.

Police Officer Stanley Kovac from the 6th Precinct arrived a short while after Norman made the call. He was with a younger officer. His experience with a rape was limited and he was a bit unsure on how to handle it. He knew he had to be careful in his questioning with a fragile young lady.

"I'm sorry you had to go through this awful experience and I'll be as brief as I can so you can go the hospital and they'll take care of you there," Officer Kovac said as he took out a small note pad and a pen . . . ready to take notes. "Just give me as best you can what happened. Describe the best you can who did this and where, so we can get some crime scene detectives over there to look for evidence. Any detail that you can remember, no matter how small, will help."

Rosemary looked around the room. There was Aunt Anna, Norman, Mickey and the two police officers. "Could we just have you and your partner here when I tell my story? It might be easier that way."

Mickey, Anna, and Norman took the cue and went into the kitchen to leave Rosemary alone with the police. She started telling the ordeal slowly, but as her anger grew, her embarrassment waned, and she told them everything she could remember including the brown-skinned arm she saw and that she heard the name 'Ali'. She also remembered scratching the neck of one of them. Officer Kovac took notes as fast as he could and asked her to repeat some of the story when he fell behind in his note taking. When he was done, he asked if the others would join him as he had something he wanted to share.

They all came back into the dining room and sat around the table as the officers stood behind them.

"Something has jumped into my head as I listened to Miss Lesko's story. I remember there was a death in the family about a year ago. On Devil's Night, to be exact, where your parents were killed in a car accident and five teens were being investigated. I was working with a state trooper on the case. My point being, I don't believe in coincidences. If there is a tie between this Georgie character and Miss Lesko's attack, then I think we should contact the State Police and maybe they can help in the investigation. I'll have to approach my commander to get his permission to get The Michigan State Police involved in a crime in Detroit. So, I'll have to see how that goes."

They all looked around at each other with question marks on their faces. Mickey was the first to speak. "If Georgie is involved in this then I'm not surprised. He's been stalking us and another thing he's involved in, is that we think . . . and I know . . . that he poisoned our dog Perro."

"Wow. Things are pilling up on this kid. Another reason to get Trooper Emery involved in this. The State Police have more experience and available expertise in this kind of stuff, so I am definitely going to make a case for his involvement. Thanks for all your help and we'll be leaving now. I'll call Receiving Hospital, where you should go Miss Lesko and they'll be ready for you to do what they do in cases like this. I will follow up with aah . . . who should be the main contact?"

"That would be me, Anna Borovic, officer. I'll give you my phone number and you can call me with any updates or questions. Thank you."

The police left. Anna, Norman, and Rosemary left for the hospital and Mickey went to his room to try to absorb what was happening to his and Rosie's life over the past year.

He decided to call Lenny and share the bad news. Lenny was there within a half an hour. Mickey gave him as much of the story as he could remember. His sorrow was showing through as he thought about what his sister had just been through. She had been so strong for him, even as she suffered her own loss of their parents.

Lenny listened quietly and shook his head as he

heard the awful details. His conscience kicked in when Mickey told him he thought that Georgie was behind not only this, but the poisoning of Perro and somehow involved in his parents' death.

Lenny couldn't hold back any more. He thought he might lose Mickey's friendship that had grown over the past year but he knew in his soul that this was the right thing to do, no matter the outcome.

"Mickey, I have a confession to make and I hope it won't destroy our friendship." Mickey didn't respond. He just waited for the shoe to drop.

"Me and Georgie and Jimmy and Mark and Stanley were all part of the prank that led to the accident that killed your Mom and Dad. I'm sorry. We never intended to hurt anyone. It was just some foolishness that we all regret – except Georgie.! He was blowing off the whole thing after it happened, even blaming your dad for reckless driving. I'm so glad to be rid of him. Jimmy, Mark, and Stanley also want nothing to do with him. He picked up with those other guys: Ali, Jimmy, and Chico and I would bet that Georgie put them up to attacking your sister. He is one sick FUCK! Can you ever forgive me Mickey? As I said, we didn't mean any harm and I'll do whatever you want me to do. If you want me to go to the police and tell them the whole story then I will. I just want your understanding and forgiveness."

Mickey listened intently as Lenny bared his soul. He too was enjoying his relationship with Lenny and didn't want to destroy it . . . but could he forgive? He knew he couldn't forget!

"I appreciate you telling me this Lenny. It's a tough pill to swallow. I've been enjoying our friendship, but with this confession I'm going to have to think long and hard. I don't want you to go to the police. That wouldn't solve anything right now. But if it comes to you telling the police what happened that might relate to my sister's attack then I might ask you to offer. For right now, I'm good. Let's leave it at that." Mickey got up and walked over to Lenny who was sitting on a kitchen chair. He placed his hands on Lenny's shoulders and squeezed out a warm, "It's okay."

15

Investigation II

Officer Kovac was waiting in the 6th precinct Commander's office when Trooper Emery arrived. Handshaking around and they all sat down. Commander Jerome Prescott was the Detroit 6th Precinct Commander.

"I understand from my commander that you might need my help in relation to a rape that happened recently," Doug Emery said to open the meeting.

"That's right Doug." Commander Prescott replied. "Officer Kovac here realized that there might be a connection to the rape of Miss Lesko and the accident that killed her parents that you investigated a year ago. Good catch Kovac. Might have to make you a detective."

"No thanks. Happy where I'm at. Just happy if I can help."

"What I'd like to do Doug is team you up with one of our seasoned detectives and you two can work on the case together. His name is Duke Wayne and he's one of our best. Any type of heinous crime such as this, is his specialty, and if it ties in with the car accident that killed her parents, all the more reason to have you two working together. I'll get a hold of him and have him meet you here tomorrow and we can discuss all the facts in both cases and go from there."

"Sounds like a plan Commander and I look forward to meeting this Duke Wayne. Sounds like a tough guy."

"He is . . . for sure!"

They met the following day at the 6th Precinct. Commander Prescott introduced the two officers and then let them discuss their situation in one of the interrogation rooms. "Make sure I get regular updates on your progress or . . . lack of progress," Commander Prescott instructed.

Duke Wayne was exactly what Doug Emery expected when he heard the name Duke Wayne. He was a tall, barrel-chested man with a military crew cut and a gait that cried out cowboy. The nickname Duke was bestowed on Marion Wayne when one of the Detroit Police Officers found out that John Wayne's given name was Marion. His fellow officers started to call him Duke. He liked it and the name stuck.

Detective Wayne said to abstain from the

formalities and call him Duke and Trooper Emery agreed and said to call him Doug. After the ice-breaking, Doug laid out as much of the case as he could remember. He brought the case file in a dog eared manilla folder that he opened on the wooden desk that they were seated at. Duke slid the photos of the car crash with his index finger and looked at them trying to understand exactly what happened that Devil's Night.

They discussed the case back and forth with questions bouncing off each other's brains. After detailing everything they could from the accident report, they shifted to the rape of Rosemary. This would be the tough part. Doug knew Rosemary from his meeting with her after her parents were killed. And now this!

"I need to go over the crime scenes, or alleged crime scenes to wrap my head around it, Doug. Can we take a ride over to the Xway site and then to that house where she was attacked?"

"Yeah sure. It will help me also to refresh my memory and I'm not familiar with the rape crime scene. We'll have to get some keys from the Commander to get into the house. The owners have been notified and it's been locked up with signs all over warning not to trespass."

They got into Duke Wayne's Detroit police cruiser and proceeded down McGraw Avenue toward the I-94 expressway. Along the way they shared their history of how they got into the police business.

Duke parked the cruiser on the service drive next to the Wesson Street overpass. The got out of the car and walked over to the fence bordering the top of the expressway. They both put their hands on the upper rail of the fence and stared down on the steady stream of cars running over the memories of the tragic accident.

Doug suggested that they walk over the overpass where they could get a closer look at the accident scene. Doug stopped at the rail and pointed down to the moving traffic. "This is where a dummy was hung off this handrail. It was assumed Mr. Lesko saw the dummy fall and thought it was a real person falling off the bridge. He slammed on his brakes, the car swerved and ran full force into that abutment." They both leaned over the rail and peered down. Even though more than a year had gone by, there was still a smear of engine oil that absorbed into the concrete pavement. The scar from Larry's beloved Catalina where the grill was split half-in-two was still evident on the bridge abutment and would remain there for countless Devil's Nights to come.

"Okay I've seen enough here Doug. Let's go over

to that house where the other thing happened." Duke said trying to avoid the ugly word of "rape."

They drove over to the Radke house on 31st street in silence. Each absorbing and thinking about what they just looked at. Each having their own way of processing. Duke as an investigative detective and Doug as someone that could relate to Rosemary and Mickey and what they had gone through on that Devil's Night.

They parked directly in front of the empty Radke house. As they walked up the steps to the brick walled front porch, they could see the sign posted on the front door with red letters reading, "DO NOT ENTER by ORDER OF THE DETROIT POLICE DEPARTMENT." In smaller black letters were the words – "violators will be prosecuted."

Doug pulled out a key with a small manilla tag attached with the address on it and opened the screen door and unlocked the front door. The immediate smell of dust and dankness invaded their noses. Each of them had police issued flashlights and although it was still daylight outside the flashlights reduced the darkness inside. They walked into the foyer and then the living room and all three of the bedrooms and then on to the kitchen. Their footsteps were echoing off the naked floors and walls as they slowly toured the house. They were aware that the rape took place in the basement so they carefully walked down the linoleum covered stairs into the basement. The moldy smell and remnants of burning wax lingered. They swept their flashlight beams across the room and noticed the open door to what appeared to be a pantry. They saw the collection of orange crates used by the teens that gathered there and some beer bottles and a bag of candles was tucked into one of the upturned crates. Crushed out cigarette butts covered the floor. It was obvious that the forensic team had been there by the number of bent index cards with numbers written on them, evidently marking where evidence had been found and or collected. Doug and Duke new the procedure and were careful not to disturb any of the cards or what they indicated.

They walked slowly over to the wooden table where the attack had taken place and stared at the remnants of the wax candles. The light cords that had been used to tie Rosemary to the table were collected by the forensic team. Silence . . . as they both were forced to imagine what had taken place there and the awful aftermath that Rosemary and even Mickey would have to face.

"Seen enough Duke?" Doug asked, as he was anxious to get away from the heart wrenching scene before them.

"Yes. I've seen enough. I'm sure you are like me when it comes to these awful crime scenes. Hard to get out of your head. Right?" Duke asked rhetorically as they turned to leave the basement.

Detective Duke Wayne suggested they stop and get something to eat before they went back to the 6th Precinct to discuss the case. He suggested a well-known cop-lunch-hangout near the precinct. It was called Bill's and was located one block away from the precinct.

It was a typical diner with booths covering both outer walls and a row of tables in the center of the diner. They sat in a booth and waited for one of the waitresses to take their order. Before the order came Duke started the conversation.

"When we get back, I'd like to go over any potential witnesses, and or suspects. We can have one of the cadet officers help us, if we find someone we want to interrogate or just question."

"Great. I had a cadet by the name of Jack Crocker help me on the original car accident and he was very helpful. I'll ask the commander if we can use him or if you have someone at the precinct then we can use him. Not a problem."

They finished their meal, left and proceeded back

to the precinct. There was an empty interrogation room so they reserved it and got some stale coffee and some notepads and sat down to strategize.

Doug was feeling more and more comfortable with Duke after the review of the crime scenes and a friendly lunch. He was thinking that his mundane freeway patrols were getting a bit boring and that working with a guy like Duke Wayne would be a lot more exciting, investigating major crimes. *A switch to the Detroit Police . . . Maybe?"* He thought.

Doug Emery laid out the file on the accident and explained to Duke Wayne that they had five boys that were thought to have been involved in causing the accident that killed the Lesko parents. He told him that they interrogated all five with no solid evidence that the boys were involved.

"I've got to say that the one boy, his name is Georgie, had an attitude that he was smarter than us. He gave four or five tell signs that he was lying, but once again we couldn't tie him directly to the accident. We think . . . my Commander and me . . . after reviewing all the evidence and talking to a Detroit Police Officer by the name of Kovac that this was a Devil's Night prank that went terribly wrong and the five boys caused the accident, even though they may have not planned it that way. Whew, out of breath on that. Any questions, Duke?"

"I notice you said he gave some tell signs that he was lying. We also use tell signs in our interrogations. And I firmly believe that they do reveal when a person is lying. Speaking of that, when and if we get some suspects in this rape case, I've got another trick up my sleeve. It's called the Reid technique. Ever hear of it?"

"Nope. Can't say I have. What is it?"

"I'll give you the *Readers Digest* version. It's a method of interrogation developed by a former Chicago cop by the name of John E. Reid. He was also a psychologist and a polygraph expert. Basically, it's this; you put some major pressure on the suspect, then when you see him at the breaking point you turn on the sympathy, you offer help but only if you can get a confession. It has proven to be very successful. However, now for the caveat. There have been cases of false confessions especially in the case of juveniles. So . . . if we're going to be interrogating juvies, we'll have to be very careful. Any questions, Doug?"

"I do. Do we have to have a parent present for teens? Or maybe even a lawyer? Also, do we only use one interrogator? I guess that's all for now."

"It's better to have a parent or lawyer present to make it more legitimate but it's not required by law. If the teen doesn't ask for someone then we can proceed without a parent or a lawyer. I've done many interrogations of this sort by myself but I also have done it together with fellow officers. It's known as "good cop – bad cop". So does that answer your questions, Doug?"

"It does."

Duke Wayne leaned back in his chair until the two front legs were off the floor. Doug was afraid he would tip back, seeing he was such a hefty specimen. Duke continued. "Here's what I propose and you can add to it. I think we compile a list of all the suspects and or witnesses that we can find and then we sort them as to importance and most likely. Then we call them in one by one and see what we can glean from them. How does that sound, Doug?"

"Sounds like a plan. I'd like to be part of the inter-rogations if you don't mind. Maybe I can pick up some tips on that Reid technique."

"Okay with me. Let's go get some help in finding all the usual suspects and witnesses."

They left the interrogation room and went back to the squad room where Duke Wayne had a desk. The desk was a thing to behold. There were stacks of papers and manilla folders. It was evident by the yellowing and dog ears that some had been there for eons. In-and-Out trays were crammed full with more papers and folders. There was a Detroit Tiger coffee mug showing evidence it never had been washed since it was bought at a Brigg's Stadium souvenir shop, who knows how long ago? There was an amber glass ash-tray begging to be emptied along with a pencil sharp-ener attached to the side of the desk with overflowing shavings. Doug grabbed a vacant chair from the next desk and set it down on the opposite side of the desk, facing Duke. He carefully cleared a small area in front of him and placed a notepad down and was ready to start note taking. He grinned as he looked at Duke.

"I know. It's a disaster. But it's my disaster. I know where everything is. If I straightened it out and orga-nized it, I wouldn't be able to find anything," Duke quipped.

They started with the victim, Rosemary Lesko, then Mickey Lesko and Aunt Anna Borovic and her friend Norman Aringa. Next were: Lenny Solack — Mickey's friend, Georgie Kolpacki, Jimmy Gorski, Stanley Kowalski, and Mark Jackson who were all part of the first investigation of the fatal car crash. They were unaware of Georgie Kolpacki switching from these friends at the time of the accident, to a new set of friends, when his paranoia and psychosis started to cement itself to his brain.

16

Soft Interviews

The first people they invited in were Rosemary, Mickey, and Lenny. Norman drove Rosemary and Aunt Anna in and waited in the main lobby. He would pick up Mickey and Lenny after they were let out from school.

They reserved a conference room as opposed to an interrogation room with its tight quarters and invasive two-way mirror — so as to put Rosemary at ease. Rosemary wanted Aunt Anna there for moral support.

Trooper Doug Emery introduced Duke Wayne to Rosemary and Aunt Anna since he had known them from the accident and the hospital visit with Mickey.

"I know this is difficult Rosemary. Can I call you Rosemary, Miss Lesko?" Detective Wayne asked.

"Yes, Rosemary, or my friends and family call me Rosie so . . . Rosie is fine."

Okay. Thank you, Rosie. We'd like you to tell us as much as you can about the attack. Start from the time just before the attack, the attack itself and what happened afterward. Once again, I know this is difficult, but as much detail as you can give us will help us get to the bottom of this and find out who did this to you. We'll take as much time as you need." Doug listened intently wanting to get as much from Duke's process as he could and he was prepared to take notes.

Rosemary sat next to her aunt. Aunt Anna reached over and held Rosemary's cold moist hand on her lap in an effort to calm her down and give her some comfort with her presence. Rosemary started her story; getting off work, taking the bus home, and how cold it was. Neither Duke nor Doug interrupted as she relayed being blindsided as she walked down 31st street past the deserted Radke house. She told them of being dragged into the basement and tied to the table and being painfully assaulted. She told them she was a virgin and the fear she had that as awful as the attack was, she was afraid she would be killed. She told them how she scratched the one attacker and that one of the names was Ali, and one with brown skin. She said she couldn't identify either one because they wore ski masks.

"What happened after the attack Rosie? After they left?"

"I freed myself from the cord they tied my hand to the table and I collected my underwear and headed home. The police have my underwear. Could that mean anything as far as evidence?" Rosemary had re-laxed and shed her embarrassment with the question.

"Who knows? It could mean something in the fu-ture . . . the way science is moving so fast these days. I'm not so sure they can find anything at this time." Duke answered.

"I think that's all we have for now, Rosie. You've been very helpful and very detailed in your account of the attack. I think that will help us immensely. Doug, do you have any questions?"

"I don't at this time. I also would like to thank you Rosie. And I know that this along with losing your parents have been very traumatic. With the informa-tion you've given us — such as the name Ali and the scratching of one of them is going to be very instru-mental in catching these animals. I think I can speak for Detective Wayne here in saying that we will do everything we can to apprehend these people and turn them over to the courts for prosecution. So, thanks again Rosie, and you Anna for your support."

Both men escorted Rosemary and Anna to the lobby where Norman was waiting. Anna introduced Norman to the policemen. Handshakes went around. Duke Wayne thought he recognized Norman. "Do you own that bar Nifty's down on Michigan?"

"I do. It's Nifty Norman's. I think I've seen you in there a few times."

"Hate to admit it but the few times I was in there was for the gratis fish dinners for men in blue. So, thanks in person for some great perch dinners."

"You're welcome detective. Glad you enjoyed. Stop by anytime for another gratis fish fry." Norman said with a smile.

"I'm going to pick up Mickey and Lenny from school and bring them here. Is that the plan?" Norman asked.

"That's the plan, Norman. We'll stay here and wait here in the lobby while they talk to Mickey and Lenny." Anna answered.

Before they resumed the interviews with Mickey and Lenny, Detective Wayne reminded Trooper Emery they should continue the meeting as an interview rather than an interrogation. They should save the interrogation and the Reid technique for the boys that they think committed the assault on Rosemary.

"Let's continue the interviews with open ended questions and see what the boys have to offer. I think we'll get more from them this way than with the hard gotcha questions." Detective Wayne suggested.

"Agree. I'll be happy to see how this Reid technique works once we get some strong suspects." Doug responded.

Norman picked up the boys from school as planned. On the way to the police station, he tried to put the boys at ease by talking and asking questions about school and sports. They arrived at the police station and Norman parked in the visitor parking space and escorted the boys inside where Rosemary and Aunt Anna were waiting.

"They just want to question both of you about what you might know about the attack on Rosie. They're pretty friendly, so not to worry." Aunt Anna offered. As she was speaking Duke Wayne and Doug Emery came out to the lobby and introductions were made and the boys were led to the conference room.

"You boys want something to drink? A pop or some water?" Duke offered with a smile on his face. He was trying his best to lose his tough interrogative persona and put on a gentle friendly air. Both boys shook their heads and declined and took a seat next to each other opposite Duke and Doug at the conference table.

"As you know, we're trying to get to the bottom of the attack on your sister and the more information you guys can give us the easier it will be to nab them. Rosie has given a lot of valuable information but if you can offer any additional info, it can only help. So, start with anything that you can think of that might be related to what went on at that Radke house. Is that what you call it . . . the Radke house?" Duke asked.

"That's it." Mickey answered. "I know who did it and why!" Mickey immediately blurted out.

Both Doug and Duke were a bit startled at Mickey's quick reply and tried to hide their surprise.

"Why do you say that, Mickey. What do you know?" Duke asked.

"Georgie's behind this. I know he is. He may not have been in on the attack, but I'll give you the story and why I think what I think."

"Go ahead and tell us your story and take your time and give us all the detail you can," Doug asked.

Mickey sat up straight in his chair and laced his fingers in resolve on the table as he began relating his story to the two police officers.

"I know – for a fact – from someone who was there – that Georgie was involved in the accident that killed my mom and dad. I can't tell you how I know. I just know."

Lenny squirmed a bit in his chair, knowing that Mickey was referring to him as the source and unwilling to give him up. Both Duke and Doug saw Lenny's reaction and were thinking the same thing.

"That's what started this whole mess with Georgie and what happened after. And then there's how Georgie poisoned my dog Perro." Mickey's voice started to shake and his eyes were welling up as he relayed the story of the poison and the butcher paper with the name Kolpacki on it. Lenny felt the tremor in Mickey's voice. He placed his hand on Mickey's back and rubbed it slightly hoping to ease the ugly memory that Mickey was conjuring up.

Mickey was feeling a bit more at ease as he felt Lenny's hand on his back and he continued with his story. He told the officers how Georgie was stalking both him and Lenny and had actually punched Lenny and gave him a black eye and how their schoolmates reacted negatively to Georgie. He told them that Georgie was supposed to go to the same high school – Saint Andrew – but he transferred to a public school – Chadsey High.

The next part of his story lit up Duke and Doug's investigative gut-sense. Mickey told them that Georgie stopped being friends with Lenny, Stanley, Mark and Jimmy and found new friends at Chadsey. When he gave the names of Jimmy, Chico, and Ali, both men leaned in when they heard Ali. It was the name that Rosie had told them that she heard during her attack. They didn't know if Rosemary had told Mickey about the Ali name. Doug almost forgot about the notes he was taking when her heard the name Ali. They continued to listen to Mickey's story and Doug continued his notes.

"Do you know where we can find these boys, Jimmy, Chico and Ali? And do you know their last names?" Doug asked.

Lenny answered as Mickey caught his breath after relaying his story and why he thought Georgie was responsible. "We don't know their last names but you can find them hanging out at Steve's pool room on Buchanan and 31st."

The street names immediately rang a bell with both Duke and Doug. "Is that close to where the Radke house is?" Duke asked.

"It's directly across the street." Lenny answered.

"Unless you have any questions for us, I think we're done here. Doug, do you have any questions for the boys?"

"Did your sister ever mention the name Ali to you Mickey?"

"No. I just know his name from him hanging around with Georgie. Why?"

"It may have some importance on our investigation. That's all. Thanks for that."

"You boys have given us a lot to go on. You can leave now and thanks for the help," Duke Wayne said.

Mickey jumped in with one more thought. His ire was raised as he told his story and thought about his sister and his mother and father . . . and of course Perro. "I just want you to catch who did this and Georgie too. I know he's involved." Mickey looked at both Doug and Duke and then to Lenny and wiped a tear from the corner of his eye with his tee shirt sleeve.

They thanked the boys again and walked them out to the lobby where Rosemary, Aunt Anna and Norman were nervously waiting.

"The boys have given us some valuable information along with what you told us Rosie. We're confident that we can wrap this up in short order." Duke looked at Doug for agreement and Doug nodded his head affirmatively.

"We'll keep in touch with you Mrs. Borovic as the central point, if that's okay with all of you?" They all agreed. As they left, Anna nudged Duke aside and told him it was Miss — not Mrs. — with a broad smile on her face as she nodded toward Norman.

17

Interrogations

Immediately after the interviews Duke and Doug sat at Duke's disastrous desk and discussed what they just heard. They decided to forego Georgie's previous friends, Jimmy, Stanley and Mark. Everything was pointing strongly toward the four names that were given by Mickey and Lenny. There was; Jimmy, Chico, Ali and of course Georgie, that were all beginning to look strongly as the main suspects in the attack. Rosemary couldn't identify the attackers by sight, since they wore ski-masks. They would have to work their interrogative magic to get some sort of confession or confessions if they were going to get to the bottom of the attack.

One of the junior detectives was tasked with finding out as much as he could about the four boys and get back to Duke and Doug with all the information by the next morning.

"Find out their full names, where they live, their families, where they go to school, any arrests or run-ins with the law, any juvenile time served, where they hang out and anything else you can think of, detective," Detective Wayne directed the junior detective. "And let us know if you need any help. If not, see you early tomorrow morning."

"I'll get right on it and I'll probably use my partner and maybe someone from the youth squad to help gather all this info. I hope I can finish it by tomorrow morning," he said.

"Let's do this, to be fair. Let's make it after lunch tomorrow. That'll give you some more time and I don't want to rush this if we don't have to." Detective Wayne offered.

The junior detective broke out in a relieved smile and a 'thank you' and left to start his assignment.

Doug smiled at Duke as the junior detective turned and walked away. "Pretty clever how you gave him a most difficult task and timeline and then relaxed it a bit. I think he'll have a positive feeling with your generous addition of time." Doug said.

The first order of business the next morning was to go over the interrogation process they would use when they had the suspects at hand. Duke poured a cup of coffee in his brown stained Detroit Tiger's cup and offered a sparkling, white, clean, visitor's cup to Doug.

They each grabbed a donut from the grease-stained cake-box next to the coffee pot and got comfortable in one of the empty interrogation rooms.

"I want you to follow my lead in these interrogations, Doug. I'll start with the tough, bad-cop questions and see if I can shake them a bit. I don't know if they'll have lawyers or parents with them, but it won't make a difference to me. Once I get them on the ropes and sweating a bit, is where you'll jump in. You, Mr. Nice-Guy-Cop will come to the rescue and show sympathy for their predicament. Offer them a way out. It usually results in a bit of relief on their part and a chance to get out of their scary future. Make sense, Doug?"

"It does. I think I'll be okay to follow through on your lead. I guess we'll have to wait and see."

"If I see it going south in any way, I'll jump in. I'll see if they got all the info we asked for yesterday and hopefully we can start the process this afternoon." Duke got up and went to look for his junior detective. Doug sat ankle-cross-legged, sipping his luke-warm coffee and thinking about what he was about to do and learn about interrogations.

The first of the boys to be called in for an interrogation was Jimmy Zafino. Knowing a bit about interrogations by the police, Jimmy brought his father in with him. Duke Wayne was not happy with this. He knew Jimmy's father's reputation as a small-time gangster and probably was wise to any tricks he may have up his sleeve. So, the good cop - bad cop may not work on Jimmy Zafino.

Jimmy and his father were seated in the interrogation room. Outside the room, Duke explained to Doug that this interrogation would just be the standard . . . just questions and hopefully he would reveal something to use on the other boys. He explained to Doug that with his experienced father there, using the Reid technique would probably shut down everything and they would not get any information.

"Jimmy, we've called you in here to find out what you might know about an assault that took place the other night close to where you hang out. Can you tell us where you were on this particular night?" Duke pointed to a day on the November calendar on the desk.

Jimmy looked at the calendar with his father leaning over his shoulder. He thought a minute and said, "I was at Steve's pool hall shooting pool. You can check with him. Maybe he'll remember."

"Who were you with?"

Hesitation . . . "Just some of my friends. Chico, Ali, and Georgie. We were all shooting pool that night. I swear."

Both Duke and Doug were looking for the telltale signs of someone lying. They noticed only that he was hesitant in his responses as if he was thinking of what to say before he answered. He also used a mild oath 'I swear'.

"What time were you there and how long did you stay?" Doug Asked.

He hesitated again. "I don't know. Most of the evening, I guess." Jimmy answered and started to squirm and look more at his father for support. Mr. Zafino looked at both Duke and Doug and said. "The kid told you where he was. Go check with the pool hall guy if you don't believe him. Can we go now? He doesn't know anything about some attack. Let's go Jimmy."

Duke looked at Doug and lightly shrugged his shoulders. He knew if he pushed the issue they would just walk out anyway, so he thanked them and led them to the lobby.

"Well Doug, what do you think? Get anything from the answers?"

"Not much. He was a little fidgety and slow to respond. At least he gave us some names that we're familiar with. I guess we need to go to that pool hall and talk to the owner and see if he can confirm the boys were there that night."

"Agree. I'll tell the detective to schedule Chico and Ali for tomorrow morning. Let them sweat a little. Maybe we'll have a little more to go on after we check out the pool hall alibi?"

It was only a short ride to the corner of 31st and Buchanan. Duke parked the cruiser directly in front of the entrance on 31st street. Steve was sitting in his usual spot on a stool behind the cigar counter/humidor. He was leafing through the latest edition of *True Detective* magazine spread out on the cigar humidor counter. His head jerked up as he saw two men enter the pool hall. One a state trooper and the other an obvious plain clothes police officer. His easy persona perked up.

"What can I do for you gentlemen? Need a rack? Lots of open tables including a snooker if you're so inclined."

"Not here for pool. Just have a few questions about some of your customers." Duke responded.,

"Sure. Whatever I can help with."

"About a week ago in the evening around 8 o'clock four boys claimed they were here shooting pool. We're checking their alibi. It was a Georgie, Jimmy, Chico and Ali. You know them?"

Steve started to work up a sweat thinking that he knew the boys were not eighteen . . . the legal age for pool halls. "I know that Georgie kid. He said they were all eighteen." Steve quickly replied.

"We don't care about their ages. We're not here for that. Not to worry. We just want to know if they were here on that night."

"They were here one night. I'm not sure which. Oh! Wait. I can check my log. I charged them the premium rate." Steve broke into a wry smile thinking that he charged them double the rack rate. "Here it is. Yes, they were here, playing on the last table back by the rear door. As a matter of fact, do you see those two guys back there shooting snooker? They're regulars. They were here that night. Maybe they remember?" Steve offered.

Duke thanked Steve and both him and Doug walked backed to the two men playing snooker. Doug's Smokey the Bear hat got immediate attention. Both men, dressed in identical blue work shirts with logos and name tags sewn over the pockets, stopped shooting and leaned on their cue sticks as the two men approached them.

Duke asked the same questions he asked Steve.

One of the men scratched his chin and replied. "As a matter of fact, I do remember the kids. They were kinda strange. Looked under age, but I don't know. The strange thing was that a couple of them left by the rear door. No big thing, but they returned about an hour later and got really loud and annoying, as if they wanted us to notice them. That's about all I remember."

The other man shrugged his shoulders and said. "Me too."

"Okay thanks, guys. You've been a big help." Doug said as they turned walked back toward a nervous Steve. "Thanks Steve. Might take you up on that snooker offer. Haven't played in a while."

"Looks like we might have those sons a bitches. Sneaking out the back door to do their dirty deed. Can't wait to get them in the hot-box tomorrow and see what they have to say. By a process of elimination, it looks like the culprits are Ali and Chico, and Georgie set it up." Duke said as he leaned over the roof of the police cruiser and looked at Doug. They headed back to the 6th Precinct.

They spent the rest of the afternoon going over all the information that the junior detective could glean on Chico, Ali and Georgie. Knowing the suspects, as well as could be by the interrogator, was one of the strengths of interrogation. Once again – they went over the tell signs of a lying person and how the Reid technique works.

They had the youth squad pick up both Chico and Ali from school. They would let Georgie think about, and stew over his two friends being picked up by the police and carted off to be interrogated.

Chico Kowalski was the first suspect they were going to interrogate. He was led into the small room with a small worn wooden table and three chairs, one against the wall and facing the two-way mirror and the other two on the opposite side.

"You know why you're here, Chico?"

Chico just shook his head as he placed his folded hands on the table in an effort to control his nervousness.

"We have information that you were one of the boys that assaulted a young lady last week. We have eye witnesses that can put you in that vicinity. Any comment?" Duke said looking directly into Chico's eyes.

"Don't know what you're talking about. Never assaulted anyone."

"By the way. What's that scratch on your neck? Who did that to you?'

Without thinking Chico grabbed the edge of his collar and raised it in an attempt to cover the scabbed over scratch. "Cut myself shaving."

"That peach fuzz is not ready for shaving. My cat could lick it off with a little milk." Duke replied with a sarcastic grin on his face. Chico lifted his collar again.

"That looks more like a scratch from a couple of fingernails, not a shaving nick, Mr. Chico."

"Let's get back to the night in question, shall we?" Duke grabbed a calendar and pointed to the date in question. Chico looked up and away from the calendar. Doug gently nudged the back of Chico's head, forcing him to look at the calendar.

He hesitated and said, "We were shooting pool that night – all night – ask my friends or Steve."

"Oh. we've done that already, Chico my friend. They said you and your friend Ali skipped out the back door and then came back an hour later. Just enough time to rape a young girl. And another thing, calling out your friend Ali by name wasn't very smart either. We know you wore ski-masks so she couldn't see your faces but we have the scratches on your neck that she bravely gave you and the name Ali that she heard. So, we need you to tell us the whole story if you want to get any break from us when we turn you over to the juvenile authorities. If you don't talk to us now, we'll do everything we can to make sure you pay . . . and pay dearly."

Duke was leaning over the table and getting as close as he could to Chico's face and as he got louder and louder and red in the face a spray of spittle shot out and Chico wiped his face with his sleeve and tried to back his chair away from Duke. To no avail, the chair back was already touching the back wall.

Duke could see his efforts were getting to Chico.

His brown complexion was lightening and a tiny drop of sweat was forming on his forehead in the cool room. He placed his once folded hands on his lap to hide his nervousness. Duke continued the pressure and the questions, increasing to the point of almost scaring Doug, who was watching intensely a Master-at-Work. Chico unconsciously continued to pull up his collar, trying to hide the scabbed over nail scratch. After a few more minutes, that seemed like hours to Chico, Duke gave a nod to Doug to jump in with the second half of the Reid technique.

"Listen Chico." Doug put on a friendly face after Duke's scary one. "We're here to help you. We already know you were involved in this terrible crime. We can help you get a lighter sentence in juvie . . . or maybe even probation or community work as your punishment. How about it? You want to come clean with us and tell us the whole story? We know Ali was with you when you slipped out the back door of the pool hall, and . . . we know Georgie was behind this. If Ali is the first to tell us your involvement, then we won't be able to help you. Do you want to be the one taking all the punishment and letting Ali and Georgie get away with their part in this?"

Chico's demeanor seemed to change. He became a little more relaxed and appeared to be thinking deeply at what Trooper Emery had just told him. He stopped pulling up his collar and put his hands on the calendar still laying on the desk in front of him.

"I don't know. I need to talk to a lawyer or someone before I tell you anything," Chico said almost whispering.

"Are you sure, Chico? If you call in a lawyer, all bets are off. No deals! We're going to talk to Ali now, so if we haven't heard from you in the next few minutes, you're on your own to suffer the consequences."

Chico remained quiet.

They left Chico seated at the table with the calendar in front of him. Giving him time to think about his predicament. They went over to the other interrogation room where Ali was nervously waiting. As in the other room, Ali was seated in a chair with his back to the wall with a table in front of him and the two-way mirror on the opposite wall.

Now that they had been through the whole Reid Technique together, they were showing signs of confidence that they could make this work with Ali, and maybe even Chico would wise up and tell them the whole story.

"Hello Ali. I'm Detective Wayne and this is Trooper Emery. We just left your friend Chico in the other room and we're going to give you the same opportunity that we gave him. Let me lay it on the line. We know you were involved in the rape of Miss Lesko. We have eye witnesses of you and Chico going to grab her. We know she heard your name called out — ALI!

We know that she scratched Chico's neck and we also know that Georgie was behind this whole criminal act." Ali showed signs of even more nervousness than Chico. He kept rubbing his hands together as, if he was Lady Macbeth, trying to rub the guilt off of his hands. Both Duke and Doug picked up on this compulsive act. Duke continued his point-blank questioning until Doug felt the moment to jump into his role.

"I'm going to tell you the same thing I told your friend Chico. The first guy that gives us the whole story is the guy we're going to go to bat for when it comes to sentencing. We can get you probation maybe and you can continue to go to school. If not, you're going to have to spend a lot of time in juvie with all the other misfits. Make no mistake Ali, right now we have all we need to turn you guys over to the juvenile courts. We just need one of you to tell us the whole story. Do you want Georgie to walk free on this while you guys are sitting in a jail for a long time . . . maybe till you're 18?" Do you?"

Ali didn't respond. He kept up with the hand wringing. Duke and Doug waited in a deafening silence. Finally, Ali spoke.

"Yeah, this was all Georgie's plan. Chico and me were just doing what he planned." Ali tried to euphemize the attack. "We were just suppose to scare her and play around with her and things got out of hand. I'm sorry."

Both Duke and Doug listened as Ali gave it up. But they needed more. They wanted the whole story and Georgie's involvement.

It only took a few minutes for Ali to settle down and think that he was doing the right thing. He felt that the second policeman with the more friendly attitude was telling him the truth. That they would help him and get a light sentence for what they had done. It was a sort of relief, now that he was telling someone that could help him. He wasn't thinking of Chico or Georgie or Jimmy. He was thinking of himself.

As he started his story, Duke took out a tape recorder from under the table. It was the size of a hardback novel. He punched the red record button, not waiting for Ali's approval. The whir of the tape seemed to add a calming effect on Ali. He started his story where he and Jimmy and Chico met Georgie in high school. At any long pauses, either Duke or Wayne would prompt him with a question or a simple, "Go on

Ali, you're doing great."

Ali told of all their walking around the neighborhood looking for trouble, of time spent in the Radke basement, smoking and drinking beer and he told them about the time Georgie prompted them to help in poisoning Mickey and Rosemary's dog. He was running out of breath as he went on and Doug left the room and brought back a paper cup of water.

Ali nodded to Doug as he took the cup and gulped it down until the cup was empty.

When he finished his story, right up to the time he and Chico went back to the pool hall, he sat back in his chair and breathed a sigh.

"Okay Ali. Is that it? Anything else you want to tell us?" Duke asked.

"Isn't that enough. You wanted the story so I gave you all I can remember. What happens now?"

"We'll be keeping you overnight at the juvenile center downtown. You and Chico will be there until tomorrow. We're going to bring Georgie in and question him the same way we questioned you and Chico. We can't let you guys go home and tell Georgie anything about what went on here. You understand?" Duke added.

"Yeah, I guess so. But I thought you were going to help me. Doesn't sound like help if you're sending us to juvie prison."

"As we said, it's only for tonight and then tomor-row after we talk to Georgie, we'll get this whole mess straightened out. We'll let you call your parents, so you can tell them what's going on. It'll be tough telling them what you guys did but . . . it should be another relief after you tell them and they can help you with some moral support." Doug said as he leaned over to Ali and tried to give him a comforting face.

Both Chico and Ali were transported to Juvenile Hall in Downtown Detroit and Duke and Doug spent the rest of the day discussing what they had just heard from Ali. Tomorrow they would bring Georgie in and hopefully, get him to confess his role in the rape of Rosemary. But Doug had his doubts, thinking of Georgie's arrogance and lying and cold personality when he questioned him on the death of Rosemary and Mickey's parents.

They called Aunt Anna and updated her on what they learned from Ali and told her she could tell Rosemary, so she could have a little peace after a most terrible act to her body and her psyche.

Aunt Anna called Rosemary and told her she was coming over to give her and Mickey an update from Trooper Emery. She said Norman would be with her.

Rosemary and Mickey were waiting patiently

at the dining room table, that seemed to be the focal point of all the news updates, good and bad. Aunt Anna and Norman arrived a short while after the phone call. They all sat facing each other.

"Well, the good news is that one of the boys confessed to the attack, Rosie. His name is Ali. I think that's the name you heard during the attack, Rosie. Is that right?"

"Yes," Rosemary replied with her head down, looking at the lace tablecloth and trying to erase the ugly picture out of her mind.

Anna continued. "The other boy they interrogated, Chico something or other, was refusing to confess. But with one confession they think they can take this to juvenile court and have these boys punished. The other facet of this investigation is that they will bring Georgie Kolpacki in tomorrow for questioning. As you said Mickey, you feel that Georgie was behind this whole ugly mess. Maybe he wasn't at the house but maybe he was the one who planned it. That's the bad news. If they can't put him at the scene then they might have a tough time charging him with anything. Those are Trooper Emery's fears. He said he would update me after they talked to Georgie. Any questions, kids?"

Both Rosemary and Mickey shook their heads. Norman remained silent and listened to the information that Anna was giving. He had his own thoughts on how to deal with these boys that committed such an awful crime, especially dealing with Georgie. He would worry about that later after all the facts were in. He did know more than one person that could help him in street justice outside of the legal world. On his mind at the present, was to give any comfort he could to Anna, Rosemary, and Mickey.

After a brief silence, Mickey spoke up. "If they don't get Georgie for this, then what can we do? We can't let him get away with this." Norman smiled and thought to himself. *Mickey was thinking exactly as me. Get revenge!* He thought about the phrase he had heard in the past but never really considered the true meaning — *Revenge is a Dish Best Served Cold.* As Mickey relayed his thoughts Norman knew exactly what that phrase meant — revenge is more satisfying when one has had time to prepare vengeance that is: well-planned, long-feared, and unexpected! He would do his homework on preparing a special dish for the guilty ones — served cold for sure!

Officer Kovac and his junior partner went to Chadsey high the next morning. They went to the principal's office and told him that they needed to speak with a student by the name of Kolpacki — Georgie Kolpacki.

The principal asked "why" and was told they couldn't tell him presently . . . police policy. He gave them the room number and pointed them in the right direction down a deserted hallway.

Officer Kovac rapped lightly on the classroom frosted glass door and opened it slowly. He walked up to the teacher and in a low voice he told her that he needed to speak to one of her students. His partner waited silently at the doorway.

"Georgie, these officers need to talk to you. Could you please come up here and go with them?"

Georgie got up, left his open text book on the desk and proudly walked up from the rear of the room. He grinned and nodded at Patrolman Kovac as he walked slowly and looked at all the faces following him up the narrow aisle. He felt proud that the police were there to see him. This would give him more street creds.

He was escorted to the police car waiting at the entrance of the school, smiling the whole time . . . more street creds!

Detective Duke Wayne and Trooper Doug Emery were waiting for Georgie when Patrolman Kovac ushered him into the interrogation room.

"Have a seat, Georgie. We need some information from you. We talked to your friends Chico and Ali yesterday and they were happy to tell us your roll in the rape of Miss Lesko. You want to tell us how you were involved? And remember this Georgie Boy, we already know you were involved, so any lying is not going to go well for you. It will only make it worse," Detective Wayne said as he leaned over the table, getting as close as he could to Georgie's smirk.

Georgie leaned back in his chair attempting to distance himself from Detective's hot cigarette-breath and an attempt to show his arrogance.

"I don't know what the fuck you're talking about."

"You use that kind of language again with me and I'm going to slap you silly. Got it Georgie Boy?" Detective Wayne shouted back knowing that the "Georgie Boy" moniker was getting Georgie's attention and not in a pleasant way.

"Got it," Georgie snapped back.

"So, once again Georgie, tell us your story about that night that Chico and Ali raped Miss Lesko?"

"I told you. I don't know about no rape. I was shooting pool with Jimmy that night. Just ask Steve. He'll tell you that I was there all night," Georgie answered.

"You seem to know the night I'm talking about. I didn't say what night it was. You must have known about it. We were told you planned it. So, fess up Georgie."

Once again, he refused to tell the officers anything.

Trooper Emery thought maybe the kind side of the Reid technique might be in play. Duke sat back and let Doug do his thing.

"Listen Georgie, we're going to give one of your friends, who told us the whole story, some assistance when it comes to juvie court. If you want the same help, you need to tell us your side of the story. We're going to find out sooner or later so you can help yourself here and now. What do you say?"

Georgie leaned back in his chair again and folded his hands over his chest and kept silent. It was obvious from his posture and attitude and silence that they weren't going to get anything from him. They waited in silence as Georgie removed his folded arms from his chest and placed his laced fingers behind his head – yet another physical sign of his resistance to incriminate himself.

With a stern warning that they were not through with him, they called in Patrolman Kovac and told him to take Georgie back to school. They would deal with him later. Georgie smiled, offered his hand, which was ignored, showing another sign of arrogance. He followed the police officers out of the interrogation room, turned his head and smartly said, "See you around officers."

"Nothing worse than a smart-ass teenager to make your day," Duke said.

"I don't know what we can do to get this smart-ass. By what Ali told us, he planned the whole thing. Whether that means anything to the juvenile courts, I don't know. I guess we'll have to wait and see after we turn over Chico and Ali. He could get away with this. What do you think Duke?"

"He may get away with the legal part of it, but in my dealings with assholes like Georgie, it's only a matter of time before he messes with the wrong person. Someone will make sure he pays for involvement in either this rape or something else. Once again . . . just a matter of time."

Detective Wayne and Trooper Emery met with Commander Prescott immediately after they released Georgie.

"Well gentlemen, how did it go with the suspects? Any progress?" Commander Prescott said looking across his desk.

"Some good and some bad. The good thing is we got one of the kids, Ali, to confess that he raped Miss Lesko. He told us his part in the rape and told us his friend Chico was the other rapist. He told us that the Georgie kid was the one who instigated and planned the whole thing. Here's the bad part. Georgie is one arrogant son of a bitch. He denied everything, said he had an alibi and refused to say anything more. We checked out the alibi and it's good. So, as we see it, both Trooper Emery and myself, is we can take these two to juvenile court and we are probably not going to be able to charge Georgie Kolpacki." Detective Wayne finished and sat back in his chair.

"I think Duke has laid it out pretty good Commander. We can turn those two over to the court and let them do what they have to. I don't know if there is anything else we can do for now, unless you have any ideas," Doug added.

Commander Prescott shook his head.

18

Adjudications

Detective Duke Wayne along with Trooper Doug Emery collected all of the documents related to the assault on Rosemary Lesko. It consisted of interview notes, police reports, witness reports, crime scene investigations, Rosemary's underwear, photographs of the Radke basement and kitchen area, latent fingerprint, and the tape recording of Ali Khan's confession. They organized everything and placed the documents in a binder and turned it over to the juvenile authorities. The ball was now in their court. (No pun intended)

It took a week for the juvenile prosecutor to review all the documentation and evidence. He filed a petition stating the charge of rape of Miss Rosemary Lesko by one Francisco Kowalski and one Ali Khan. The prosecutor then contacted the parents of the suspects. He also contacted Rosemary's Aunt Anna, and the police commander in charge of the investigation. He told all involved that there would be a pre-trial hearing at which he would present the evidence to a referee appointed by a juvenile judge to hear the evidence and see if the suspects would plead guilty or if there needed to be a formal trial. He had to tell Anna that because it was a juvenile hearing that no one would be allowed in the court during the hearing. The prosecutor then told her that he would fill her in on all the details after the hearing was over, and that Trooper Emery would also be present as a witness and he could answer any questions she or Rosemary might have.

She was disappointed on one side and relieved on another that her or Rosemary or Mickey would not have to hear any of the disturbing details. So, it was probably a good thing.

Francisco Kowalski, aka Chico, arrived with his mother, a strikingly attractive light skinned Latina woman. Ali Khan arrived with his father, dressed in a business suit and tie, looking like one of the lawyers that congregated in the hallway of the court.

The referee called the court to order and proceeded to ask the prosecutor to read the charges. Both Chico and Ali were sitting at a table across the aisle from the prosecutor. They were separated by a court deputy, sitting between them. Their attending parents sat next to a rail directly behind them.

As the prosecutor read the petition and spelled out the charge of rape, both parents hung their heads at the words "Rape of Miss Rosemary Lesko". The courtroom fell silent for what seemed like an hour after the reading. The referee asked the boys what their plea was. They were not represented by lawyers. There was an ad hoc court appointed lawyer available if needed. Lawyers were not required in juvenile cases unless they were remanded to an adult court for prosecution.

Ali spoke first. "I'm guilty Judge". He hung his head with his chin touching his chest.

Chico saw no way out. "Me too, Judge."

"I'm not a judge gentleman. I'm a referee. But you can refer to me as Your Honor. And Mr. Kowalski, do you also plead guilty. 'Me too' is not sufficient."

"Yes, Your Honor. I plead guilty."

Mrs. Kowalski stood up and raised her hand. The referee saw her standing with her hand raised and asked her who she was and what did she want to say.

"I'm Mrs. Kowalski. I'm Francisco's mother and I would like to say a few words on the behalf of my son. Is that okay Your Honor?" The referee nodded and replied it was okay.

"Hearing what my son has admitted to — breaks my heart. I know this is going to sound contradictory to what we all just heard, but my son is a good boy. He was not brought up like this. We are a responsible Catholic family and we have taught all of our children to respect one another. I am sure there is more to the story, but I accept the fact that he has pleaded guilty. I support whatever punishment you hand out and I will do everything in my power — to right this wrong and — I speak for my husband also.

"I know that what he has done has overwhelming consequences for Miss Lesko. I apologize for him and I expect him to apologize to Miss Lesko and all the people he has hurt. So, Your Honor, do what you must." She hung her head, grabbed a tissue from a box on the wooden railing in front of her and dabbed tears from her eyes.

The referee took a short recess to review all of the evidence and give thought to the confessions and weak apologies, while he pondered what a fair sentence would be — fair to the teens and most of all — fair to Rosemary.

"I've given your cases some thought and the fact that both of you have confessed contributes to this case being adjudicated — meaning both of you have been convicted and there will be no need for a trial. That being said, I am sentencing you to six months in the Juvenile Detention Center in Plymouth, Michigan. After you have served your six months, without any serious violations of the rules of the facility, you will be released. You will then be on probation for six months with community service, as determined by your parole officers. You will start your sentence to-morrow. I'm giving you today to settle any affairs you need to and to say your goodbyes. One caution and — this is the most important one. If you violate any of the rules of the juvenile facility and do not fulfill your community service, then you will appear before a juvenile judge and will probably be sentenced back to the facility to remain there until you are 18 years old. This will be my recommendation to the judge. Is that clear?"

They both nodded their bowed heads.

"I need a response, gentlemen."

"Yes, Your Honor." They replied in unison.

Rosemary, Mickey, Anna and Norman waited ner-vously for the prosecutor and Trooper Emery to come back and tell them the outcome of the trial. They were waiting in one of the small conference rooms used by lawyers, suspects, and families when privacy was needed. There was a small conference table and six desk chairs evenly lined up against the walls.

The prosecutor and Trooper Emery slowly opened the door and entered with serious looks on their faces. They looked at the four dire faces anticipating their update.

The prosecutor spoke first. "Well folks, it's over. Here's the verdict. Both of the boys pleaded guilty so there will be no need for a trial before a juvenile judge. The referee in this case gave a lot of thought to what he heard and reviewed all the evidence very carefully. His decision and sentencing goes like this." He looked across all of their faces and then zeroed in on Rosemary's solemn face with teary eyes. "The boys will serve six months in the juvenile reformatory in Plymouth, Michigan. After they are released – if they serve their time without any serious problems – they will then serve six months of probation and communi-ty service. If they violate any of the probation officers' guidelines and get into any trouble whatsoever, they could go back to the reformatory to remain there until they are 18 years of age. So that's about it. Anything to add Doug?"

"Just to say that I don't think that justice was served entirely. I think they got off with a very light sentence. Of course, they will be going through some trauma when they face all of the liberty that will be lost. Their lives will be one of routine and obeying the reformatory officers to a "T." And the other part that is lacking in this hearing is that Georgie, that we all know was the mastermind of this awful assault, is getting off scot-free. As the lawyers would say – Georgie Kolpacki is *non compos mentis* – INSANE!"

Anna looked at Rosemary with sad eyes. "I guess that all we can do now is accept the sentence and try to move on. Thank you for all your help, Mister Prosecutor and to you Trooper Emery. You've done all you can and we thank you for that. Rosie, would you like to say anything?"

"No. I guess it is what it is. And like you said Aunt Anna, we need to try and get on with our lives. Both me and Mickey will give comfort to each other and we'll pray to Mom and Dad to help us through this." She grabbed Mickey's hand and smiled a weak smile and Mickey returned the smile.

Norman sat quietly through the discourse. His mind was churning. He was appalled at the light sentence for two teenagers that ruined an innocent young girl's life. His mind would continue to churn as he thought about *the dish served cold*.

They all left in silence after thanking the two men once again. Anna and Norman trailed behind Rosemary and Mickey. Anna suggested to Norman that they drop off Rosie and Mickey at home and the two of them go down to Norman's bar. She said strongly that they needed to discuss the matter further! Norman agreed.

Nifty Norman's was quiet, being that it was late afternoon, and before the after-work crowd would invade. They sat in Norman's booth and Norman went to the waitress wait-station at the bar and brought back a glass of tap beer and a Coke for Anna.

"Well Anna what do you think about the sentencing?"

"I don't know. I just think about Rosie all the time and what she went through.

And those fuckers get away with six months." Before their meeting and her exposure to the bar life, Anna would not say "shit" if she had a mouthful — that was un-ladylike — but since she was spending more time at the bar the shock of hearing salty and rough language had subsided. She felt more comfortable using a salty word when called for, especially when talking to Norman. "I know that 'Revenge is mine sayeth the Lord' and all that, but I want a little more revenge than what I heard today. What do you think?"

Norman was smiling and thinking that Anna was expressing his thoughts exactly when it came to revenge. "I'm with you Anna. Those fuckers have got to pay more than just a six-month vacation in juvie. I've got some thoughts, but I'll save them for later, when I work out some details."

"I don't want anyone hurt. There's been enough hurt to go around already. But there should be some other way to punish these fuckers. There I go again with the language. Sorry Norm, but when I think about what they did to Rosie."

Norman let out a small giggle at hearing Anna saying 'fucker' and then apologizing. "If I come up with something I don't think you'll like I won't tell you the details. I'll just tell you the deed was done and — justice was served. A wry smile broke out on both of their faces.

"Okay. That's enough revenge talk for now. Let's go upstairs Norman and have a glass of wine and some cuddling."

Norman and Anna, both with lingering smiles on their faces, proceeded up the back stairwell to Norman's apartment. They had been enjoying each other's intimate company for a few months. At first Anna felt a bit guilty — not being married and her being a devout Catholic — but that subsided as the encounters became more romantic and intense. Norman would turn on the record player with an assortment of soft romantic music by either Frank Sinatra, Tony Bennett or Vic Damone. Sinatra's "To Love and Be Loved" was her favorite. Anna would light the candles on the night-stand in the bedroom alongside two chilled glasses of Chianti wine. After this latest love making Anna thought how much mental pleasure she felt in giving up her virginity to Norman. She thought about Rosie and how she would never have the choice of giving her virginity to someone she loved. Her virginity was taken in the most horrific way! *Someone had to pay,* she thought.

Officer Kovac arrived at Chico and Ali's homes early the next morning. He placed both of them in the back of the squad car and proceeded to drive to the Juvenile Detention Center in Plymouth, Michigan. It was a short ride of less than a half an hour. Officer Kovac didn't have to tell the boys no talking. They remained silent the whole ride – alone with their thoughts.

As he escorted them out of the squad car and up the front walk, he cautioned them that for their own good – to listen to all the instructions they would get upon being registered and to obey all orders to a "T." "It will be for your own good to do as your told." He tried to keep a positive and warm lilt to his voice.

Both boys listened unconsciously, as they walked

up to the entrance of the building. It was a somber grey-brick building, square and without character. It matched the boy's mood as they anticipated what was yet to come. Officer Kovac brought them to the front desk and waited for a juvenile officer to take control of them.

"Good luck and you'll need it." He warned them. "Just remember what I told you about listening and obeying – it will be a lot easier." He turned and left them to their future for the next six months.

The induction officer/guard, Joe Morgan, was a man in his fifties that would fit the role of a Marine Drill Instructor. Barrel chested, white-wall brush-cut and a voice they felt vibrating their bones. There was a strong resemblance to Ernest Borgnine's character, Fatso (Sergeant Judson) in the movie "*From Here to Eternity*", right down to the gap-tooth. The resemblance was not lost on his fellow guards but the nickname "Fatso" was never said to his face. If it was said in his earshot, a beating would be in short order. The name was even shared by some of the juvenile inmates, but once again – never to his face!

"Here's how it goes boys. You're going to strip down and I mean strip to your birthday suits. You and your clothes will be searched for any contraband. You better hope we don't find anything. If we do, then you'll already be started on the wrong step. Now follow me to the shower room."

They did as they were told and sheepishly followed in the shadow of guard Morgan to the locker room next to the open shower room. They stripped down as told and stood with their hands spread at their groins, trying to hide their embarrassment and shaking from the cold damp room and their nervousness. Another officer arrived pulling on medical latex gloves as he walked. He grabbed their clothes, shook them, checked the pockets, and felt for anything else that might be in the clothing. He checked in their mouths and told them to bend over so he could see if anything might be in their nether orifices. They were feeling just a hint of what Rosemary felt!

They were given orange jumpsuits until their clothing could be washed and returned to them. They were told that their parents could bring other clothing after a week or so. The next stop on their indoctrination was the sleeping area. It was not what they expected. They were expecting prison cells with iron bars. Instead, they would be sleeping in one of the open-bay wards.

Twenty steel framed cots with peeling olive drab paint lined both exterior walls. Narrow slits of inescapable windows allowed slivers of light into the ward. Along the center of the ward, olive-drab wooden footlockers were lined up in perfect military style. They were directed to two cots in the center of a row of beds and told to make the beds the best they could with the sheets, blankets, and pillows stacked on thin rolled up mattresses. They would learn to perfect the art of taut-military-bed-making in short order.

They hadn't spoke to each other, except for a few words, since the interrogations. They were trapped in their own thoughts and how this whole thing started and the dire situation they were in now.

"Chico, I don't know about you, but we need to listen to that Kovac cop and toe the line. And . . . when we get out of here, we need to do something about that fucker Georgie. I know we did wrong and we should pay but if it wasn't for him, we wouldn't be here right now."

Ali sat on his cot next to Chico's cot with his elbows on his knees facing Ali. They were a mirror of each other, even to the look of depression on their faces. "You're right. All we can do now is keep our time here clean and decide later what to do about Georgie. That son of a bitch is probably laughing at us right now. Let's try to forget about him for now and just do our time." Chico nodded.

The first week was a week of informal indoctrination. A few of the fellow inmates took it on themselves to tell Chico and Ali what they could do, what they couldn't do, and what to expect. They were assigned to the lowest ranking chores: latrine duty, garbage patrol in the kitchen after meals, mopping and dusting the hallways and the mess hall. It would be a few weeks or the arrival of newbies, to get them to more likeable duties.

The lack of privacy was unsettling. Their bunks were in the middle of the bay. Bunks against the walls and especially those in corners with a little more privacy were only to be wished for. The most affronting to their privacy was the shower room. No stalls, just a wide-open room with shower heads along opposing walls and a tiled six-foot long bench in the middle of the room. To add to the embarrassment, a guard, or guards, stood watch in order to speed every-other-day showers, but more importantly to prevent any misbehavior of a sexual nature. There was a long list of varied charges among the inmates so the guards had to be wary; from petty thievery to assault, to auto theft and to the rare charge of rape that Chico and Ali were serving time for!

The knowledge of their adjudication on rape charges quickly spread throughout the detention center. They were either admired and prompted to tell all the sexual details or they were loathed and shied away from. They didn't quite know how to handle either situation. Request for details of the rape might help them make some friends, but after they thought about it and talked to each other about it, they decided the best thing to do was to keep their mouths shut and just do their time.

"I think the best thing for us is to keep our traps shut Ali. If we start telling our story about that bitch then it'll get back to the guards and who knows what they'll do. What do you think?"

"I think you're right. We don't know these fuckers and we don't know if they're using us in some way to get in good with the guards. We don't know who are trustees, who's on the guard's shitlist or anything else about our fellow inmates. So yes, you're right. Let's just keep quiet until we find out who's who. Even then, I think we keep our mouths shut." Ali responded.

Getting use to the routine took a while. Up and out of bed by 6 a.m., make bed per requirements, breakfast at 7 a.m., start daily chores, school in afternoon, dinner, then free time, and lights out by 9 p.m. . . . then, start all over again the next day. By the end of the second week, they were getting the hang of things. They started to talk to other inmates and getting their stories. They were still nervous and embarrassed about telling their story so the usual response was "No big deal, some bitch accused us of feeling her up." They tried to leave it at that even when the horny inmates pressed for the details like, what did she look like? How big were her tits? etc., etc.

They still tried to keep their distance from most of the inmates and only listened if someone was telling them about the procedures, either formal or informal. They were dreading the next six months and how they were going to make it out unscathed. The only reasonably comfortable time of their days was spent in the dayroom. There were two ping pong tables, usually occupied, a grainy color TV, and chess and checkers sets. There was a bookcase with dogeared paperbacks, and stacks of *National Geographic*, and *Boys' Life* . . . mostly untouched.

Nighttime was the worst part of their days. When lights went out it would only be a short time before the snoring started and then the coughing, the farting, giggling and no doubt masturbation under the covers, as evidenced by the stiff, stained sheets the following morning. Both Ali and Chico would lay in bed with their eyes closed trying not to think about their life now and what would happen in the future. They would whisper comfort-words to each other across the narrow aisle that separated their cots.

"Ali, you doing okay? I can't stop thinking about

how we got in this mess and thinking about Georgie. How about you?"

"Yeah, I'm the same. Hard to fall asleep with all the racket in here. I'm tired as a bitch and I do have the same thoughts about Georgie. Let's try not to think about him anymore, at least till we get out. I don't know about you but I also have some thought about that girl, Rosie. I'm feeling a little guilt every now and then. I wonder how she's doing and I'm starting to realize what a terrible thing we did. Thoughts?"

"Same. I also feel that guilt creeping up. Oh well, we'll have to live with it for now. Goodnight, Ali."

The stain would stay with them for longer than they thought.

19

A Meal Served Cold

The next morning at breakfast they both had contented looks on their faces. Norman was fixing a breakfast of French toast, bacon and scrambled eggs – his specialty. Anna was freshening up and combing out her bed-head hair.

After the delicious and welcome breakfast, Anna told Norman that she had to work until 6 p.m. that day.

"What's the plans for today? I have to work until 6. "

"Why don't you come and meet me at the bar. I'm going to talk to some people today and I may have some plans to deal with those two punks in juvie. I'll tell you what I come up with . . . or not . . . depending on the plan. Is that good for you?"

"It is. And, like I said before. I want them punished even more but I don't want anyone seriously hurt. There's been enough hurt to go around. I don't know what you're thinking and maybe I don't want to know, so just do what you have to and we can discuss tonight."

Anna gathered her belongings, gave Norman a passionate kiss and a broad smile and left for home to get ready for work.

Norman cleaned up the kitchen, washed the dishes and took a shower and waited for late afternoon to go downstairs to the bar. He knew Anthony would be there. His plan for Chico and Ali and maybe even Georgie was swimming around in his head and he wanted to discuss it with Anthony and see if he could help with the *Meal Served Cold!*

Right on cue, Anthony came into Nifty Norman's and sat at his regular stool at the end of the bar. Norman walked over and patted Anthony on his silk-shirted shoulder.

"Anthony, how they hangin? I need to talk to you a bit. Follow me back my booth. Bring your drink."

Anthony followed Norman back to the booth, slid in and took a swig of his bottled Stroh's beer. "What's up Norm? You look serious. What can I do for you?"

"I may need you to help me out with a problem. It's for Anna. Her niece was raped a little while back. I don't know if you heard."

Anthony's jaw dropped as he stared at Norman's

sad eyes. "Oh my God Norm. No, I didn't hear. I do remember reading about an assault on a teen-ager a few weeks ago. But you know they never put any names or details into rape reports. So maybe that was about Anna's niece. So, what can I do Norm?"

"The two assholes that raped her have been caught and sentenced. They're in the Plymouth Juvenile Center."

"Are they Mulignans? I'll kill those black mother-fuckers if they are. That's how I can help."

"No Anthony, they're not niggers. One's an Arab and the other is a mix of Polak and spick. They got six months in juvie and then some community work when they get out. Me and Anna think it's a pretty light sentence for two assholes who ruined Rosemary's life, not to mention her brother and her Aunt Anna. Here's what I need to know. I know you have a lot of connections. Do you know anyone at that Plymouth facility? A guard or something?"

"As a matter of fact, I do know a guard there. His name is Joe Morgan. We served together on The Detroit Police Force. They kicked his ass out after too many hands-on beatings of perps he didn't like, es-pecially the niggers. There was a lawsuit that finally put the nail in his coffin. The crazy thing about Joe is that he looks exactly like Ernie Borgnine. You know the actor in *"From Here to Eternity"*? In fact, he picked up the nickname "Fatso". But nobody calls him that to his face. He's even got the gap-tooth grin. So, Norm, what's your plan? How can I help?"

"Here's what I'm thinking Anthony. If you think this guy, Joe. Is that his name?"

"Yeah. Joe Morgan, aka, Fatso." Anthony let out a little laugh and Norman returned his own little snicker.

"If you think Joe would help us get some revenge on these two, like a beating or worse then why don't you give him a call and have him meet us here tomorrow and we can discuss what I need. Tell him that there would be a nice reward if he helps us. And that goes for you too. Deal?"

"Deal. I'll call him later and set it up for tomorrow here at the bar."

Late afternoon, after Joe Morgan got off work, he walked into Nifty Norman's. He had gone home and changed into mufti. He didn't want to stand out in the bar in his guard's uniform. Norman and Anthony were waiting for him in Norman's booth at the rear of the bar. Anthony waved him over as Joe swiveled his head looking for Anthony. Joe Morgan smiled and nodded to Anthony and walked slowly to the booth.

Norman had a tough time suppressing a laugh

when he saw Joe's face. He and Anna had recently seen a revival showing of the 1953 film "*From Here to Eternity*" at the Kramer Show.

He had the Ernest Borgnine character "Fatso" fresh in his head. As he approached the booth with a gap-toothed smile, Norman whispered to Anthony. "That son of a bitch could be Fatso if I didn't know better."

"Shhh. He'll hear you."

Joe Morgan slid into the booth next to Anthony. Anthony made introductions and Joe got right to the subject. "I understand you need my services at the joint? Is that right?" Joe said looking at Norman and side-glanced Anthony.

"Right Joe. There are a couple assholes in there that raped my girlfriend's niece and they got away with light sentences. I just want to make their time a little tougher. You get me?"

"I do. But I'll tell you this. I know exactly who you're talking about. Ali and Chico and I knew they were in there for rape. I won't do any beatings myself. I'd get out of control especially knowing what they did and now knowing you, makes it personal. Anthony, you know what I mean and how it got me in trouble as a cop." Anthony nodded his head with a wry smile. "I can have a couple of the juvies I give special favors to, take care of it. How does that sound?"

"As a matter of fact, I wasn't thinking of a beating. I was thinking of something more personal, so they could feel the shame and pain of being raped. Get my drift?"

"I do. It can be arranged. What about the money? I'll have to grease some palms, like other guards to turn the other way and give a few 20's to the them helping."

"I can give you 10 C-notes."

"How about 15? That will take care of the payoffs and leave a little for me," he smiled.

"15 it is. You want pay now or after the deed is done?" Norman asked.

"Now would be great so I'll have the money to set up the deal with the other guards and juvies."

Norman excused himself and went to his upstairs apartment. He closed the door to the stairway. Halfway up the stairs he pushed on one of the risers of a step. The riser popped open. Norman reached in and pulled out a small grey-metal cash-box. He opened it and grabbed a handful of 100-dollar bills. He counted off 15, put them in an envelope, placed the rest back in the box, placed the box back in the opening and carefully closed the riser.

Norman sat back down in the booth and slid the envelope over to Joe. "15, like you asked. I'll take care of you later Anthony." Anthony smiled knowing

Norman was a man of his word. "Just let me know when the deed is done and I might want to know some details like how they reacted."

"I can do that. It'll probably take a week or so. I'll get back with Anthony when I have everything taken care of. Nice meeting you Mr. Norman and it's a pleasure doing business with you."

"Likewise." Norman answered.

Joe left and Anthony looked at Norman and said. "Well, what do you think?"

"I like. I think he'll get the job done. Looks like a bruiser. And I can't believe how much he looks like Fatso. Anna would get a kick out of seeing him. We went to the movies and saw that movie about Pearl Harbor. Maybe I'll have her waiting in the wings when he gets back to us about getting everything taken care of."

Joe Morgan had a smile on his face all the way home as he constantly felt the wad of $100 dollar bills in his shirt pocket. He was thinking of what he would do with the money. *Need a new hunting rifle and maybe a nice gift for the old lady, a new vacuum or some new clothes. Yeah, that would be nice*, he thought.

The next afternoon, at the start of his shift, he gathered his fellow guards for that day and asked them to meet in the cafeteria. "I've got some good news for you guys and not so good news for those two that raped that girl. You know . . . that Ali and Chico. Here's the deal." He pulled out 5 of the bills Norman gave him and gave one to each. "I need you guys to turn the other way while I take care of those two in the shower room on Wednesday. We're going to let them know how it feels to be raped, if you get my drift?" All five of the guards seated at the table looked at the rarely seen $100 bills, smiled and nodded.

"I'm going to use our most trusted and capable trustees here to do the dirty deed. I'll give them a couple 20's and some extra privileges. It's not like it would be the first-time justice was enhanced in the shower room for some of the low life's we get here. Any questions?"

None of them said anything. They all had been at the juvenile center for many years and knew how the justice system worked in the facility. As long as no one was killed or seriously hurt it was accepted as okay. They all kept the code of silence whenever someone wanted to do something outside the rules. And the extra cash would seal their mouths even tighter.

Wednesday had arrived and the usual routine for showers in Chico and Ali's ward had started. The boys marched into the locker room and stripped down and hung their clothes in two of the unlocked, empty wall lockers. They grabbed a washcloth and a bar of small motel soap and made their way into the shower room and parked under unattended shower heads. The rule was . . . wash as fast as you can, because the 20-minute rule was strictly enforced.

As the clock ticked down and the boys started to vacate the shower room, Joe Morgan entered carrying a wooden baton with a leather rawhide strap. He watched as the shower room quickly emptied.

"You two, Ali and Chico, you stay here."

They looked up at Joe, holding a baton and slapping it into his palm. They knew immediately this was not good. They were suddenly aware of their nakedness and their vulnerability. Even in the hot humid air of the shower room they both started to shiver. They didn't question Joe Morgan. They knew better. They just stood with their crossed open hands at their crotches . . . and waited.

It seemed like an eternity as they waited. The silence was interrupted by two of their fellow inmates — each carrying a wooden-handled rubber toilet plunger and wet washcloths. The two inmates Joe had selected and paid with cash and the promise of more privileges were two of the biggest and meanest in the ward. When the guards weren't around . . . they were in charge.

They told both Ali and Chico to kneel down at the ceramic-tiled center-island bench. They each grabbed their hair and lifted their heads and forcibly stuffed wet soiled washcloths into their mouths. They looked at Joe Morgan and waited for a signal. Joe nodded and slapped the nightstick forcibly into his palm.

Chico and Ali were not thinking of Rosemary at the moment. They were only thinking of their pain and trying to scream but could only let out muffled cries of agony and loss of dignity. The inmates stopped when they saw blood trailing down their thighs and mixing into pink water droplets on the shower floor. Chico and Ali could feel the warm blood as it trickled onto their thighs.

Joe motioned for them to leave and take the soiled plungers. "Okay guys. I hope you got the message. You can feel a small taste of what you did to that girl. Now clean up and get dressed and get the fuck out of here." They walked gingerly out of the shower room after washing the remnants of their rape from their bodies. Washing away the memory would take longer . . . if not forever!

Joe Morgan wasn't feeling any guilt at the moment for what he just did. But as guilt slid into his head over the next few days, he would feel the wad of bills in his pocket and smile and the guilt would quickly melt away.

They spent the rest of their six-month sentence in virtual isolation. When the word got out that they were raped in the shower room as retaliation for their raping of a young girl, no one wanted anything to do with them. So, they spent their days doing their chores, avoiding the dayroom and not mingling with the other inmates and speaking very little to each other. As the physical hurt healed, the mental hurt started and became more intense. As hard as they tried, the brutality they inflicted on Rosemary constantly invaded their thoughts. And as it persisted more and more; their thoughts were starting to get more intense on Georgie's roll in the drastic change to their young lives.

Joe Morgan called Anthony the following day and told him the deed was done and if he would like a recap, he could meet him at Nifty Norman's. Anthony agreed. He called Norman and told him that Joe would give them an update this evening.

Norman knew Anna was working and he couldn't reach her by phone, so he drove over to Federal Department Store to tell her the news. She was talking to a fellow employee when he entered the store. She introduced him with a proud smile on her face. The other employee got the hint and left them alone.

"I've taken care of our little problem over at the detention center. The fellow who helped us out along with Anthony will be in the bar tonight to give us any detail we might want to know. I don't want you to hear all that went on. But I would like you there to see this guy. I'm not going to tell you who he looks like but you have got to see him. I think you will get a kick out of his resemblance to someone we both saw in the recent past. I'll leave it at that."

"Why don't you want me to hear what this guy has to say? Is it that bad? I told you I don't want anyone seriously hurt."

"I know. And I can give you some info once I talk to him. Are you going to come down after work? You can sit in another booth while Anthony and me get this guy's story. Okay?"

"Okay. I'll be there after work. I can have something to eat also. I'm famished and still have a few hours to go. See you then. I got to get back to work or get fired. I see some customers over there." Norman gave her a peck on the cheek and left.

Anna arrived at Nifty Norman's shortly after her shift ended. She nodded and said "Hi" to all the customers she had met and felt comfortable with over the past months. Norman greeted her with a hug and a kiss and directed her to a table facing directly to 'his booth' but far enough away so she wouldn't be obvious to Joe Morgan when he arrived,

"Just sit here and sip on your sloe gin fizz or whatever, as if you're waiting for someone. You won't be able to hear us. I just want you to see this guy."

"Okay. I'm going to order a burger or something and eat and sip while I wait. This better be good, the way you're talking about it."

Joe Morgan arrived shortly after Anna's burger and fries were delivered to her table. She did as Norman instructed and nonchalantly munched on her burger and fries and sipped on her Coke. He was wearing his khaki guard's uniform with a Sam Browne belt which made the resemblance even more striking.

Anna covered her mouth to conceal her grin and whispered to herself, into her hand, "Oh my God! He looks exactly like Fatso. Norm wasn't lying. I can't believe it."

She wiped the grin off of her face and continued to shoot glances over to the booth, trying not to be obvious. She could see them talking but the din of the now crowded after-work-crowd muffled all of the conversation. The look of surprise and shock was evident on Norman's and even Anthony's faces. It was evident that Joe Morgan was giving them some not-so-pleasant details of the revenge that Norman had orchestrated. She lost her appetite!

Joe Morgan's belly crushed against the edge of the table as he slid out of the booth and turned to leave. Anna caught one last and lasting glance as Joe Morgan looked her way and gave her a friendly smile and a nod.

"Well, what do you think?"

"Fatso for sure. What did he tell you?'

"I'm not going to give you the details. I'll just say this. They were dealt with — in kind — for what they did to Rosemary. I'll leave it at that. And I'll leave it up to you to decide on what you might want to tell Rosemary and Mickey. It's your family. If you want me to be there if you decide to tell them anything . . . then I'm okay with that."

"I get the drift on what happened to those two. And now I hope we can start to get over this. I think I'll tell Rosie and Mickey that those two had some trouble in juvie and were punished. I'll leave it at that."

Anna went alone to Rosemary and Mickey's house the next day. She sat them down and relayed to them, using as many euphemisms as she could think of, to describe that justice had been served. Both Rosemary and Mickey squeezed out brief smiles. Mickey was thinking about Georgie's role and his justice, but kept quiet, not wanting to upset Rosemary even more! So, the elephant in the room was not addressed. Georgie's justice!

20

Lucifer

Chico and Ali returned to school shortly after being released from the detention center. They were given strict orders to meet regularly with their parole officer as scheduled and to perform whatever community service they were assigned. It was emphasized more than once that any violation, no matter how small or seemingly insignificant, would be punished by returning to the detention center until they were 18 years old. They got the message loud and clear. It was also reinforced by their parents who were present at their release and meeting with the parole officer.

Georgie knew of their release and planned to welcome them back. His friendship with Jimmy, the other one that escaped conviction, waned over the six months that Chico and Ali were in detention. Jimmy felt for Chico and Ali and his reluctance to participate in the rape, saved him from the same fate. His intelligent-self told him *Keep away from Georgie — he's trouble.* So he did!

After a collection of snubs from Jimmy, Georgie got the message. "Fuck you, Jimmy. You should have been with those other assholes up in Plymouth. Who needs you anyway?" Were the last words that Georgie had with Jimmy.

Chico and Ali walked sheepishly into their first class back after release. They knew full well that the well-oiled grapevine in school had certainly spread the story of their rape of Rosemary. For the first week or so they kept to themselves, relying on each other for some semblance of companionship. No one blatantly avoided them. It was just a feeling they were being isolated. When they talked in their loneliness, they shared the same thought. They knew they deserved this treatment and they understood it. The six months was more than enough time to think through their actions and make them realize what a horrible thing they had done. So, their treatment by the other students, some of who they thought of as friends, was understandable and accepted with regrets.

Trying to connect with Jimmy was even more difficult. Jimmy knew the whole story and how Georgie talked them into the rape. He felt they were certainly responsible for what they had done, but he knew that if they hadn't taken Georgie into their circle of friends — this never would have happened.

"Hi guys. Good to see you back. I'm not going to ask you anything about what happened or how bad it was in juvie. I'm just going to say this . . . I'm still your friend. I haven't spoken to Georgie since you left and I don't intend to speak that fucker ever again."

As Jimmy greeted them, they both thought about the terrible price they paid in the juvenile center and . . . they were somewhat relieved that Jimmy wasn't going to ask them about their time in juvenile detention.

"Thanks for that Jimmy," Chico answered and Ali nodded, looking into Jimmy's eyes.

"I think I can speak for both of us when I say that we fucked up royal. Georgie started it and planned it and we probably would never have done such a thing, but he has got to take some responsibility – but knowing him a little better now, we don't think he will. He's got to be punished somehow, but that can't be up to us. If we stray, even a little, we can have our asses back in Plymouth until we're 18. And I never want to see that place again, except if we have to go back to get a final release after probation." Chico said.

"I'm with Chico. We got to walk the straight and narrow. If you want to hang with us, that would be great. It seems like no one wants to be near us. And who could blame them?"

"Yeah, I'm here for you guys. After all, it could have been me too."

Georgie approached Chico and Ali the day after they spoke with Jimmy.

"Hi guys. Good to see you're out. Wanna do something after school?" Georgie asked as if nothing had ever happened.

"Get the fuck away from us, you piece of shit. Because of you, our lives are ruined." Chico said as he pushed his face as close to Georgie as he dared and poked his finger firmly into Georgie's chest. His spittle sprinkled Georgie's face. Georgie nonchalantly wiped his face with his shirt sleeve.

"Hey. . . just trying to be friendly. It's not my fault you got caught. Okay, if that's the way you want to play it. I don't need you guys anyway. I did just fine while you were mopping floors and cleaning shitters."

"You're gonna get yours Georgie Boy. It may not be from us but someone is going to ring your bell. And, once again, stay away from us and Jimmy. He doesn't want anything to do with you either – you sorry-ass piece of shit." Ali gave Georgie another shower of spittle.

Georgie shrugged his shoulders, stuck up both his middle fingers and said, "fuck both of you and the horse you rode in on." He turned, shrugged his shoulders and walked away.

Georgie had been avoiding and denying the treatment he was getting. At first, he thought he was being shunned because of his friendship with Chico and Ali and it was their fault — not his. They were in juvie for raping a young girl — not him. He could feel eyes on him wherever he went. Now he was being rejected by what he thought of as friends and that dug in even deeper. It wasn't the loneliness. Loneliness had been part of his life for a long time. It was the rejection and the penetrating stares and the whispers that he knew were about him. That's what was rearing in his psyche. It was taking hold of every waking moment. Any encounter was fear of what they were thinking and what they were planning. The words that Chico said, "You're gonna get yours Georgie Boy", stuck in his head. He was sure there was a plan to get him. He didn't know what. He would have to be extra careful and watch every little thing . . . *before they get me*. He thought.

As he walked home alone, he thought and talked to himself. "*I don't need those fuckers. I don't need Jimmy. I don't need Chico. I don't need Ali. I can make new friends. They just got me in trouble. They brought that fucking dog to attack me with that big nose Wop. I'll fix them. I'll ignore them. I'll find some other friends. There are plenty of kids looking for a friend or two.*" His unconscious walking had brought him to his front yard. He looked at the dire condition of the house and the yard and felt even more depressed.

"Hi Mom. Georgie said as he saw his mother sitting at her usual spot at the kitchen table, smoking, and sipping from a tea cup. She was holding a nub of a pencil in her gnarly hand, with the eraser chewed off, and staring at a half-finished crossword puzzle. She nodded with a "Hmmm" and dropped her head back to looking at the newspaper.

What was a routine and an accepted part of Georgie's life was now taking on a magnification of the rejection he was facing at school? His mother's close-to-ignoring attitude multiplied his already broken-window mind of paranoia. *Not only are my so-called-friends ignoring me but my mother is also ignoring me. And my father . . . who knows about him? At least he doesn't ignore me. He can't. He's never here!* He thought.

He walked slowly back to his bedroom. The hunger pangs he had before he talked to Chico and Ali had left and were replaced by a leaden ball in his stomach. The dank condition of his bedroom did nothing to lift his spirits. He looked at the transistor radio he had stolen from a grade-schooler while walking to school. He thought that turning on the radio would ease his mind a bit. Bad timing! *The Shadow* broadcast was just beginning. The announcer echoed out "Who knows what evil lurks in the hearts of men? The Shadow knows!"

His heart dropped into his stomach to join the leaden ball already there. This was a sign. This was proof. He was right. People were evil and plotting against him. Another reason to be careful and wary of everyone around him. He drifted into an uneasy sleep as the radio program ended.

Norman was sitting in his booth with a scattering of white and yellow paper slips covering most of the table in addition to a small adding machine and a pad of paper

Anthony walked over to the booth with a half empty bottle of Goebel beer. "Watcha doin Norm? Counting all your profits?" Anthony said as he looked down at Norman.

"No, I'm trying to figure out your bar tab Anthony." Norman laughed. "What do you need. Kidding about your tab. I erased that when you helped with Joe. I'm busy with yesterday's chits and bills."

"I was just wondering about our little project over at juvie. Joe told me those kids are out."

"Sit down and let's talk." Norman motioned over to the bartender to bring him a drink. "You need another beer?"

"No. I'm good." Anthony said as he slid into

the booth, careful not to disturb the piles of paper. Norman collected the piles of paper and slid them over to the end of the table next to the wall. His glass of Coke arrived. He seldom drank alcohol during the day. Only in the evenings to be sociable or take the edge off a busy day . . . or a glass of romantic Chianti with Anna.

"What's on your mind Anthony? What did Joe say? Is there a problem?"

"No. Nothing like that. Joe said everything was cool. I was just wondering if now that we're through with those two that raped Anna's niece — is that it? I was wondering about that other motherfucker . . . that Georgie kid? The one you told me that was the instigator in this whole rape thing. Are we through with him? He got off without even a slap on the wrist." Anthony asked as he looked at Norman shuffling some of the papers and listening.

"As a matter of fact, Anthony my dear friend, I have been playing around with that unfinished business. You're reading my mind. Great minds and all that. Georgie is the rest of the cold meal. The desert!"

"What the fuck are you talking about . . . cold meal?"

"Just a saying. Revenge is a meal best served cold. Never mind that. Listen Anthony, I've got to take care of all this paperwork, receipts, bills, etc. etc. It's the end of the month. Let's do this. You come by tomorrow afternoon and we'll talk. I'll give you my idea on what we might want to do with that bastard. Okay?"

"Okay Norm. See you tomorrow. Get back to your bill paying. I'm out of your hair until tomorrow." He raised his now empty bottle of beer and turned and left.

The next day Norman was sitting in his booth, deep in thought when Anthony broke into his thoughts.

"Thinking about your cold meal Norm?"

Norman's face contorted into a wry smile. "As a matter of fact Anthony, I am. Sit down and we can discuss."

Anthony slid into the booth and waited for Norman to speak. "I got all my paperwork done as you can see by the cleared off table. So . . . Anthony, this is what I've been thinking. We got some justice on those two in juvie. I think they'll remember what they did for a long time. Maybe they'll even develop some remorse, if they haven't already. As we discussed briefly, that kid Georgie who was the instigator in this whole mess has walked off scot free. Anna told me she's glad we took care of those two and she wanted it to be over with. Me . . . I'm not so sure? So, here's what I think. And, I want your input."

"Good. Shoot. Give me what you got and I'll give you my thoughts."

"You told me that when you approached that kid Georgie with Lucifer by your side, he almost shit his pants. Along with the rape of Rosemary, they think that he poisoned their dog Perro. So, if you've got some free afternoons and maybe some evenings, I was wondering if you might pay Georgie Boy a visit. Just give him a boost from the first warning. What do you say? There's some extra cash in it for you."

Anthony smiled and rubbed his chin. "I don't need any extra cash, Norm. I would take great pleasure in giving that kid a boost. And I know Lucifer would also take some enjoyment out of scaring the shit out of him. I'm in."

"Here's what I'm thinking Anthony. Just follow him around a couple of days or so. We know where he goes to school and where he lives and he hangs out at that pool room on the corner. So, mix it up. One day school. One day his house. One day the pool hall. He'll go crazy trying to figure out when the next meeting with Lucifer will be. Agree?"

"Agree!"

"Bring Lucifer by tomorrow. I haven't seen him for a while. I just want to refresh my memory on how scary he might look to someone that doesn't know him. Okay? Can you do that?"

"I'll come by tomorrow late afternoon. I've got some other business in the morning. You can give me the info on where he lives and the school and the rest of it tomorrow. Okay?"

"See you then."

Norman forgot that he had invited Anthony back the next day as Anna entered the bar and spotted him behind the bar.

"Just got off work and didn't feel like cooking so here I am. Can someone rustle up a burger or something, Dear?"

"Yes Ma'am. I'll go back to the kitchen and see what I can find. Head over to my booth and I'll bring it out with a Coke pronto." Norman smiled at Anna and she returned the smile and headed toward the booth.

Norman was bringing a cheeseburger and fries and a Coke over to the booth when Anthony came through the rear door with Lucifer leading the way. As Norman set down the plate with the food and the Coke, he saw a startled look on Anna's face. She spotted Lucifer!

"Oh my God, Norm! Look at that dog."

Norman swiveled his head and saw Anthony and Lucifer and he let out a laugh. "That's just Lucifer. He's the friendliest Doberman around. He won't hurt you. I just asked Anthony to bring him around cause I haven't seen him in a while. I'm glad you're here to meet him. Lucifer say "hi" to Anna. Anna say "hi" to Lucifer."

"Anna sheepishly raised her hand and said, "Hi Lucifer. What a scary name you have."

Lucifer looked at Anna and walked slowly over to the booth. His toenails tapping on the tiled floor. He looked at Anna and slowly laid his head on her lap as she cautiously leaned back in the booth.

"He likes you, Anna. He's smelling the French fries. One of his favorite treats. Give him one and you have a friend for life."

Anna picked up the end of the largest fry she could find with two fingers and cautiously brought it close to Lucifer. Instead of a lunge for the fry as Anna expected, he gently grabbed the end of the fry and popped it into his mouth. It was gone in a second. Back to staring at Anna. She took the cue and produced another fry. This went on for a few minutes until the plate of fries was nearly empty.

"I'll get another plate of fresh fries for you Anna since Lucifer made short order of yours," Norman said and headed back to the kitchen. Anthony sat on a chair next to the booth and held on to his leash as Lucifer and Anna slowly became friends. His head on her lap and Anna petting his head and chin and feeling the spikes on his collar. A bond was formed!

The first encounter with Lucifer happened the next day. Georgie spotted Lucifer as he turned the corner and started to walk toward his house. Anthony didn't say a word, but held on to the strained leash as they approached Georgie. Georgie was silent. He picked up his pace as Lucifer's snarls got closer to his heels. He could feel and almost hear as his heart began to beat faster and faster. Lucifer could smell the fear and strained harder to get closer as Anthony held fast onto his leash. Georgie quickened his pace even more as he looked back and saw the spiked collar and the slobber dripping from Lucifer's teeth.

As they approached Mickey and Rosemary's house, both Anthony and Georgie noticed Lenny sitting close to Mickey on the top step of the porch.

"Who's your new friend Georgie Boy? Where's your other friends, Georgie Boy?" Mickey shouted and both he and Lenny giggled loud enough for Georgie to hear them.

Anthony joined their giggles with a laugh and said to the boys with a small wave of his free hand. "Hi guys. Just taking Lucifer for a little walk. See you around."

Anthony and Lucifer followed Georgie all the way to his front yard. Georgie began to run up to his house, hoping Lucifer was not going to follow.

Anthony remained quiet as he watched Georgie disappear into the front doorway. He smiled and thought to himself. *Day One – Mission accomplished!* He left and headed to the bar to update Norman.

Georgie rushed into his bedroom, without even noticing that his mother was not in her usual spot at the kitchen table. He laid on his bed and his nervous cold sweat slowly blended into the dankness of his bed-sheet. Now he knew for sure that they were out to get him. They had kept his friends from him. Everyone was talking about him. He was by himself. No one to turn to. No one to protect him. What was he going to do? He thought about going down to Steve's pool hall, but quickly dismissed that idea. He was afraid that the hood with the dog would be outside waiting for him. Being by himself and thinking about his dire situation was becoming a pattern. His bedroom window faced the street. He pushed aside the dirty grey muslin curtain, that had once been white, and peeked out the window. Just as he thought . . . he could see moon shadows of the hood and the dog waiting for him next to the naked apple tree. He laid back on his bed and fell asleep until he was wakened by his father and mother returning home after the bar closed. He got up and went back to the window and carefully slid the curtain open with his index finger. They were still there!

It was Friday, last day of school. After that he wouldn't have to worry about the kids in school talking about him and that dog following him and walking past Mickey and Rosemary's house. As soon as he got out of bed, he once again peeked out the window. *They're gone — for now,* he thought. The walk to school was becoming a walk of trepidation along with all his other routines. The fear was imbedding itself into his every action.

He spent the weekend at home — afraid to go out and encounter a Doberman Pinscher nipping at his heels. He laid in bed listening to the radio and trying to occupy his mind reading comic books. *Tales from the Crypt* was one of his favorites. There was no escaping. The issue he picked up and started to read was of a demon dog devouring rotting corpses — a Doberman Pinscher! He ripped the comic in two and threw it across the room, hitting the curtains and bringing one panel down to the floor. There was no escaping. Even the comics were out to destroy his sanity.

After a long weekend of doing nothing but staring out the window, he almost welcomed the walk to school. In an attempt to prevent all of the classmates staring at him and whispering, he very politely asked his homeroom teacher if he could sit in one of the rear seats of the room which were unoccupied. He told the teacher he was coming down with a cold and sitting nearer to the radiators might help him keep the chills off. He obliged. Now they couldn't stare at him without craning their necks – especially Jimmy, Chico and Ali! His walk home, that was usually filled with laughter and pranks was now lonely and scary – waiting for the dog to appear. This day there was no dog.

That evening with a rare dinner with his mother, she asked him to go down to the pool hall and get her a package of Lucky Strikes. He hesitantly agreed.

"Okay Mom. But I may stay a while and shoot some pool. Are you okay with ciggies till I get home?"

"Yeah. If I run out, I'll steal some of your dad's. No hurry. Enjoy yourself. And I've been noticing that you've been spending a lot of time at home alone. Where are your friends that use to come around every day?"

"They're pissing me off lately and I'm looking for some new friends. Some of them just got out of juvie and I don't want to be seen with them. They raped that Rosie girl. That girl whose her parents got killed when the old man drove into the expressway bridge. Probably drunk on his ass. Anyway, I'm good. See you later. He grabbed a dollar bill off the table and left.

Steve was sitting at his usual stool behind the cigar counter.

"Hi Steve. I need a pack of Luckies for my mom and give me a pack of Marvels. I save the coupons. And a rack for the last table."

"I got the ciggies for you but no racks, Georgie. After those two of your friends got caught raping that girl, the cops have been keeping an eye on this place. You're not eighteen, so no racks. Sorry Georgie."

Georgie paid for the cigarettes, stuffed them in his pocket and abruptly turned and left. *Another one against me*, he thought. He stopped outside the pool room and leaned toward the wall with one leg bent and his foot supporting him. He took out the package of Marvels and unzipped the cellophane wrapper, rapped the package against his palm and shook out a cigarette. He hadn't used his Zippo flick-open trick in a while and when he tried it the Zippo fell to the ground. *Another failure.*

As he bent to pick up the lighter, he noticed three set of feet approaching. It was Jimmy, Chico and Ali. "You guys can't go in there and play pool. Steve said the cops are bugging him since you guys got caught." Georgie said in hopes of getting some sort of conversation going with his old friends.

"Fuck you, Georgie. You don't tell us what to do. Those days are over. Just keep your remarks to yourself. We'll take care of each other." As Chico was finishing his response to Georgie, they all heard and saw Anthony approaching with Lucifer straining at the leash.

"Here comes your four-legged friend, Georgie Boy. He's the only friend you've got and even he might bite off your balls if you get to close." Ali said and they all laughed.

"Hi guys. Nice day for a stroll. Wouldn't you say?" Anthony greeted them. Georgie backed against the wall again as Lucifer first sniffed the other boys but his sniffing turned into a blood curdling snarl as he approached Georgie. Georgie thought of the picture of the Doberman Pinscher with blood dripping from his fangs in the *Tales of the Crypt* comic book he threw across his bedroom.

Anthony grinned as Georgie tried to disappear himself into the wall. "He doesn't seem to like you very much Georgie. Maybe he knows about your poisoning his friend Perro. Or . . . maybe he knows about your role in the trouble these guys got into because of you." Anthony swiveled his head over to where the other three boys were standing in awe. Georgie kept his silence. There would be no challenges to the man with the dog. Georgie started his walk home with Lucifer as an unwanted companion.

He was thinking through his next walk home from school and dreading it. Where would the dog appear? He thought hard and realized that the hood and his dog were following him and appearing where he normally would walk. They knew all of his usual ways home and to the pool hall. What if he went a different way? They might not bother him. He would try it.

It was late October and the daylight was being squeezed out between the darkness. He hung around school that one day, sitting on the playground bleachers and watching football practice. He thought if he altered his regular routine and the times he walked home, they wouldn't find him. As daylight was starting to leave the sky and practice was ending, he could see the blood red Hunter's Moon peeking over the horizon. Time to head home.

He walked his usual route along Buchanan Street until he got to 30th street. He didn't see any sign of the dog. He decided to walk down the alley instead of 31st street in case Mickey and Lenny were sitting on Mickey's porch and maybe the dog would be there. As he walked down the alley the daylight was completely gone. The moon and an occasional light from a garage were all he could count on to light his way. The night was quiet, with only the whirr of a distant passing car to break the silence. He was constantly looking behind his back to see it anyone was following him. No one. Before he realized it, and he had never considered it, he was at Mickey's back yard. The low cyclone fence and Perro's vacant dog house came into his view. A cold sweat broke out on his forehead. A flashback to the poisoned hot dog jumped into his brain. He looked over the fence and jumped back – startled. He gasped. It can't be. How did they find me?

He was seeing Lucifer laying beside the dog house. *It can't be*, he thought. *It must be some sort of trick. Are they keeping that dog in their yard now?* He had to look closer. He leaned his elbows on the rail of the fence and strained his neck as far as he could. The Doberman growled, leaped to his feet and lunged toward Georgie. He backed up, turned and ran as fast as he could down the alley. When he reached the end of the alley, he could see the shadow of the dog rushing toward him. He turned at the corner of the alley, hoping to beat the dog to his house and safety. He stumbled, got up and looked down the alley again to see if the dog was gaining on him. No dog. It was gone. Or was it even there? He was starting to doubt his own eyes. *What the fuck is going on?*

He stopped running. He was out of breath. He walked fast. Just in case! As he approached his house, the moon was now fully in view and projected a silhouette of the naked branches on the apple tree in front of his house. He rubbed his eyes just to make sure. Leaning against the tree, swirling a leash was the hood. The dog was unleashed and the spikes on his collar were sparkling in the moonlight. He didn't dare walk up to his house with them standing there. He turned around and went back down the alley to get to his house from the rear. As he turned the corner of the alley, the Doberman was there waiting for him. He woke up!

It was morning. He had trouble sorting out the real from his dreams. This last dream or so he thought, was about Rosemary. She was dressed like the scarecrow he and Lenny and Jimmy and Mark and Stanley threw over the expressway railing. Her hair was bloody and streamed down in knots from under the Detroit Tiger ballcap. "You wanna kiss me, Georgie Boy?" she said as she moved closer and he could smell death on her breath. All the boys were laughing and shouting "Kiss her Georgie Boy. She won't bite . . . maybe just a little?"

He struggled, but finally got the nightmare image out of his head. The dream of Lucifer chasing him with Lenny and Mickey riding on his back came in flashes and he pushed the flashes away until they faded. Rosemary's face and voice would not fade.

21

Devil's Night III

Anthony kept bringing Lucifer to Nifty Norman's even as his little chore of delivering that extra desert 'cold meal' was ongoing. He saw how attached Lucifer had become to Anna and vice versa. If he came in without Lucifer and Anna was there, she would always ask, "Where's Lucifer? I need someone to share my French fries with."

It was Friday evening and Anna was sitting in Norman's booth, munching on French fries and sipping on a Coke. She was waiting for Norman who was in the kitchen taking care of some personnel business.

"Here's your friend Anna. He's hungry and wants some of those fries." Anthony said as Lucifer quickly snuggled his head on Anna's lap and gave her that begging look. She obliged with a steady stream of fries while she petted his head and neck — feeling the spiked collar!

Anthony slid into the seat across from Anna. Do you mind?" he asked.

"No. Not at all. As long as Lucifer is okay with it." Anna smiled and Anthony returned the smile.

"I have a small favor to ask. I already talked to Norm and he said it's up to you."

"I'm all ears. Just like Lucifer." She giggled.

"I have to take a short trip for a client of mine and I'll be gone until next Tuesday, the day after Halloween. My regular dog sitter is in the hospital, so I need someone to watch Lucifer for a few days. Since you and Lucifer get along so well, I thought that you might want to help me out . . . and Lucifer. I understand if you don't want to or if you can't because of work or whatever. No problem. I have a few other friends I can ask. I just thought you might enjoy spending some time with him. And I know he would like your company. Think it over and let me know by tomorrow, Anna."

"Oh, I don't have to think it over. I'd be delighted to have him for company for a few days. As a matter of fact, I have the weekend off, including Monday, Halloween."

"Great. I was hoping you would say yes and I brought some Alpo along. I see you're parked next to Norm out back, so I can put the food and Lucifer's bowl in your car. Okay?"

"Okay."

Norman finished his business in the kitchen and

joined Anthony and Anna and Lucifer in the booth. "You two settle the dog sitting job?"

"We did. So, you might not see me a whole lot this weekend. I'll be spending some time with my new boyfriend here." Anna reached down and petted Lucifer's head.

"That's fine. And as a matter of fact, I'm going to be extra busy this weekend with some Halloween costume parties on the weekend and Monday, Halloween. You two have fun."

Anna was wakened by a wet kiss on the cheek and it wasn't Norman. She opened her eyes and was greeted by her new bed partner. Anthony had given her advice on when and how much to feed Lucifer. She jumped out of bed and before she took care of her morning routine, she filled the monogrammed doggie bowl with Lucifer's breakfast.

Anna was excited with her new friend and wanted to show him off. She got dressed in some comfy walk around clothes, grabbed a light jacket, and a babushka and attached Lucifer's leash to his spiked collar.

"Let's go Lucifer. Let's go visit Rosie and Mickey."

Rosemary and Mickey were sitting at the kitchen table along with Lenny. Lenny had spent another sleepover, that was becoming routine on the weekends.

Anna knocked loudly on the front door and easily opened the door and shouted, "Anyone home?"

"In here Aunt Anna. We're having breakfast," Rosemary answered.

They all had a look of surprise. Both Mickey and Lenny had spoonfuls of Cheerios in mid air along with their mouths agape.

"Meet my new friend, Lucifer. I'm dog sitting for Norman's friend for the weekend." Lucifer was sitting dutifully on his rear haunches next to Anna.

"He's beautiful Aunt Anna." Mickey said. "I've seen him around the neighborhood a few times with some big guy. I guess that's his master?"

"Yes, that's Anthony, Norm's friend. Would you boys like to take him for a walk? He loves to walk and exercise."

Mickey and Lenny held out their open hands and Lucifer calmly walked over and let them pet him.

"Let's get dressed Lenny and take him for a walk around the block."

Both boys hurriedly dressed. Mickey grabbed the leash from Anna and they hurried out the door. "Not too far boys. Just around the block once or twice."

"What's the matter Rosie? You look kinda down in the dumps."

"I don't know. I guess it's because another anniversary of my mom and dad's death is coming up in a few days. I was thinking that I want to take a walk over on Sunday to where they died and say a few prayers and then go to the cemetery. You want to join me?"

"Of course. That's a wonderful thought. What about Mickey?"

"He's been spending a lot of time with Lenny. They're busy with school, sports and games and I don't want to remind him. That's Devil's Night, so they'll probably be out and about with their friends . . . hopefully not getting into any trouble. But I trust both of them and I'm not worried. So, just the two of us." Rosemary said.

"I can make dinner Sunday and we can go after that. How about some galompki?"

"Sounds good Aunt Anna. Thanks."

They rounded the corner and unconsciously arrived in front of Georgie's house. They both stopped as Lucifer tugged at the leash attempting to head toward Georgie's house.

Georgie was sitting on the edge of his bed staring out the window. The curtain panel he knocked down with the torn comic book remained on the floor. He saw movement outside as he walked up to the window. He could see both Mickey and Lenny and Lucifer standing in front of the apple tree and both boys were staring at his window. He quickly moved to the side of the window behind the remaining hanging grey curtain panel. He was afraid they already spotted him looking out the window. He cautiously pulled the curtain to the side and continued to look out. They were just standing there and he could see the strain on Lucifer's leash. It seemed like an hour before they continued to walk away from his front yard. He didn't notice the cold sweat that had formed on his brow.

He hadn't had a bath in over a week. His body odor and the dank smell in the house blended together. He hardly noticed. His appetite dwindled down to a few pieces of toast in the morning and a piece of fruit after school . . . if there was any that wasn't rotting on the kitchen table.

His mother barely noticed his demeanor. Every time she mentioned that he needed a bath or why he wasn't eating, he ignored her or gave her a trite answer like, "I'm good. Just not feeling well, quit bugging me and drink your tea, ha-ha."

He was at his lowest level since Chico and Ali were released from juvenile detention and he realized that their friendship was over. Paranoia that had started slowly was steadily increasing as the weeks went by. Now, here he was on the cusp of the second anniversary of that Devil's Night's and he knew he had to do something.

He knew exactly where to find it. He walked into the garage with a dim flickering flashlight and found what he was looking for. The bottle of COWLEY'S RAT POISON was still hidden behind the paint cans. He thought about the ugly death throes that Perro suffered and maybe a human would suffer even more. Was he that desperate to solve his situation? *It took care of that bitch Perro . . . so maybe it'll solve my problem,* he thought. He ignored the cautions he used when he poisoned the hot dog for Perro and grabbed the bottle, looked at the skull and crossbones, and slipped it into his jacket pocket.

He didn't have to think where he was going. It was automatic. It was Devil's Night and there was only one place to be. He walked slowly down to Wesson Street. A cold shiver went up his spine as he passed the house. It was dark except for a light in the rear of the house and a porchlight. There was no Jacko 'lantern. There was no scarecrow. Only a vacant swing. He continued to walk feeling the cold bottle in his pocket.

Just as they had planned, Aunt Anna made a generous pot of galumpki with Rosemary's help. Mickey and Lenny's mouths were watering as they smelled the cabbage, tomato and beef aromas drifting from the kitchen. After they all had their fill, Mickey and Lenny were assigned to the chores of cleaning up the dishes, pots, and pans, etc., before they set out on Devil's Night. They had strict warnings from both Aunt Anna and Rosemary to make sure they didn't get into any trouble. They assured them they would be careful. Rosemary didn't want to remind Mickey that it was the anniversary of their parents' death, so nothing was mentioned. She was also aware of Lenny's role in the tragedy and since he and Mickey had become such close friends, she didn't want to open up the wound for either of them. Both Mickey and Lenny were aware. It was also in the back of their minds and they had discussed it the day before. They had the same kind thoughtfulness of not reminding Rosie of what day it was.

As soon as Mickey and Lenny were out the door, Rosemary grabbed a jacket. Anna told Rosie she had some roses they could take to the cemetery after they visited the accident site. She had snipped off two of the last roses of summer — one red and one yellow.

They followed the same route Georgie had taken

only minutes before. They weren't aware of the house with the vacant front porch swing, so it went unnoticed as they passed. They unconsciously looked both ways before crossing the service drive with Anna holding Rosemary's hand and Lucifer's leash with the other hand. Rosemary held on to the two roses that Anna had brought. Sorrow jumped into their core as they heard the din of the racing cars and trucks down below.

As they approached the crown of the pedestrian bridge, still holding hands, and Anna holding on to Lucifer's leash, they saw a figure leaning over the railing of the bridge and staring down on to the oncoming traffic.

Georgie turned as he heard footsteps echoing on the walkway. Anna shouted "What the fuck are you doing here?" She then let out a tirade of the worst language she had acquired at Nifty Norman's. Rosemary was more agreeable — than shocked, when she heard the obscenities bouncing off of Georgie's face. He leaned back as far as he could so that the small of his back was pressed tightly against the ice-cold railing. He remained silent. His stare went from Anna to Rosemary and then to Lucifer. There was a new emotion in him now. He was numb with fear.

Georgie looked at Anna and Rosemary with surprise and at Lucifer with fear. It was a fear fueled by
paranoia that had been hardening and invading his
every waking moment. Their sudden appearance had
thwarted his plans for the bottle in his pocket. He felt
its coolness as he squeezed it harder in his attempt to
ease the fear.

He barely knew the woman holding Lucifer's
leash. He had seen her around both Rosemary and
Mickey and had guessed she was a relative. It was the
harsh words that she was throwing at him that had
caught him off-guard. What was his next move?

He looked at Rosemary and thought that he should
attack her to take the verbal assault off him by the
woman holding the dog leash.

"Haven't you had enough, Rosie? Looking for
more? This is where your drunken old man piled into
that bridge down there. Have a good look." He pulled
out the bottle from his pocket that had warmed from
his grip and shoved it close to her face. "This is the
little treat that I gave to your little bitch. I guess he
didn't like it too much," he said with as much sarcasm
as he could muster.

Rosemary was stunned and felt her hatred boil-
ing up as the hateful words poured out of Georgie's
mouth. She wanted to do something but was lost as to
what was the right move. She clenched her fists and

could feel the thorns from the roses. The pain moved up into her brain but she didn't react. Anna was in control of Lucifer and she would act.

With this counter attack by Georgie, Anna took a step closer to Georgie and Lucifer pulled even tighter on his leash, trying to get at the pungent body-odor-smelling target. Georgie felt the railing biting into his sweat soaked back as he attempted to move further away from Lucifer. It was no use. He could only bend backward!

Anna felt the strain on Lucifer's leash. He growled, stared at the reeking catatonic target, and his growls turned to snarls. Anna reached down and unclipped the leash. Lucifer lunged!

Bruce Fink had been hauling cars for twenty years. He enjoyed his job, even the long hauls. Talking with his 'good buddies' on the new CB craze for truckers, made the time go by faster and more enjoyable. They talked about everything that came to mind: their families, the weather, best truck stops, diesel oil prices, sports, and women — especially when they looked down from their semi-seat-perches and spotted skirts hiked up and showing thighs and nylon tops.

Bruce was informed by his dispatcher, on that day before Halloween he would be delivering cars to a new auto dealership. He would be delivering a truckload of new Pontiacs to Hell, Michigan.

He let out a hearty laugh when he heard the destination from the dispatcher. He couldn't wait to get on the CB and tell his buddies he was going to Hell. And . . . when he got home, he would tell his wife and friends, he went to Hell and back.

Bruce barely heard the thud, as Georgie's head implanted itself into the windshield of the Pontiac Catalina. He swiveled his head to both side-view mirrors in time to see a small bottle hit the side of the trailer and grey diesel smoke trailing from the twin vertical exhaust stacks.

He wouldn't realize he had taken on a passenger until he and Georgie both arrived in Hell!

The End

CPSIA information can be obtained
at www.ICGtesting.com
Printed in the USA
JSHW032309280922
31120JS00006B/91

9 781977 257413